Dedication

This book is dedicated to my family.

My husband, Peter who has helped, encouraged and supported me through this exciting process, and my amazingly understanding children, Jenny and Tom.

..and to my beautiful daughter Lucy, for without her there wouldn't be a book. She was and is my inspiration, I was so proud to be your Mummy. This book is for you kiddo, you were incredible, strong and wonderful, and I love you. xx

~ ~ ~ ~

At first, my journey seems certain,
my destination in sight,
calm and ready for a new golden light.
When my heart's near at journeys end,
a quiet but building ripple pulls me
from her grasp again.
I am being transported to a different shore,
to a place where loss is present
and where searing pain is at its innermost core.
The shore is shallow and dark.
When the ripples rise they spit and engulf.
"you cannot leave us sweet child,"
they say, "you cannot!"
You are our soul now, to do with as we wish.
If we choose to be cruel,
you will embrace us and cheer"
With the Devils sneer,
I hear them cry you cannot come close.
You cannot come near, to the simpering love that
you hold so dear. Others too are caught in
the silent scream, as their future is
not as believed, a quiet stream.
They arch with the agony of the dying whale.
They thrash against the rocks.
Caught up in evils movie, in a battle they have lost.
Still in vain they search for love,
for the essence of their souls,
but as the sailor they are sinking,
as we pray "save their souls".
Sadly, they are drifting to a torturous goal.
They walk in the darkness in a soulless dawn,
enveloped without end. The Devils spawn.

For an eternity they believe,
surely love will prevail, yet the all-encompassing
evil, always laughs and lowers its veil.
Thrashing in vain to save their souls,
and steal one last breath, they can only abhor.
I am not afraid of the deadly threats,
and so to them I make no bets.
I have chosen a broken mind,
with a joy they cannot cajole,
with love pulling me closer to my Mother's soul.
To never be able to roam on the earth,
will be worth all the pain,
as it will still lead me swiftly to my Mother's name.
A final call to the Gods "please do as I ask"
Whatever the pain that life has in store,
do not spirit me away from the one I adore.
She waits for her angel, as innocent as a lamb,
unaware of our choices, we are both truly sailed.
For the fate I have chosen. I tread a different path.
To reach it requires destruction in its aftermath.
They must break my soul into a thousand pieces,
tis the only way. My body although useless will
reach its goal. To leave my love, I cannot do.
So to be destroyed is my accepted due.
So take me to her, in my broken form.
In shattered scorn I will be earthly born.
For whatever my pain, her light shines bright.
A Mothers love in the failing light.
To her very core I must descend.
I have made the choice, I cannot amend.
I fear it not, as I know she is with me.
In life as in death we shall always be.

~ ~ ~ ~

Prologue

Was it day or night? I do not remember,
I am sure I looked at the clock in front of me.
I believe it was about eight thirty,
All I knew now was a darkness had enveloped me,
like no nightmare I had ever known.
I thought, why had this happened to us?
But then I thought, why should it not be us?
We were not special, or immune to pain.
I knew this day would change our lives forever.
Whether I survive this, or am destroyed by it,
I will do whatever I can to love
and care for this child.
Which is all a mother can do....isn't it?

Chapter 1

I've heard people say that they can remember being in the womb, or remember being born! Personally, I remember nothing. No struggle, no cries, just silence. The first things I can remember though, are strange sounds. Beeps if you like, almost like music, soothing yet with an air of panic surrounding it, so confusing in fact that I closed off, to a more peaceful place, a place I would visit so many times in my life to come. Sometimes I would be nudged out of my reverie, not just to the sounds, but to a strange yet comforting feeling. I didn't know what it was, but when it came near, I felt my heart beating with a strange longing. A warmth that made me feel scared, yet more alive than at any other time. The beeps became annoyingly louder, yet it didn't detract from the feeling the……… Love, yes that's what it was.

The Love enveloped me, it made me feel so warm and so safe. My closeted world in those early days was a mixture of sounds, pain, Special Place. sounds, pain, Special Place. The pain was short-lived, thankfully, and throughout it all The Love was there, tinged with a tangible agony, that thankfully was not me, but it pained me, as I knew it was connected to the warmth... The Love.

When I said I didn't remember my birth, that was true, yet the reason it was true was different from others who claim to remember this traumatic event. The truth for me was that when I was born, I couldn't remember, because I wasn't alive! I had died.

Chapter 2

It was a relatively uncomplicated pregnancy, Yes, I bordered on gestational diabetes, threats of pre-eclampsia, and a severe case of swollen … well just about everything!

In the summer of 1991, leafy Kent was unbearably hot, and a seriously badly timed pregnancy on my part, meaning that not only was it hot and humid, but, when I got my annual attack of hay fever I Couldn't take any antihistamines, which in future planned pregnancies, I would never repeat.

I was happy, however, expecting my first child, soon after marrying Michael. I'd met him whilst at work. I wasn't really a career girl, and I felt guilty as I wasn't really interested in becoming one. The job for me was just "coasting", I had no real idea what I wanted to do with my life, or any real ambition to achieve anything in particular. I'm sad to say, I was one of those little girls, embroiled in my own femininity, and flourished in the role expected of my gender. I played with dolls, and I was surrounded by pink, despite the amused horror it produced in my Mother..., as I got older, my dreams were simple. I just wanted to, fall in love, to a handsome Prince, and have a family of my own.

I was an only child. My mother, Samantha Burns, was so diametrically opposed to me, as I was a girly girl, and she was an ardent feminist. She gave birth to me at 35, ancient in those days, and out of wedlock a disgrace in the sixties. My mother was never ashamed; however, she was disowned by her family, and she rarely ever mentioned them. If I pressed her she became irritated and gave clipped answers to any question. She had trained as a primary school teacher, (a job which she loved). and we lived a comfortable (but insular) life. She had friends, and was extremely popular with them, as she was with her pupils, whom she occasionally invited over to our home for tea. I, however. always felt a little jealous that they were having Mum on "my time", so I wasn't always particularly friendly to them. Our house was a happy one though and often filled with fun and laughter. Unlike my Mum though, I was not gregarious, and basically a loner. It wasn't that I didn't have friends, it was just, that I really didn't mind being on my own. In fact, I felt happier in my own surroundings, and fantasising, about what my future would be. I had simple wants and desires. I was a dreamer, but the dreams were always simple ones.

As I got older my thoughts and personality never really changed, in fact, I became more introverted, and single-minded Whilst I was in my teens, Mum began having dreadful headaches, and balance issues, from which she was eventually diagnosed as having an inoperable brain tumour. I was 16, at the time, and went into free fall, after her diagnosis. My life would be changed forever.

Despite persistent nagging about concentrating on my exams I never really applied myself with school work again. I would often lie to Mum about doing well at school, and makeup stories about, how my A levels were going, and careers I was interested in. It was easier for me, and as she weakened, the questions became less, as I was needed more and more as her carer, a role I know she never would have chosen for me voluntarily. Mum never lied to me about the extent of her illness, and in the later stages, we had many discussions about death. Deep down though I'm not sure if I truly believed she would die and leave me. Our last few months were filled with her physical pain, which increased, and as the tumour grew, her mentality changed, which caused her to have blackouts, hysterical outbursts, and delusions. Yet despite this, there was still laughter in her more lucid moments.

Sadly, Mum never divulged much information about her own family. It was difficult and unfair to press her given the circumstances, yet I couldn't believe that they wouldn't want to know or see her, but she refused any information, saying that it wouldn't make any difference to them and that she didn't want them in my life, now or ever. She was adamant, but at the time I couldn't help but feel resentful, feeling that she was being selfish, as when she was gone, I would have no one.

A few months after I turned 18, Mum deteriorated rapidly, she needed round the clock care. Thankfully Macmillan Nurses came to help. They were invaluable to both of us, and they helped me a lot emotionally, I will always be grateful, as they cared as much for me, as her. They found the time for tea, and a chat, about my own grief and uncertain future.

Mum was eventually admitted into a hospital. She was having seizures, which never seemed to stop. She had barely arrived in the A and E department when she had a cardiac arrest. While I stood in

shock, they administered C.P.R. Incredibly they brought her back, however, she soon slipped into a coma, and we never were to speak again.
Mum clung to life for 3 days, and I never left her side, I knew that praying would be fruitless. Although it was inevitable, I still held out some hope, that a miracle would happen, but at 3 pm on a Friday, her eyes flickered for the last time, before passing peacefully. The inevitable, that I feared would never happen, had happened. I was alone now. Some of Mum's friends helped me organise her funeral. There were lots of people there. The children from her school cried, but I was in shock, and hardly cried at all. Did it mean I didn't really love her? I felt guilty. A bad daughter. After the funeral, all, but a few of Mum's friends had a disappeared from my life. I was a loner of course, so although a little hurt, I didn't mourn their loss to any great degree. I sold our house, as it was ridiculous for me to have a three bedroomed house. After selling I bought a small flat, in central Ashford, and put the rest of the money, into a savings account, and wondered, what on earth I would do next?
Having failed most of my A levels, as expected, I had no thoughts about my future. I needed to get a job, but as what I had no idea. I just started looking at the local papers, as it seemed the best place to start. After some months scouring the locals, I eventually saw a position advertised, for a cashier in my local Bank. It sounded promising, and as maths was my best subject, I decided to apply. I got an interview and secured a post at Barclays in Ashford.

I met Michael three days after getting the job as a bank cashier. He was the branch manager and appeared much older than me, he seemed very grown up, and I was far too shy to have more than a cursory attempt at conversation. After about 8 months I felt more home and had settled well into the daily workings of the bank. The six other people in the small branch were all very kind and helpful to me. I went out occasionally with my workmates, but no meaningful relationships flourished. As time went on, however, my friendship with Michael Schaffer, became closer, and I realised we had things in common. He too was an only child, and we had a lot of similar interests, in music, especially Elton John, books and life.

He was ten years older than me at 28, actually younger than I had originally thought. He was, I found a really nice down to earth guy. He was very funny. I found after a while that he was making lots of excuses to see me or ask for my help specifically in the branch. I didn't, for a long time consider that he was "interested in me" romantically, probably because, I was still waiting for my fantasy prince and my silly childish dreams of romantic love. That didn't mean It wasn't romantic love, but it was safe somehow, and I really needed to feel safe. He was gentle, and when he smiled at me, I became flustered and shaky. When Michael, eventually asked me out on a date, I was delighted. Being with him, I felt happy and more secure than I had for a long time. He was the one, I decided quickly, yes definitely. We married in a little church in the Kent countryside close to Canterbury, I was only twenty.

This was what I had always wanted. A loving husband, and after six months of marriage, I was pregnant, and looking forward, to having my own family and realising the only dream I had ever had. It was the beginning. Everything seemed perfect! Pregnancy had brought out the most stubborn part of my character, I decided I wanted a high-tech hospital birth. I loved my mother but, maybe there was a part of me that desired to go against the feminist ways that I know my Mother would have wanted for me. I wanted to feel I was in control, as in my life so far, I had found that difficult. My mother I knew, would have wanted me to have a natural home birth. She loved to regale me with the story of my birth, which only made me cringe, and made me determined that that wouldn't be for me. I didn't bother to go to any birthing classes, as I had already decided, no natural birth for me! soon as possible, it would be an epidural and goodbye pain, hello baby.

Life of course very rarely goes to plan. After being a week late, I was forced into a hospital to be induced. I had put this off for a day, as it was Michaels Birthday, and I just wanted to be at home with him. Thankfully the hospital relented, and I came into the hospital on Sunday the 11th of August 1991. Typically, as it was a weekend, there seemed to be a skeleton staff, meaning that there was only one anaesthetist, and he was on an emergency, so couldn't be there to perform an epidural, there and then. I was suddenly given a crash course in, so-called "natural birth" consisting of breathing, and consuming vast amounts of gas and air!

To be honest I don't remember much about the birth, just lots of pain and confusion. I felt myself slipping in and out of consciousness, with a strong sense of foreboding, which sadly turned out to be for a good reason. Melissa was born, flat and blue, there was no crying, no sound. Even in my semi-conscious state, I knew my baby was not alive! If the birth was confusing, the next few hours were equally so.

At one point a kindly looking woman joined me in the birthing room, only to tell me my child was dead! I remember the screaming, and begging, that it couldn't be true. The unbearable agony, and the inability to believe! There was a gap in time, where I remember nothing, and when I did and became aware, the woman was gone! I wish I could remember her name, or what she looked like, but I can't.

Later I was still alone in the Labour room, when the doors flapped open and a large incubator was wheeled into the room, with an Asian looking doctor, and two nurses with him. "Well," he explained in an almost jolly fashion, "your daughter gave us a quite a fright. We've got to take her to SCBU, as she is still very unwell" I could hardly catch my breath, or speak, as they disappeared as quickly as they came. I remember trying to crane my neck to see what was in the incubator, but all I could see were wires, tubes and nothing else.

The next thing I remember was lying in a private room, with Michael in a put-up bed next to me. I remember feeling so so tired, but felt so guilty of wanting to sleep when my baby was…. somewhere! I did sleep that night. I slept very deeply.

The doctors came to see me, in the way that they would for weeks to come. They explained that our baby was very sick, and had, through inhaling meconium into her lungs, been starved of oxygen, and as a result had suffered a significant brain injury during the birth. They told us that if she survived the first few months, which was unlikely, she would have very little quality of life, and would die young. We had many of these similar meetings over the next few weeks. Each time Michael and I would hope beyond hope that they had something new to tell us. To give us hope for our Melissa. Sadly, this was not to be. Many tests were done, and each one just gave us more and more devastating news to try and process. She was blind, that I already knew. She was paraplegic and epileptic. She also had a condition called nystagmus, which resulted in her eyes never being still. They moved up and down and side to side. I knew blindness was inarguable. Every test showed massive damage throughout the brain.
One sense, however, appeared not to be affected, was her hearing. It was obvious to us she could hear. She often attempted to move her head to sounds. If you clapped, her body jumped in surprise. If I spoke to her, I felt her trying to concentrate, despite the fact the doctors said this was unlikely. It was impossible to know what she understood from her hearing, or how her brain processed the sounds. But to us, it didn't matter. She could hear.

Chapter 3

I could feel it, The Love all around me, even when I went away to my Special Place!
The feeling, the warmth, almost all of the time, when I came back I felt it!
Once, when The Love came, I remember a voice saying "she knows you're here, every time you touch her, her heart rate increases, she knows you are her mother"
That was the first time I heard the word mother! The Love was my mother, and although there was 'other love', there was nothing like my 'mother love'!
In those weeks and months or years, I tried to talk to mother! It didn't seem to matter what I did, or how often I tried, Mother could never hear me.
I felt a strange feeling when I heard The Love cry. Sometimes loud cries, begging me, begging me to, "talk to mummy, mama, mama, please say mama"!
I wanted to cry out "but mama I hear you"!
Sometimes I was just too tired to try. I got used to mummy talking to me, and asking me to do things I knew I could never do. It was often easier to go to the "Special Place" It was calm there. I felt no pain at all, even when the people with kind voices, were doing things to me! Things that caused pain. I just went to the "other place" and all the pain just slipped away.
Mummy would cry, but she also would laugh. She would talk to me and say lots of things I didn't understand. I did understand The love though. The wet kisses on my face. The stroking of my hair. The best was the singing. The Love sang such lovely,

funny songs. If I could have sung and laughed, I would have. But I couldn't, so I didn't, but I did hear.

After what seemed like an age I heard other sounds. Strange sounds, a bit like Mummy when she cried, but much worse. It was so loud I wanted to put my hands over my ears, but of course, I couldn't. The strange thing was that The Love in Mummy's voice was still there. The love said all the things she said to me. The same sounds, the same songs. In time I realised that the loud sound laughed like Mummy, laughed, and said "mama, mama".

After a while, the loud sound talked like Mummy, and always wanted things from Mummy. The loud one made Mummy laugh, and I so wished that I could do the same.

When The Love told us stories of things, the loud one always knew the words that Mummy would say. It made me feel bad, that she could do that, so I went to "the Special Place" where I didn't have to hear her"

At times I knew Mummy was angry like me too. Sometimes she shouted or cried, and it scared me. I didn't understand, so I went back to "the Special Place". I was spending more and more time there. I don't know why, but I felt very tired. It was calmer when I was there, yet when I was there, I missed The Love.

I didn't understand sadness, but I knew The Love felt sad. She was tired like me, and when she laughed it wasn't real. Her pain went through me as she touched me, and I hated it because it made me feel the sadness too.

Chapter 4

Life with a beautiful yet severely handicapped child was like entering a special, kind of alternate club, that nobody wants to join. We didn't really have any "regular friends" most were other parents with handicapped children.

Most of the people I knew before Melissa was born, seemed to slip from my life. I never went back to the bank, but Michael needed to work for us all, which he always did without complaint. I used to think most people were afraid to be friends with us. Maybe tragedy was catching. I often believed they thought: How can we talk about our own children's accomplished milestones when your child will never achieve any?

Life for us now consisted of going through a metaphorical revolving door. From the hospital, physiotherapists, specialists and back again! Living with a special yet completely immobile child who could and would never recover was at times almost unbearable. The most important person I met, however, was at a Cerebral Palsy family meet up, she was a wonderful woman named Suki Kaur. She had a loud voice, with a personality to match, she was Asian, but often wore African inspired clothing, which more than matched her personality. Her own thirteen-year-old son Ramon, had a brain injury that resulted in limited movement and speech, but, gifted him with immense intelligence. She set up the group when she realised the isolation that having a handicapped child inflicted on parents and carers. Everything we suffered, she had too. She was so strong and positive and confident. I always wished I was like her. Her friendship with me was genuine. No matter what the issue, if she could help she would. Sadly, I didn't always take up the invitations, as it was difficult for me to admit how I struggled to cope. Thankfully for me, Suki didn't take my pride lying down. She would often turn up at my house unannounced, with flowers, food, or both. I would tell Suki things, especially about my past, things about mum and her illness, that I didn't really discuss with anyone. Not even Michael.

I can't deny there were many times of denial. A refusal to admit that my Melissa, my child, would never see, never speak, never walk, feed herself or call me Mummy! The most frustrating and upsetting thing, was not truly knowing what Melissa understood if anything. Sometimes I was sure she could understand. There were times when I truly believed she was trying to communicate with me. In those early days there was a part of me that was so confident that one day we would be able to understand each other, and eventually, I suppose that did happen, but not in the way I could ever have envisioned it.

After having Melissa, it took my husband Michael and myself a while to contemplate having another child. The fear that history would repeat itself was all consuming. When I became pregnant with Jessica, Melissa was two, I was never truly relaxed. It was an easier pregnancy but filled with worry and strain. Looking after Melissa whilst being heavily pregnant was not easy. My relationship with Michael went on the back burner, yet we were both still excited at the prospect of having another child and curious as to what life would be like if this baby was without problems. I always tried to avoid using the word "normal" when talking about Melissa. This, in some way, seemed an insulting thing to say, about her, as it implied that Melissa was abnormal. Melissa was just different! Sometimes like a beautiful porcelain doll. God knows I used to think in later years, I pray she isn't aware and isn't suffering!

I was determined this time there would be no delay in my new baby's birth. An elective Caesarean was my option. I don't think emotionally I could have ever gone through a natural birth again! After Jessica was born, on a snowy November day, in 1993, I was still haunted by the belief that my new baby, may have "problems". It took constant reassurance from the doctors that she was "absolutely fine".

Melissa had never cried. Never demanded my attention. How I longed to hear her cry. Jessica's cry's filled me with a joy I can't put into words. To hear her demand food, attention, a cuddle, a nappy change. It was all new. So wonderful, but still induced so much pain that I would never know these experiences with Melissa. Jessica adored her quiet, beautiful older sister. She babbled away to her, and I'm sure sometimes I could almost see, a slight smile, from Melissa, and equally a look of irritation and even disdain, from her, but I guessed that was just my imagination. The doctors told me Melissa's understanding was no more than a 3-month old baby. I was, they said, just imagining the things I told them about Melissa. In the end, I stopped telling them, they just pitied me and thought I was deluded understandably of course.

Having two children that were almost immobile was a struggle, and as Jessica grew, there was an increasing rumbling of resentment, from her, as she began to realise how our lives were dominated by the needs of her big sister. Jessica was often affected by, various medical emergencies that I couldn't protect her from. The cancelled days out were numerous because Melissa was sick again. Melissa having epileptic seizures in front of Jessica, which resulted in us rushing to the hospital by ambulance. No holiday's because no one could be left to take care of Melissa's needs! By the time Melissa had reached her fourth birthday, and Jessica was an active busy toddler, the strain was becoming more and more difficult to cope with. I felt depressed and sad, I had no energy. I felt a failure for not being able to cope. Michael was wonderful, and his relationship with Melissa was so special. He had accepted her, and her issues immediately. He like me adored her, and that had not changed. Sleep was a rarity, as one of us had to stay awake at night in case Melissa had a seizure. It was mostly me, as Michael needed his sleep, so he could work. I often went about as if in a constant state of hangover, heavy and exhausted, it was impossible for Michael to give up work as we needed him to be making the money, and we needed the money!

One day a routine appointment for me at the doctor's surgery changed the course of all our lives in a way no one could ever have imagined! I booked into the reception area, and sat down, waiting for my name to be called. I waited and waited. Twenty-five minutes, thirty-five minutes, forty minutes! Being typically English it took me this long to go back to the receptionist and ask why I had been waiting so long. "Did you sign in?" Said the surly woman at the desk, barely looking at me. I wanted to scream "of course I fucking signed in! do I look like a fucking idiot to you?" Of course, I didn't say that. I just smiled thinly, explaining yes, of course, I had signed in.

"Well" she drawled, "you'll have to wait a bit longer I'll get you in in the next ten minutes". God how I hated that woman. If I'd had a gun I could picture myself shooting her through the head, without hesitation!

I walked back through the packed waiting room to the chair where I had been sitting, only to find a threatening looking man with all manner of tattoos and piercings, staring at me, with a look that said, he was just wishing for me to challenge him for the seat. Fuck, I thought he wouldn't't' be so fucking cocky if I had that bloody gun! I stood in the corner feeling absolutely and utterly defeated.

After about fifteen minutes, my name was called and I headed off to see Doctor Shah. I hadn't had much to do with the G.P. myself, as most times when Melissa became unwell, I took her straight to the local Hospital's Children's ward. This was a blessing, that the Paediatric Consultant had allowed me to do, avoiding the delays at the surgery or suffer the agonies of A and E.

So, it completely threw and embarrassed me that as soon as I entered the room I burst into uncontrollable tears. I just couldn't stop. The Doctor

seemed in no hurry for me to stop either. He touched my arm gently as I sobbed and sobbed until I could hardly breathe anymore.
Dear Doctor Shah, he listened to me, once I had got my powers of speech back. He listened and listened as I poured out the pain that I had been holding back for so long!
When I had finished he asked me why I had not asked for help before? I didn't know how to answer. I didn't know I could ask for help, and even if I did, what help would I be given? Dr Shah informed me that I had to have help with Melissa, or I would become more depressed and be useful to nobody.

Whilst I was relieved and realised I did need help, the thought of anyone but my husband or myself looking after Melissa seemed unthinkable. How would they understand her? We had an unspoken code, that only we knew. How could I trust them? How could they love her? She needed love. She needed to be held. I wasn't really sure if I could cope letting someone else into our alternate lifc? The trouble with that was, that I knew I was going to have to, or else I was going to go insane!
Doctor Shah gave me the name of a Nursing Agency, where I could get help with Melissa's basic needs, they would also come in and stay awake with her at night, in case she had a seizure. This would mean Michael and I could sleep, without having to get up every few hours to check on her. The doctor also told me he would help us to get financial help to pay for this from the local authority.

I went home feeling excited and scared at the same time. At last, I thought everything will change. We will be able to be more like a normal family. Maybe we could go on holiday! If the person caring for Melissa, was someone we trusted? All sorts of things were whirring in my head. I couldn't wait to get home and tell Michael. Things were going to get better. I just knew it.

I got a call from the agency about two weeks later. A lady named Gemma, told me gleefully and excitedly "Mrs Schaffer, we have a great lady on our books. Her name is Julie Ward, she is amazing with children including those with special needs, and we would love you to meet her. We have told her all about your family and Melissa's requirements, and we think she would be great with Jessica too"!

A few days later I was pacing the living room floor, with nerves and trepidation about meeting Melissa's potential new carer. I was more nervous as I knew we had an appointment at the hospital in a couple of hours, and wondered if the carer would start immediately, and come with us or stay at the house?

We were told by the agency that Julie Ward, was an experienced carer, with excellent references, and had been with the agency for two years, working in hospitals, care homes, and with families, and was one of their most popular employees. I was so worried! Would I like her? More importantly, would Melissa take to her? Could I trust this complete stranger with my special girl?

While I was pondering the doorbell rang, and I nearly jumped out of my skin. I gingerly went to the door.

When I opened it, a rather severe-looking woman stood on the doorstep. She was smiling though, which was good. I would say she was about fortyish, with very short dirty blonde hair, which I thought emphasised her narrow rather lined face. Her eyes were a piercing blue. She had thin lips, and I could definitely smell cigarettes, on her breath and clothes. She had a general look about her, of someone who had not had an easy life. This was purely first impressions of course, and rather harsh ones I thought on reflection.

"Hello," I said brightly "You must be Julie"?
She smiled broadly, and in that instant, I liked her.
"Yes, I am, and you must be Rebecca"
"Yes, I replied, but please call me Bex!
"It's so lovely to be here," she said, as she shook my hand warmly, and walked in. I led her into the living room where Melissa was snoozing in her adapted wheelchair, and Jessica was engrossed in Beauty and the Beast, her favourite film on the video recorder. Julie looked straight at Jessica and waved. "Hello little miss, you must be Jessica" Jessica gave her a cursory glance, and a shy smile, and then went back to watching her beloved movie. I suddenly felt guilty. "Sorry about that," I said. "She's obsessed with that film at the moment" You don't need to apologise Julie said kindly, looking genuinely unconcerned. She turned and walked over slowly to the dozing Melissa.

"My my," she said in a whisper, "this is obviously Melissa", and as she said it she gently took hold of

Melissa's hands. "She is absolutely beautiful; you must be so proud" Now no one had ever said that to me before (the proud bit I mean). She was often described as beautiful, but mostly in a pity way, in that ", she's so beautiful, what a shame she is like this". Julie seemed oblivious to my presence, for a few awkward minutes (on my part anyway). She just smiled at Melissa and gently stroked her soft hands, that in sleep were not caught in the spastic grip that was ever present when awake.

After a while, Julie seemed to snap back to the present and looking up at me asked me what plans I had that day? I told her I needed to go to the hospital with Melissa in about an hour and a half. Well, then she said. Just show me the kitchen and I'll make us a cup of tea, I'm parched, what about you? "Umm Yes, I yes that would be nice, and off she went not really even asking me where anything was, she just got on with it, and soon I could hear the rumblings of the kettle heating up. Wow, I thought this feels good, this feels really good! During tea, we chatted about various things (Melissa mostly), and when we all set off in our adapted vehicle about an hour later, Julie was chatting away to Melissa and Jessica in equal measure, I felt what I can only describe as hopeful. Things can only get better I thought. Just for a second though, it crossed my mind that, doesn't she seem too good to be true?

Don't be silly I told myself.

Chapter 5

The day The Hate came I was in my Special Place, but I was struggling to ignore the danger surrounding The Love! I felt the darkness cloaked in loving words. A smell that I'd never experienced before enveloped me. I didn't want to come back, but I knew the people I loved were in danger, but how could I help? I knew nothing I said, could be heard or understood in Mummy's world!
Sadly, The Hate didn't leave. It seemed now to be a part of our lives. I couldn't understand when I heard The Love laughing with The Hate! Couldn't she feel it?
The hate didn't hurt me, (at first), she looked after me. She bathed me and washed my hair, and spoke kindly to me. The Hate loved Jessica, but that love was something alien to The Love that I knew? She would hug Jessica so hard that I would hear Jessica cry "let me go". "I want Mummy".
For a long time, life held a familiar pattern, The Hate would come every day. She would look after us, and play. She took me to the noisy place with mummy, where the doctors would talk, and an annoying woman would do strange things to my body that I did not like or appreciate. I think they called it physiotherapy. What it was supposed to achieve I have no idea. I don't think even The Love felt it really helped me. I remember once she whispered to me, "Don't worry my angel we will finish with this crap soon".
To be honest The Love seemed happier than she had for a long time. When she laughed there was a freedom in her I hadn't heard before. She seemed

less tired, and she took us out to places, that held no interest to me at all, but I could tell Jessica was having fun, and so it made it worth the physical discomfort. I could always, of course, go to the "Special Place", but I was still aware that the people I loved were in danger and obviously were unaware that The Hate was just biding her time.

As each day came I could feel The Hate's loathing for my Mummy increase. How could The Love not understand? How could I tell her that for every kind word, for every seemingly caring act, was just a cover for The Hate! I had to spend less time "there", and more time here, and listen, as listening was all I could do to protect The Love.

As I did not understand about time, and how long things took, I was unaware of how long The Hate had been with us? One of the most troubling times for me on this side, was when for some reason Mummy was not there. I was surrounded by The Hate, it was everywhere! There was no love. I wasn't frightened of The Hate, but I did spend most of the time with "my special people". It was only when I felt the kind of stabbing physical pain that I usually found when I went to the place where there were many sounds, and where there seemed to lots of voices, all talking at the same time. This time I felt my body doing strange things that I could not understand. There were others around, The Hate, who was making a fuss in front of people, as I could hear them telling her not to worry. That Melissa would be all right, and that it wasn't her fault, and that she was a wonderful carer. I heard the loud sounds that were almost deafening. I could hear The Hate crying, but I knew the cries were lies. She

was enjoying for some reason, all the people telling her how kind and good she was. She sounded like she was crying, however, inside she was smiling! I remember, later I knew I was back, where love was. Mummy was back. She was crying, but she was also angry, and for the first time, she was angry with The Hate. I was back to where The Love was. For a while, I hoped that maybe that was the last of the danger. Sadly, I was wrong.
The Hate remained!

Chapter 6

For the next few months' life went on in a much happier light. Julie seemed to love both the girls equally and encouraged me to get out more on my own, which I wasn't used to. I saw more of Suki, and our friendship began to grow deeper, and more meaningful. I began to trust Julie with the girls, and so I went out, often just a bit of shopping. To suddenly have a little time to myself, was something I felt very grateful for. She also would offer to babysit in the evenings so Michael and I could go out together for dinner or a movie. We were having "date nights". We actually started to feel like normal people again. We laughed more, had sex more, and generally, it was felt by all that Julie was a real godsend. If Michael and I went out, Julie helped me pick a dress, and jewellery, although, I'd given up on fashion a long time ago, and a lot of my clothes were looking dated. Julie would pick out something for me and say, "Well this is the best, out of a bad lot. I couldn't help but laugh and didn't feel she ever said anything intentionally to hurt me. I had never really had much Jewellery either, so usually, I would wear my necklace that my mother had bought me. I wasn't bothered about having lots of jewellery, and besides, it was always my favourite. Of course, there were the odd times where, I felt Julie was overstepping the mark, and being slightly controlling. She would often do things without asking me first.

On a few occasions, she would take the girls to her house, in Hythe, which was quite a drive away, without asking me. Sometimes I would come back from shopping to find a note telling me where she had taken the girls, and when she would be back. Another instance that stands out was when I was having a meeting at the house with some of the medical experts, to discuss Melissa and her progress. These meetings were always a bit stressful for me, especially, as I never really approved or agreed with what they had to say about Melissa. I was usually too polite to argue with them though. I mean most people would feel intimidated with one Consultant in the house, never mind four or five! On that morning particularly, Julie turned up in Horse riding clothes and blustered through the house, ushering Jessica to change her clothes as they were going horse riding. I knew it seemed a little ungracious, as she was, after all, taking Jessica out for a fun day, and at her own expense. I just felt she should have asked me first, and I told her so, a little bit more forcefully than I meant to, probably because of the stress I felt that morning. Her attitude was to become very cold, and I have to admit the look she gave me, made me surprised, and not a little well.......... Scared!

I now found myself feeling very guilty, and apologising profusely. "How stupid of me". "Of course, you can go horse-riding". I was still getting the cold shoulder, as she replied. "You're in charge of course, but I thought I was doing you a favour, and that it would help you, but if you don't want Jessica to go horse-riding? Jessica looked at me in despair, her bottom lip trembling. "No, of course, you can take her I said, feeling like the wicked Queen. "You are helping me; I can't believe I made such a fuss". "I'm sorry". I was tied in knots, as the dirty looks from them both made me blush ferociously with embarrassment. I could see her noticing this, but instead of helping, she just stared even harder. "Well if you're sure," she said finally. "I don't want to push my boundaries as the hired help! "No No", I said alarmed, "I would never consider you as the hired help, you are our friend. "Please Julie, forget what I said earlier". "I really didn't mean it! Her cool eyes bored into me, increasing the colour in my already red face. Suddenly, she took Jessica's hand and announced "we'll be back before five," and off they went.

Later that evening I cringed, as I related the story back to Michael. "No wonder she was annoyed" He announced in a mocking tone". "I would be furious as well if someone offered to take my child horse riding. "What a Bitch". "Very funny", I replied with an embarrassed smile. Michael carried on, "let's face it, Bex, you were saying the night before, that you were worried that Jessica would get bored, and start to misbehave with all the doctors here". "I know I said that," now feeling even more like the most ungrateful bitch ever.

Michael laughed and gave my arm a gentle squeeze. "Don't feel so bad Baby he said, you can't turn off your feelings just like that. He gave me a wink. I threw a toothpick at him, and I realised, what a fool I was, and how much I loved him. Thankfully the next day Julie acted like nothing had happened, which I was grateful for. Michael and I had arranged to go to an Elton John Concert, at the

weekend, and we were buzzing with excitement. We were both fans, but Michael wasn't far off being a super fan. He had every album. He often sourced out special imports, and thankfully, when it came to buying presents for him, which was always difficult, I always knew that something connected to Elton, would ensure, a very happy husband.
 Julie would be babysitting of course. When Saturday came It was fun dressing up, for a change, and I'd decided, as usual, I was going to wear my rose quartz pendant that my mother, gave me. Even though she was so unwell at the time, she, with help from a close friend, had chosen and bought me this special gift for my Eighteenth Birthday. It was so special to me, at the time, and as she was so ill I hadn't really expected anything from her. I cried when she gave it to me. "Oh Mum," I said through tears, "you really shouldn't have. This is too much" I remember Mum laughing, and in a croaky voice said: "Do you honestly think I would let this special day go by, without getting you something". My mother and I knew it would potentially be the last birthday celebration, we would have together. I always had the belief, that even after her death, that if I wore it when I did something special, somehow, she would be there, and enjoy it with me!
As I opened my black and gold highly polished jewellery box, a loved QVC purchase, I lifted out the velvet lined inner boxes holding a few treasured, and not so treasured items. I picked out the velvet pouch that I always kept the necklace in, and put my two fingers in to prize out the necklace... I felt nothing! The necklace wasn't in there? It must have dropped out of the pouch I

thought, so I started digging. With each touch, I became more and more panicked. It must be here somewhere? I felt tears pricking my eyes, as my anxiety, panic and fear grew by the second. By now I was throwing everything from the box onto my bed. I wasn't just crying now, I was sobbing hysterically, so much so, that Michael ran into the bedroom with a more than worried look on his face. "What's happened"? I was in such a state, I don't think Michael understood half of my ranting's, I must have sounded like a mad woman! Eventually, I managed to make sense enough to explain to Michael, that my necklace had disappeared. He was panicked enough himself, to start going through the same searching techniques as me. Eventually, without success on either side, he grabbed my shoulders and started kissing my face. "Its ok baby, "we'll find it. You must have just not put it back the last time you wore it". "No, I sobbed I always put it away, back in its pouch,". "Always".

Eventually, we both sat on the edge of the bed, Michael hugging me until I stopped crying, and my breathing went somewhere back to normal. It's going to be ok said, Michael. Don't worry about it. I promise we will find it. At that moment Julie appeared in the doorway looking concerned." Is everything ok Rebecca"? "It's ok", said Michael, for me. Bex has just misplaced a piece of jewellery her Mum gave her." But its ok we will find it". "We haven't found it" I barked. "It's missing. Someone must have taken It! "No Bex that's impossible," he said. Looking at Julie, in an apologetic manner, as if I had already blamed her. "Please Julie, when we are out, could you please take a look around the house for it? Maybe Jessica took it without meaning too. "Out" I spluttered "I can't go out! Not now!" Julie piped up: "Of course you have got to go out, you've been looking forward to this concert for months". Look when you are out I will look around the bedroom just in case. I'll look everywhere, including Jessica's room, and her cot". "I'm sure it's not far away Julie said reassuringly. I really didn't want to go, but I couldn't let Michael down. I looked up at her, tried to pull myself together, just managing to produce a weak smile. "Thank you, Julie, that's good of you".

I lowered my head again as Michael said, "yes thanks Julie that would be good of you". I managed to get up and try to adjust my old dress, that now was not only old but wrinkled as well. I quickly checked myself in the mirror. I looked a complete sight. Looking at myself, almost made me want to start crying again. With a tissue, I wiped the mascara from off my face and added some more lipstick. Using my hands, I tried to flatten my hair, that now wouldn't have looked out of place on Worzel Gummage's head. I turned towards the door. Julie was in the hall, and Michael in the doorway. I put on a fake smile and walked out of our room. Michael took my hand and we started to walk downstairs. I remember thinking where on earth are you necklace? and as I did, it made me turn around, to have one last look. As I turned and looked up the stairs. Julie was turning away, so I could only really see that one side of her face was visible, despite that, however, I thought for one fleeting moment, that I could detect a faint, but obvious smirk on her face!

The Elton John concert came and went in a blur. I was trying not to let the loss of my pendant upset the evening, but it was impossible. I spent most of the evening racking my brain to try and think of the last time I had worn my necklace, and where I could have put it. Beyond this, but just as uppermost in my thoughts, I just kept thinking of seeing Julie's face, real or imagined, and that "smirk", I thought I saw on her face. Surely I was imagining things? She was a friend. On the way home in the car, Michael was pumped with excitement after the concert. He was chatting away excitedly when I found myself just blurting out "Julie smiled as we left the house tonight"! "Well she's allowed to smile isn't she", said Michael, then carrying on with his chatter. "That's not what I meant I said feeling irritated. "So, what do you mean Bex", he asked in a measured tone. "What I mean is that when we're leaving the house, I turned around and I saw a definite smirk on her face". "What stuttered Michael"? He turned briefly to look at me. "What?". He repeated! "When we were going down the stairs after losing my necklace, she smiled when she thought I wasn't looking"! Michael was looking ahead and made a sort of a cough or laugh. "Bex, he said in a tone, most common in television shows, when someone is talking to a lunatic. "There's no way Julie was smiling. "Why would she"? "Exactly", I replied. "Bex, Julie was as upset as we were. Why on earth would you say this?"

Hearing Michael, I was beginning to feel embarrassed and stupid. Why had I blurted that out? Why didn't I keep quiet? "Michael," I said desperate to defend myself, "I'm sure she did" I was starting to stutter, feeling silly (again). "Bex, you know this sounds insane, don't you? Julie has done so much for us. She loves the kids, and I thought she was a good friend to you, why are you saying such nasty things about her." He paused for a moment. "I mean, Bex when it happened, you as good as accused her of stealing the necklace." "No, I didn't", I said affronted. "Well, that's what it sounded like." "If it did, I never meant it," I said. "That was never my intention". "Yes, I know she has been a great help to us". "I'm not for a minute saying I'm not grateful ", but something is not right, I just feel it! "Look, Bex, Michael said patronisingly, I know Julie has been great with us, but it doesn't mean that she's better at looking after Melissa and Jessica than you. Remember you are their mother, nothing can change that".

"My God," I thought, he thinks I'm jealous of her! "It's got nothing to do with it" I cried a little too hysterically. I'm not jealous of Julie, I'm just…. well, I'm just, oh shit forget it". "Bex". "Michael", I said, "forget it".

We travelled the rest of the journey in silence. On arriving home, I brushed past the waiting Julie and went straight up to my room. The jewellery still lay scattered on the bed. I picked it up and threw it into the jewellery box, feeling utterly miserable. I changed quickly and went to bed. It was a long time before Michael came to join me. He settled beside me. After a few minutes, he touched my shoulder gently and whispered. "Bex, can we talk"? I pretended to be asleep. I was feeling angry and foolish enough!

I lay there for a long time, feeling more and more annoyed with myself. How could I have thought such things about Julie? She was my friend. Could it be true that I was jealous of her? "NO" I knew one thing, whatever I had misunderstood, I was not jealous, I was grateful. I had made a mistake, I know, but I just needed to move on and not be so sensitive.

The next day when I woke up, Michael was gone. He had left early to avoid me, and to be honest a part of me was relieved. Julie turned up at her usual time, and pottered around, fussing over the girls, and making tea. I was just feeding Melissa (a long and laborious task) when Julie appeared with Jessica.

Rebecca, she said brightly, I'm just taking Jessica into town to get some bits and bobs, is there anything you need. Here we go again I thought! She's doing things without asking me first. I also felt she was starting to forget, that she was being paid for, to care for Melissa. I sighed and looked towards Jessica. "Do you want to go out with Julie? I asked as good-naturedly as I could. Jessica pulled a face, and exclaimed! "No want to stay with mummy". Julie shot an annoyed look at Jessica and said in a more clipped tone. "Of course, you want to come out". "We could get you a new dress". "Don't like dresses", said Jessica pulling away from Julie and snuggling next to me and Melissa. I can't deny there was a part of me that felt a river of pleasure at Julie's obvious discomfort, at the rejection. "Well, I said flatly maybe another time then". "Yes, ok said Julie through tight lips. I'll just get on my way then. "I'm only going into town for a short while". "I won't be long". Julie was smiling, yet despite the calm look on her face, the flashing red welts that appeared searing her neck told me a different story. I think after the Elton John concert, there was a definite shift in my connection with Julie. There was a change in the way I looked at her relationship with myself and the children.

I found myself watching her more closely than before. I trusted her less, and I think she knew it! Situations between us were becoming more strained, even though I was aware that I didn't really know why I mistrusted her? Was I being a Bitch? Did I really have any concrete evidence that there was something wrong? No, I didn't. I didn't, but I just felt deep inside me that I could not trust her, and maybe I just needed to watch, to see, to understand, and feel why it was that suddenly she felt like the smiling enemy.

I don't know if Julie felt my changing feelings, but there was definitely a prickly air between us. I always felt she was holding her feelings back! Another more unsettling feeling though was that I felt that she didn't actually like me. About a month after the necklace incident, which still hadn't been found, despite hours of searching the house, from top to bottom, I got a call from Michael. As soon as I answered the phone, I knew something was wrong. His Father, Jack had had a heart attack! This was a bolt out of the blue. Michael's father was one of the fittest people I knew. Michaels parents had moved to Portugal about three years ago when Jack retired early at 55 and decided to "live the dream". They sold up, lock stock and barrel and had moved to a converted farmhouse, overlooking the beautiful scenery of the Algarve.

Michael's Dad had no intention of taking life easy, however, he worked out every day. He hiked, ran, used his bike for transport, and spent the rest of the time with Angie, Michaels Mother, playing golf and cooking fresh healthy foods. I hadn't got to know them very well before Michael and me married, but we all got on well from the beginning, and I could tell with satisfaction, that they approved of me. I think there were relieved also, as Michael, had not had a long history of dating, so they were happy he was settled before they left the U.K. In Portugal Jack's health regime would put most people half his age to shame. Sadly, we hadn't seen much of them since they had moved, mostly this was due to the difficulties of transporting Melissa, anywhere, never mind abroad. Not that I had considered it much. Travelling was a nightmare anyway, "I have to go to Portugal today" explained Michael, trying to hold himself together, I could feel though, he was on the point of breaking! I need you to come to Bex!

"Michael I can't," I said perhaps a little too quickly. "You know I can't leave Melissa" "Please" pleaded Michael. "Ask Julie If she can look after the children?" "No" I almost shouted down the phone! I realised how this must have sounded to Michael. "I'm sorry Michael, of course, I want to come, but we don't know how long we would need to be there, and we can't expect Julie to look after the girls, 24/7." "Okay," said Michael sounding dejected, "I understand. I've just got to come home and pack. I'll be home in about half an hour." I put the phone down, consumed with guilt. I suddenly realised Julie was standing by the door. "What's happened," she said slowly. Through tears, I explained the situation. "But you have to go," she said in an almost accusatory tone. "Michael obviously needs you. I'm more than happy to look after the girls. I promise I will talk to you every day, and let you know how the girls are? you could call every evening". "No……. "I don't know, no I don't want to leave Melissa", and It's not fair on you" I lied. I wish I had the guts to say what I really felt. I just felt like screaming I don't want you near my fucking kids. I was amazed at my own ignorant mistrust of someone who had only ever done good things for us.

I looked directly at Julie and saw not just disappointment, but hurt in her eyes. "It's not that I don't trust you with the girls" I found myself saying, but I realised this was just what I was saying. I flopped on to the sofa, sad and confused. Julie sat beside me and put her arms around me. "It's okay," she said gently, "I understand completely, you not wanting to leave the girls. but it will be okay, I promise. You must go, Michael needs you." With tears blurring my vision I nodded, and leaned into Julie, just like I used to with my Mother. I felt that perhaps I'd been wrong about Julie all the time. What an idiot I was. "Are you sure?" I said? "Of course, I am," she said in a motherly tone. You start packing and I will look after everything here. When Michael came home, he fell into my arms with relief, when I told him I was coming to Portugal with him. I talked to Jessica, and told her, as simply, as you can to a two-year-old that we

were off to see Grandad, who was ill in hospital, and we were just going to make sure he was alright. Jessica looked confused. "me come Mummy"? "No baby, not this time, but we will be back soon."
I picked up Melissa, and I cradled her in my arms, smelling her fresh vanilla scent. "Mummy and Daddy will be home soon my angel" Melissa, as usual, showed no response, other than a slight stretch, and a bodily spasm twitch. "Auntie Julie will look after you, and we will be back soon."
Julie appeared in front of me. Looking towards Jessica "You know what" she said in a "come on let's go" fashion, why don't we go upstairs and have a bath, with all your toys? Jessica didn't seem so sure. In a grumpy tone, she said "Grover too? "Well, said Julie with hands on hips, Grover will have to sit on the side of the bath, or he'll get wet. Is that ok? Jessica scowled but nodded. "Come on then" enthused Julie, "let's go" Jessica grabbed her beloved Grover, and ran like the wind up the stairs. Julie gently took Melissa from my arms and headed towards the door. She turned back, and with a smile, said "off you go. Everything is going to be alright". I Smiled back, and I truly believed her. How wrong I was!

Chapter 7

With the dark energy of The Hate all around, I felt happier "in my Special Place". It was calm and relaxing there, and as Mummy and Jessica seemed happy enough around The Hate, I felt no pressure to listen. This began to change when Mummy disappeared, and no matter how I listened for her voice, it was gone. I was feeling an unpleasant experience, which was called "having a bath". To Jessica, however, it seemed to produce a joy in her, that was infectious, and made me feel happy for her, although I was aware that this was not detected by anyone. The warm water rippled over me, making me shiver, Jessica and The Hate were in conversation, with only some of it that I understood. "Woo squealed Jess, look at Mr Crocodile. "Yes, said The Hate, isn't it wonderful without Mummy here? "No Said Jessica, I miss Mama. "Oh don't worry Jessica, we are going to have so much fun without her! Your Mummy doesn't want you to have any fun. She wouldn't let Grover come in the bath, now, would she? No, she wouldn't, and you know she loves Melissa more than you don't you?

I could hear a tremble in Jessica's voice. Mama loves Jessica? She said it like a question, and it made me feel so bad. "Oh, said The Hate, Mummy says she loves you, but she doesn't, she only loves Melissa! I love you more than your Mummy, and I always will. You are my special girl, aren't you Jessie? And you love auntie Julie don't you Jessica?" "Yeeeees" said Jess, elongating the reply. "Jessica loves Julie?"

The joy coming from The Hate was tangible. I shivered and was so cold. The Hate was so strong; I just couldn't keep warm.

Time went by (I don't know how much). The feelings between Jessica and The Hate, seemingly stronger by the day. I was dragged along, to many places, without knowing where. I was often left alone though, and The Hate (I noticed), spoke very little to me directly, but I knew it was still important that I listened.

One time I remember knowing we were outside, where it was cold on my face, but my body was covered, so it didn't feel so chilly. "You know Jessie, wouldn't it be lovely if it was just you and me together, without Melissa around" There was no reply from Jessica. "Imagine all the things we could do without her? Can you think of any Jessie? I waited, feeling a pain, that I did not understand. "Well," said Jess slowly, "Drisliland" "Yes replied The Hate in an excited tone, yes you and me, we can go to Disneyland, and meet Belle, from Beauty and the Beast! We could go to America, and not just see Belle, it's also where Grover comes from" This excited Jessica. "I love, Belle. I love Grover" and she stomped up and down, bashing my wheelchair as she did.

"You are so beautiful, said The Hate. "Come and cuddle Mummy". I heard Jessica giggle, as I heard loud kisses, that were not meant for me .... MUMMY!!

Chapter 8

When we arrived at Faro airport, despite the circumstances, it was so refreshing to feel the warm sun, and the gentle breeze, enveloping me. I called the hospital, to let Angie know we had arrived and were on our way. Michael had organised a hire car, so we went to pick it up, then headed off on the short journey to the hospital, Particular do Algarve. The second we parked the car, we ran to the reception to find where Jack was. we found Angie by the reception, just outside the ward, as soon as she saw us, she broke into tears and hugged us both equally. "Where's Dad, said Michael? Mum held onto Michael's hand and led us to his room. The room was small, with a tiny window, that let in minimal light. Contrary to what we were expecting though, Jack was propped up in bed, on two pillows, and gave us a reassuring smile as we entered. It was all too much really. We all burst into tears, whilst hugging Jack, and feeling relief, that he didn't look as sick as we had expected. After a few minutes, Jack said "come on now stop crying, everyone. Tell them, Angie, it's going to be ok. Angie nodded through tears. "Yes, it is going to be ok". "Dad's heart attack was a mild one, so the Doctors have said, that although he will need to take beta blockers, apart from that, He just needs to take it easy, and carry on eating healthily, and maybe cutting down the amount of EXERCISE he's been doing. She jokingly frowned in Jacks direction. "Oh God," said Michael, I'm so glad". He started to choke up again. We were so worried, I was so scared, that we might not see you again, and we would get here too late! "Michael calm down", soothed Jack, I'm not going anywhere lad, at least not yet. Michael put his head on his dad's shoulder, and Jack just held him, just like he was a small boy. Angie and I looked at each other, tears of love and relief in our eyes.

The next few days were so special to us all. jack being his usual stubborn self, kept nagging whoever would listen, that it was ridiculous, for him to still be in the hospital, and that he wanted to be discharged. After the third day, and perhaps because the doctors were desperate to get rid of him, he was discharged, with drugs, prescription, and various guides, in English, on a healthy diet, which he didn't need, and a gentle exercise routine, which he did.

During the three days, I made numerous calls to Julie at home. Strangely Jessica seemed very distant when we spoke, and seemed keen to get back to whatever she was doing as soon as possible. Julie, however, reassured me that everything was going well and that Melissa, although sleepier than normal was well. I felt so grateful, that the kids were happy and safe. I didn't feel worried, although of course, I missed them both dreadfully. When we got Jack home, it was so wonderful to be with them, as we hadn't seen them for so long. We spent three more days together, catching up, about life, and the children. I hated to admit it, but being free, of responsibility, even for a short while was amazingly liberating. After Jack's heart attack, it made me think, that I hadn't spent much time in the last few years looking after myself. I looked at myself in the mirror, in the guest room at Jack and Angie's home, and realised that I looked dull and dowdy. I hadn't been to a hairdresser, or even worn much makeup since we had the children. I was twenty-four, but I looked sad and old. My hair lank, just flopping there, with no style, my skin pale and drawn. I thought I looked more like someone who had just got out of the hospital, more than Jack did. I was determined that I would try to do better when we got home, I mean I was amazed that Michael could even fancy me anymore!

Living with Jack and Angie, was so relaxing. Eating lots of fresh fruit and vegetables. Walking along the beautiful beach, and sitting in their beautiful Garden, well into the early hours, drinking wine, and Jack, sipping fruit juice and just relaxing. I had not realised how stressed I was, until luxuriating in the calming warm atmosphere of Jack and Anna's beloved Portugal.

We knew we had to return home, and although it was tough to leave, it was a relief knowing that Michael's Dad was going to be ok and be with us for hopefully, a long time to come.

We all cried as we left Faro airport to head back home. Michael and I were determined, and told them so, that we would be coming back, as soon as we could, and bring Melissa and Jessica.

Arriving back at Gatwick, we waited impatiently for our luggage. It was always frustrating, how long every procedure seemed to take when travelling abroad. Whilst waiting I decided to call Julie to let her know we were back in London. As soon as Julie picked up, there was a hesitancy in her voice, and I knew that something was wrong. "Julie

I said is there something wrong? Rebecca, please don't be alarmed, there is nothing seriously wrong, it's just ....Melissa!
"What do you mean, I stammered, my stress levels rising, and my body temperature lowering to ice cold. "Melissa is ok now, but she had an allergic reaction. "A what"? I said. "A reaction to what exactly, and where is she? By now I sounded hysterical, and people were noticing and watching me. "She's safe, here Rebecca, at home". The Doctor says that Melissa had an allergic reaction to sunlight. "To what? I said, with a grunt of disbelief, and trying to make sense of it. "Melissa has never been allergic to sunlight". "What on earth are you talking about"? "Apparently, you can get an allergy, even if you've never experienced it before, she said almost pleadingly. "She's had some swelling but has been given antihistamines, and the doctor said, she would be ok in a couple of days. "Rebecca I didn't tell you, as I didn't want to upset you". "You and Michael have been through enough". "You know what Julie, I said that really wasn't your call to make": "I am her Mother"! "Yes I know Julie said quietly, I should have let you know.

At this point Michael was heading towards me, with the cases, his face ashen. He, like everyone else in the bagging area, had heard my hysterical outburst. "Come on, said Michael, let's get home. "Julie I said, we are on our way, and without waiting for an answer, I slammed the phone down. Michael and I quickly went on our way, to the long stay car park to pick up the car.

Whilst driving back I tried to fill in the blanks, to Michael about the situation. "If it's just an allergy, why are you so angry Bex? "It sounds as though Melissa is ok, and I'm sure Julie knew it wasn't serious, or she would have tried to contact us. I could feel myself getting angry, stress levels rising again, this time with Michael, with all the calm relaxation of Portugal all but gone. I could see Michael, looking at me, strangely, his new slight tan fading before my eyes. I didn't see the point in carrying on the conversation, as we were almost home. I was the baddy again.

As we pulled up at the house Michael parked outside, not bothering to put it into the Garage. Julie was looking out of the window, waiting for us. She was there opening the door, with a nervous smile on her face. I raced to get in, but she stopped me by holding onto my shoulders with both hands and looked straight into my eyes. "Melissa is fine, really"! This action seemed to calm me somewhat, but I wasn't unaware of its patronising tone. She released me, as I tried to calmly walk into the house. I went straight to the living room where Jessica was eating, some fruit from her Sesame Street breakfast bowl. Hi, baby I said feeling a rush of love. Jessica looked up at me almost coldly, but then Jessica had always been one to make you suffer if you left her, for any length of time, so I wasn't surprised, upset or too disappointed.

Have you missed us? MMMMMM replied Jess in typical, I'm not letting you know I missed you. I turned to Julie "Melissa"! I said where is Melissa"? She's in bed having a nap, Julie said warmly. Michael was setting down the cases. Jessica ran out to him, and wrapped her arms around him, she covered him in kisses, whilst yelling "Daddy

"Daddy". I wasn't too concerned by this blatant rejection, as Jessica was moody and adorable, though at times difficult. I left them to it, as I started moving up the stairs to see Melissa. The door of her room was pulled to, but not closed, so I slowly opened the door, not wanting to disturb her. As soon as I entered, there was an arched figure, bent backwards lying there, and if it wasn't for the flowing golden hair tumbling over the duvet cover, I wouldn't have known it was Melissa. I got closer to the head of the bed, and nearly fainted with shock. Melissa's face was unrecognisable. It was bloated and red. Her eyelids were so swollen, they covered her eyes. Her lips were protruding and puffy. "Oh God" My poor baby. I scooped her out of the bed and wrapped her in my arms, whilst checking for further swelling. It all seemed confined to her beautiful face. Julie, looking concerned suddenly appeared at the door. I can honestly say I had never been angrier in my life. "I don't believe this", I bellowed. "When did this happen, and why do we only know now"? "Please, exclaimed a desperate sounding Julie, I didn't want to add to your stress. I knew she was going to be alright, there was no need in bothering you, as you were going through enough, but then I told you that on the phone. I ignored the sarcastic backlash. "I need to speak to the hospital, and Doctor Shah," I said. "I need him to tell me what happened here"? Julie looked guilty. "Rebecca, I didn't take her to the hospital. I guessed it was just an allergic reaction, so I just took her to my own G.P. It is just a reaction, the swelling will go down within twenty-four hours, honestly"

Michael appeared nervously at the door and looked visibly shocked at the sight of our gorgeous girl. "What the fuck", he stammered. What's happened to her? Julie looked desperately at Michael. "Honestly, I was telling Rebecca, it is an allergic reaction, and nothing more". "She's not in any pain, and all the swelling will go down in a day or two"! Michael nodded in Julie's direction. "You must have had one hell of a shock Julie, said Michael, going over to me, and taking Melissa from my arms. He stroked her hair, and smiling at her he whispered "hey beautiful, have you been getting into fights while I've been away. He turned to Julie, and they both smiled slightly. "Fuck I thought, even now he's sticking up for her". "Lucky you've had Auntie Julie to look after you", and Michael, looked almost in thanks at Julie.

I nearly swallowed my own tongue with fury. "Lucky, "Lucky is she"! "Well God help her if she was unlucky". I was really losing it, and I knew it. I couldn't believe Michael wasn't as furious as me. "Come on Bex" Said Michael looking at me like I was a silly child, having a tantrum. Julie's said Melissa's going to be ok. "I mean, thank God she was here and didn't panic. "I mean, do you remember Bex, when you got that allergic reaction to shellfish in Rhodes, on our first holiday together? You looked just like, what Melissa looks like now! You spent two days crying in the hotel room, then the hotel doctor gave you a shot of antihistamine, and we were back on the beach the next day. You looked like shit, but you were okay being you? I couldn't fathom how Michael, could find amusement in this situation and would stick up for

Julie rather than his own wife. Julie was enjoying this, I was sure of it, and I was completely sure it wasn't my imagination. She had lit the fuse and stood back to watch the fireworks. Her simpering look belied her pure enjoyment of the show!

Suddenly Julie started crying. I rolled my eyes. "Oh God Bex," said Michael full of concern, "now look!" Michael looked at me accusingly. "You are overwrought and tired Bex, and you're getting upset for nothing. Please don't cry Julie" he said, gingerly, putting his arm around her bony shoulder's. At that moment I could have put my hands around her scrawny neck and throttled her. Really this was too much for me. To be honest, deep down I was starting to feel ridiculous, and outnumbered. Was I really overreacting? If so, what the hell was the matter with me?

Trying to think logically I thought that Melissa's attack could have in no way been Julie's fault. How would someone even know how to do something like this, and the major question I asked myself was, why would anyone want to do this? I knew I was being really stupid, but I still felt strongly that Julie was wrong in not telling us, and I was furious that Michael, so quickly took her side over mine. I took Melissa back from Michael, in as calm a fashion as I could, and walked out of the door. I grabbed my keys to the people carrier and fled out of the house. I opened the car, and as gently as I could, put Melissa, with into Jessica's car seat, and drove off swiftly. I was suddenly feeling tired and tearful. Maybe it was just tiredness I thought, as I drove, having no real idea of exactly where I was going. I realised I had made a mistake, by putting

Melissa in Jessica's car seat, instead of bringing her in her wheelchair. It wasn't adapted to her, which was obvious as Melissa arched her body in discomfort and annoyance. "I'm sorry" Melissa I cried, feeling the tears fall, I just had to get away from that woman. "No one understands", I said out loud to myself. "Oh god, I don't think I understand".

I drove on for about 10 minutes, not thinking of my direction, or destination, but found myself driving down Canon Street, where Suki Kaur lived. I drove slowly along the quiet, beautiful tree-lined road. The large houses were all a mock Tudor, which was not very Suki at all, but the house had been bought and adapted to Ramon's very special needs when Suki had been married to Rajesh. Although Suki was divorced from her husband, who was a very successful clinical Psychiatrist, Suki had done well in the divorce settlement. To be honest, Rajesh, whom I had met on a few occasions, seemed like a nice enough guy. Their divorce had not been a bitter one, although both sides of their Muslim families did not take the divorce well, Suki and Rajesh were determined to make it amicable. This was I think, especially as they had Ramon to think of, and I felt from conversations with Suki, that although Rajesh never admitted it, he had found it very difficult to cope with Ramon's disabilities, especially early on. It seriously affected the marriage, and also as even Suki admitted, after having Ramon, she had no time for anyone else. He was her life, but both her and Rajesh had managed to forge a good friendship. Suki and Rajesh often came together for various school functions. Despite

Rajesh's difficulties, initially coping with Ramon, he was now incredibly proud of his son. Ramon, although, unable to communicate verbally, had learned to use a customised computer monitor with a joystick attached near his chin so he could work the keyboard to speak. Ramon was extremely intelligent, and although sometimes moody, and with a giant chip on his shoulder, which often looked more like arrogance. He was aware of his own immense intellectual abilities, trapped in his excess of inabilities. The irony was not lost on him, and occasionally, his anger overflowed, and mostly the brunt of his anger centred on Suki. Of course, she understood and took no notice of his frustrations. I once heard her say loudly, "once you've finished your Angelica Pickles moment" a spoilt cartoon character from Rugrats, "let me know if you'd like any dinner, and with a dismissive wave of a hand she swished and swayed, in her flowing sari, into the kitchen. She was an admirable woman, with an extraordinary son. When Ramon was in a mood, everyone knew it, however, he also had a cheeky sense of humour, and an ability to sense the uncomfortable feelings of others in relation to his disability. Sometimes I cringed, at how he could embarrass others so acutely, without uttering one word from his lips.

Eventually, I pulled up outside Suki's home. I turned off the car engine. For a moment I just sat there, not sure what to do. Melissa still furious and full of indignation, of not being in her own chair, arched and spluttered in rebuke. Trying to think, what I was doing there, and why, I still found myself walking up the flower-lined path, to the large, black, ultra-glossed front door. Up close the house looked imposing, screaming, money at me. I gently rang the doorbell. There was no immediate answer. Almost relieved I started walking back down the pathway, and eventually get back home, to probably grovel and end up apologising for my behaviour, once again. I was halfway down the drive, and almost at the car, as the front door opened and a rattled, and frazzled looking Suki, appeared, wearing a comic relief apron, and wiping her flour-covered hands on a tea towel. The rest of it looked like it had been wiped on her hair too. She looked surprised to see me but smiled warmly. I turned and moved faster, as I carried on in the direction of the car. "Bex, wait" cried Suki, as she hurried towards me, sorry I couldn't get to the door quicker, I've been baking for Ramon's school, and I'm covered in Betty Crocker. She started laughing, but all I could hear was crying. It took a few seconds to realise, that the crying was me. Suki put her arms around me, engulfing me in cake mix. "Bex, my god what's happened"? She had looked over my shoulder, seeing Melissa in the car seat. She was shocked at Melissa's appearance but didn't comment on it. "Ok she said firmly, give me the car keys, go in the house, now and I'll bring in Melissa!" I had no strength to argue.

I slowly entered Suki's Home. I entered a large but airy vestibule area, with floor to ceiling frosted windows, and beautiful thick curtains, in various shades of gold, with elephants on them. Even before I entered the main hallway of the house, I could smell the baking, Suki had alluded to. It was glorious, and reminded me so much of being a child, and how Mum and I would bake glorious cakes, and bread together at the weekends. The wonderful aroma made me miss her, like this kind of reminders always did.

  The house was mostly open plan, and the main focus, of the large imposing hall, was a stunning balcony. With a sweeping "Tara" like staircase. There was a crystal chandelier, hanging from the middle of the ceiling, the light, was supremely Suki. It was covered in crystals of every colour. I had occasionally seen it on a sunny day, and the colours it produced, in every direction made me feel the excitement of a child, entering a magical world. It really was spectacular. Despite the eccentric opulence, the house was very homely, with nick-nacks scattered all over the place. On a sideboard, I noted ornaments that ranged from a Chinese waving cat to an art deco statue. The paintings on the walls were all abstract. All different, some painted by Suki, others not. I wasn't very versed in art, but I liked them anyway. It could have been pretentious, but it wasn't. I remembered the living room was on the left-hand side. I slowly walked into it. Everything was a mish-mash of styles, Just like Suki. I found my way and walked past various pictures of Ramon, which I remember her once saying jokingly, you know I'm off to hell for these pictures, but I'm damned if anyone will stop me putting pictures of my own son on the wall. She explained later that this was because human pictures or statues, were not allowed in Muslim homes, the reason being about loving the virtues, and the essence of a person, and not their physical likeness. There were also various baskets full of half-finished items, from projects that Suki had either crochet or knitted. Suki was extremely creative. There were various handicapped aids for Ramon, dotted around. Some helpful and some not. There was of course much electronic equipment. It was actually quite untidy, which made her home even more cosy, so homely that the untidiness didn't matter.

I was feeling like the orphan that I was, and utterly alone, I sat in Suki's plump, comfortable multi-coloured sofa which could never have been found, at the local branch of DFS. I soon became aware of Suki's warm sunny voice chattering a mile a minute. She entered the living room with Melissa, relaxed in her arms. "Well she exclaimed, how are we to get you, comfy young lady". This was obviously a rhetorical question, as she started adjusting the large fur bean bag, near the sofa. She spent a while adjusting and plumping, till Melissa stopped arching her back, in spasmodic annoyance, and began settling down, enveloped in, grey, white and brown wolf fake fur. "There you go said Suki feeling satisfied, now do you want tea or coffee, Bex"? "Coffee please I whispered, feeling silly for bothering her. Ok she smiled, and now you're here you have to try the organic, no sugar banana butterfly cakes I've made. I better test them on you first, I don't want to kill the whole school in one go. "I thought you said it was Betty Crocker, I said matter of factly. "Well yes she said, these are my own version, inspired through the genius of Ms Crocker! Even in my sorry state, I couldn't help laughing. "Well I don't mind I said, and, to be honest, I'd be quite happy to be knocked off by one of your cakes, at the moment. We both laughed uncomfortably. "Well you get comfy and I'll get us something to eat, then we can have a chat, and Suki disappeared and busied herself with making the coffees. I sat in numb silence, but, with the smell of the freshly brewed coffee, now mixing with the wonderful baking smells, I realised I was starving. After not too long, Suki wheeled in an old-fashioned, but large two-tier, trolley. I imagined a very rich old lady would have once owned this trolley, in the thirties maybe. It was laden with fresh coffee in a bright blue cafeteire, and a selection of beautiful cakes, sat on very art Deco style plates, all with different designs. Knowing Suki, they would have been all searched, and bought with love, from the antique markets, she loved to frequent. It all looked so lovely, I was so glad I had come. Deftly Suki Played, being "Mother", and added cream and sugar to our cups, "one, spoon for you she smiled, and three for me, to add to my ample backside! We both laughed a little too loudly, disturbing the sleeping Melissa. Melissa frowned at the disturbance, stretched out then flopped back down, back into delightful sleep. She popped two cakes on one of the smaller plates and put this beside my steaming cup of coffee. She took one cake for herself, then looking up at me she said slowly, so now Bex Schaffer, I need you to tell me everything. I don't know how long I talked, an hour, maybe two, all I remember really were, eating the amazing cakes Suki had made, and the calming sounds of Melissa snoring gently on the beanbag, close, and safe beside us. After a long while, I stopped talking, there were, a few minutes where nothing was said, and Suki looked intently at me, seemingly trying to assimilate everything I had told her. I was the one who broke the silence. "You think I'm crazy don't you"? Of course, she would think that. Michael obviously did.

"Crazy," said Suki looking surprised, and I realised sounding a little angry. "To be honest, she carried on, I'm amazed you have allowed that woman to stay in your house, as long as you have"! One thing you and I have learnt, Bex, in having handicapped children, is that we have had to use our other senses and instincts more, if we weren't attuned to them, and listened to the bullshit of so-called experts how would we ever be able to communicate with our children. "Look, even if there was no ill intent from this "Julie", your instincts and feelings about her, should be enough for you not to have her in your house, for one more minute! I can't deny I was ecstatic someone believed me. "Look said Suki you don't have to do anything now if you don't want to, but whatever you decide, it's your decision. No one else's. "One thing I would say though is don't be too angry at Michael". "Remember he's not the one who has to stay at home with Julie". "He doesn't know her in the way you do, also he's a man, and men are idiots"! Again we were laughing. "Whatever you are feeling Bex. Confused, unsure, guilty". "It doesn't matter if your suspicions are fact or fiction". "This woman does not make you feel good". "If it feels wrong to you, you're allowed to feel that way. "She is in your house". "You are her boss", "so if it's not working out, it's time to say goodbye".

"She's not the only caregiver on the agency's books, I'm assuming, so just find someone else, period".

I hadn't felt this relaxed in ages. All the anger seemed to have left me, and the wise words of Suki, made me realise, I had to get rid of Julie from our lives, and the sooner the better. Suki and I chatted a while longer, before Melissa, having risen from her sleep, was, with her body language showing me that it was time to go.
Suki bent over the beanbag and lifted Melissa up, and cradling her in her arms exclaimed! "Melissa Schaffer, you are the bossiest child I have ever met"! Melissa grimaced as if she understood she was being reprimanded. "You know, said Suki, this child, is more than she seems to be". "She's an old soul". "Don't ever let anyone convince you otherwise Bex". "There is something very special about this little girl". "I know, I almost whispered in reply "I know.

Chapter 9

I pulled up at our house at ten thirty pm. There was no night carer for Melissa tonight, so I brought her in, ready to prepare her for bed. As I entered, I could hear the television in the living room. "Oh god I thought for a moment, I hope Julie isn't still here. I headed off to the living room, to find a snoozing Michael, with the local news going on in the background. As I put Melissa in her wheelchair, Michael stirred. I looked at him for a moment and realised that we were drifting apart. Sometimes I felt we were like strangers. Before I could think any more, Michael woke up and seeing me leapt out of the chair. "Oh, Bex he said, "I'm so sorry, I've been so worried about you both. "are you okay? I realised then that I was absolutely exhausted. Yes, I replied I'm fine. "Bex, said Michael pleadingly, let's talk? "No Michael not tonight. We are both tired, let's just get Melissa settled and then go to bed. "Ok said Michael softly. "You know I love you don't you Bex. Yes, I replied, I know you do, I love you too". Michael gently picked up Melissa, switched off the lights, and we headed upstairs. The next morning, despite a fitful night, and still feeling exhausted, I got up earlier than normal, dealt with the early morning ritual, with Melissa and Jessica, and waited for the inevitable arrival of Julie. She arrived dead on time, at eight thirty. She smiled warmly as she entered, waved at Jessica, and went into the kitchen. This was it I told myself, it's now or never. I followed her, feeling nervous with every step. There were some cups and plates in the sink, which Julie was dutifully washing up, her back towards me. "I blurted out, Julie we need to talk"! Julie slowly turned to look at me, and, in a patronising tone, she said. "Oh, Rebecca please let's not talk about what happened any more". "I know you overreacted, but it's ok I forgive you". Forgive me! I thought. she really was something. "No Julie, it's not about that, "well it's not just about that". She turned around completely and dried her hands slowly on the tea towel. She looked at me, annoyed at being stopped from doing, whatever it was she was pretending to be doing. "Well she said, are you going to spit it out or what? To be honest, she had not been so openly hostile to me before, so in fact, Julie was really making this too easy for me. "Julie I've been thinking for a while now, that "I don't think things are working out". "What things are these she said, her eyes narrowing, and boring into me. "Well," I started to stutter, losing my confidence suddenly. Why hadn't I called the agency instead? "Things are not working out with you looking after the children. Julie's demeanour changed, and her look became very dark, and for the first time I realised, I was actually frightened of her. "What exactly are you saying, Mrs Schaffer"? For a moment I looked down at my feet. It took all of my strength to lift my head up again. I looked into her ice-cold steel blue eyes and blurted out. "I don't want you to work for us any more"! For a moment or two, her look didn't change, then she slowly folded the tea towel, and put it down. Her coat was behind the kitchen chair, and her bag on the table, her set of spare keys to our home sitting on the top. She picked up both items and headed towards the door, but not before slamming the keys

on the table in front of me. My heart was beating so fast, I thought I was going to have a panic attack. Was she really leaving? "is this the end? As Julie reached the door, she slowly turned around to face me. Her cigarette lined upper lip was turned into the tightest evil grimace. "You know", she said finally, "you will find Rebecca, that I make a very bad enemy".
"My name is Bex I said!... Then louder. "MY NAME IS BEX"!

Chapter 10

The Hate had gone. My Mummy was happy again. She smiled and laughed. I'm sure she was glad. The Hate, however, was very strong. Her energy still filled the spaces around us. Her force was intense; I could feel it within the very walls. The Hate had made Jessica love her. The Hate had told Jessica that The Love was bad. Jessica was cruel to Mummy now. The Hate, made Jessica hate. I couldn't understand how I knew, but I did, and Jessica didn't?

It was so clear. The Hate hadn't really gone, though, Mummy just thought she had. Mummy and Jessica were more in danger than ever before. The Hate was not close,
but it would never leave us.

Chapter 11

I was so relieved that Julie was out of our lives. In fact, I was ecstatic. I was in no hurry to get more day help, especially as the night carers still came 3 nights a week. Melissa also seemed brighter than she had in the last few months, and although that may have been my imagination, it made me really happy. A few days after Julie had left us, I was bathing Jessica, and she was playing happily with her toys. She suddenly looked up at me and said. Can we go to Drisliland? I couldn't help but laugh, she sounded so cute. Do you mean Disneyland sweetie? "Yes, she said seriously, obviously annoyed at being corrected. "Drisiland" "Well I said, I would love us to go, but it's difficult because Melissa wouldn't like such a long journey, at the moment but yes I'm sure we will go one day. Jessica suddenly looked really angry, and throwing the wind-up shark she had into the water she burst out. "I hate you. Wish Issa was dead, and I want Muma Julie!"

I was speechless. I felt like I had been slapped across the face. I even touched my cheek, as I felt the heat rise. I could feel the tears pricking my eye's, but I refused to let them come. "Jessica," I said as calmly as I could, you mustn't say things like that about your sister. She can't help being the way she is, and I'm sorry you are missing Julie, but she had things to do with her own family" I said, cringing at the lie. Jessica slowly picked up her shark and began playing with it. In a petulant tone, she spoke without looking at me. "Don't care".

For the next few days, I tried to put our bathroom conversation behind me. I was still hurt, but I rationalised it, as probably normal. Our life was difficult, and I could see now, that Jessica was affected by her surroundings and our different lives. I understood that she would become attached to someone, who had obviously cared for her, and who in many ways showed a favouritism towards her over Melissa. This was, I assured myself another good reason to lose Julie.

As the week went by my relationship with Jessica was frayed. She wanted her father more than me. She wouldn't let me read to her, and at bedtime she only wanted Daddy. It was ok though I convinced myself. It's just a phase.

Chapter 12

A week after Julie left, the telephone rang, on a quiet morning, after a difficult night with Melissa, who had a chest infection again, I was praying she wouldn't have to go into hospital. It was Sue Harrison, our social worker. We didn't hear from her very often, but it was always nice to talk to her, as she was nice, friendly, and seemed to care about us. This time however her tone was different. Not unfriendly, just a little distant. "Bex she said after the usual pleasantries. There is a problem" "Oh, I said surprised. What kind of problem?"
There was a silence then Sue replied. "I'm Sorry Rebecca, but there has been an allegation of child abuse made against you". I suddenly felt as if I was about to faint. The floor was coming up to meet me. There was a ringing in my ears that was deafening. As the panic rose, I spluttered, "I don't understand. "I've never hurt the children. "What am I supposed to have done. Who has said these terrible things?"
"Please please Mrs Schaffer, please calm down. I know you are shocked."
 "Let me explain to you what information I have at the present time. Oh God, it all sounded so official.
 "The only thing I can tell you, Bex, is, that an allegation from a former employee, claims you sacked her after her discovery of the abuse had been made. She has intimated that the abuse concerns the overfeeding of Melissa, by you, and the starving of Jessica, by you. Of course, it was all clear now. I knew Julie had let me off too easy that day. Now she was out for revenge, and what better way, than

to accuse me of being a bad mother, the thing in life that she knew deep down was my Achilles heel. My deepest fears were that I couldn't cope, and I wasn't good enough. It was obvious Julie knew me too well. "This is crazy I screamed down the phone. "It's that crazy bitch Julie! She's done this to get back at me. Surely, Sue, you must know it's not true, I love my kids, you know I love my kids." I was sobbing now. "I know it's awful said Sue sounding empathetic. "I don't believe personally for one minute that you hurt the girls, but I'm so sorry Bex, there is a procedure and process that we have to implement. There is nothing I can do." "What will happen" I wailed. "Are you taking my girls from me? "No No said, Sue. "First Bex, we will talk to all the health professionals involved in Melissa's care, and anyone, G.P etc., who has access to Jessica. I know it doesn't help to say try not to worry, but please try not to. I'm sure this all just a misunderstanding that will be sorted out very soon." "A misunderstanding," I said bitterly. "I knew Julie was strange, but now I know she must be insane, to even think of doing something like this."

I know now the depths of Julie's hatred for me, but what had I done, and where did all this stem from? "I can imagine how awful this all is for you, but please be patient, leave things with us, and as soon as I have any more information, I will let you know by phone, and before you get any official letters from Social Services, Bex I will speak to you soon". And with that, the line went dead. I sunk to the floor, pulling over the phone as I did so, it crashed onto my ankle, but I didn't feel a thing. I was in shock. I didn't know what to do. Who could I call? Slowly in tears, I rang Suki's number.

Chapter 13

Through tears, I explained what Sue Harrison had told me. At first, Suki laughed, as if she thought I was joking. When the realisation set in that this was no joke, Suki told me to hang up the phone as she was coming straight over. She took fifteen minutes to get to the house. It was the longest fifteen minutes I could remember. She rang the bell, and I ran to the door to meet her. I flung myself into her arms. "Come on she said gently, let's sit down. We went into the living room. Jessica, who had been having an afternoon nap, suddenly appeared in the doorway, rubbing her sleepy eyes, hair in a dozen different directions, and holding tightly onto an ever-grubbier Grover. Hello, gorgeous said Suki. Someone's been sleepy. Jessica looked slightly confused and looking at me said gently. "Mummy why you cwying? "I'm ok," I said as brightly as I could. "I've just watched a sad film that's all." "Are you hungry said, Suki? "Milk," said Jessica in a demanding tone. Even though Jessica was nearly three, she was still attached to her bottle. The only time I now allowed it was after her nap. I headed off wearily to the kitchen to get one for her. There was no need I felt to rush getting her to stop drinking from the bottle, especially as we had now cut it down to once a day. I still felt guilty. "There I thought. More proof of my bad mothering technique".

I could hear Suki chatting to Jessica, and Melissa, who was as usual asleep, in her chair. As soon as I returned, with the bottle, Jess snatched it out of my hand and headed off back to her room. "She's been miserable since Julie left," I said bitterly and apologetically. "She has been a real brat to me since she left. I get the feeling that Julie has been trying to turn Jess against me, and I think she's succeeded." The tears were welling up. Suki looked at me and smiled. "Don't worry said Suki, she'll get over it. Now let's see, what we can find out about Miss Julie Ward?" Suki and I talked for a long while. "Have you got her address?" said Suki? "Yes, but no," I said panicked. "Please Suki, don't get involved, I'm telling you Julie is dangerous. I don't think I knew it until now, but whatever you do, do not go to her house. I'm in enough trouble as it is, and Julie would love the opportunity to make things even more difficult for me, and when I tell you she's dangerous, I mean that I feel that she would hurt anyone who got involved, so please Suki, as a friend, keep away from her." "You know Bex, this woman is obviously a nut job. We can't just sit back and let her get away with all this." "Well if she is a nut job," I said, "then all the more reason not to go anywhere near her. I need to stay calm and let social services sort this out. I know they will find I'm innocent. They have to find me innocent don't they?" "Yes, yes, of course, they will, you are a good Mother," said Suki, not really sounding very convincing. "You know, whatever happens, you can't let her get away with this. What if she does it again, to someone else?" "yes I know" I whispered, "but I can't think about that now." Suki stayed with me for the rest of the day, only leaving to pick up Ramon from school. She arranged for him to stay with a friend of hers, then onto his Dad. she said she wasn't leaving till Michael had come home, and we had told him everything. Suki spent the day, helping me with the girls. Playing upstairs with Jessica in her room, even vacuuming the whole house. She wouldn't listen when I told her not to. Bless her. I was in a constant state of anxiety. I couldn't help fearing the worst. Every insecurity I had ever had, rose to the surface. I felt wretched and worthless. When Michael eventually came home, like Suki, he almost laughed when I told him about Julie's accusations. "This is fucking insane, are you sure you've got this right, Bex? Why would Julie say that about you?" "Well I don't know Michael" I said sarcastically, "maybe I've just made this all up, to fill up my dreary miserable existence" Feeling my anger rising even further, "and maybe it's because she's always fucking hated me, and now you can see, that she was the bitch I said she was I'm sorry Bex, this is crazy, I thought she cared about our family?" "Well, obviously not I retorted in unapologetic disgust. When things had calmed a little, Suki said her goodbye's, said she would call me later, and left. There was an uncomfortable air between Michael and I that evening. Instead of bringing us together, there was another thing that highlighted our differences and lack of closeness. He was as shocked as I was, of course, but as usual, we coped in different ways. Sadly, not together, as we should of. When problems arose, there always seemed an increased creation of distance between us. When he wanted to talk, I found I wasn't interested, and vice- versa. There seemed to be a limit in our ability to communicate effectively together. Although I believed I still loved Michael, I was sometimes aware that we weren't always each other's best friend. Later, in the evening when I was absent-mindedly cooking us something to eat, I noticed that the paperwork from the care agency, which I had, I thought, left on the kitchen table, after Suki had insisted on seeing it, was no longer there. Suki had an idea that perhaps, within some of this paperwork, there might be a clue or evidence that would show Julie in a bad light. In the end, though there was very little of anything interesting to see, just details about Julie's address, C.V. references etc. I had shown this to Suki briefly, and we discussed perhaps contacting her previous employers, but we eventually reasoned that, if her references had been bad, she wouldn't have got on to the care agencies books. There was a slight feeling of worry, but I brushed it aside, as I reasoned, I must have put it back in the box where they had originally been and had just forgotten I'd done it. To be honest, it wasn't the most important thing on my mind, and it was very hard to think straight at all, at the moment.

Chapter 14

Mummy was unhappy again I could feel it. I could not help. I knew that, so I felt safer being in the 'Special Place' now, however I could hear a 'guiding voice' and wouldn't let me be. Please leave me alone I said, I come here for safety. Don't make me hear. Don't make me see! I didn't understand. Were the visions real? Were they dreams? I knew, however, that they would not let me go. The voice was gentle yet firm. It said, "Melissa, I will help you to watch, as well as hear, it is very important".

I hoped the voice would not let me see unless I needed to, but as the mist cleared, I was made to see a woman. It hurt me to see her at first. It confused me that I could now see and hear. In my Special Place, I could see, and it was bright too, but here the brightness hurt my eyes and made them water. It hurt enough to make everything blurry so I couldn't see clearly. I had to blink a lot, and after a while, this helped me to get used to the light, and help me to carry on watching. The lady's light seemed brighter than anything else on earth. At first, it was so bright I found it difficult to watch. It did clear after time, and at last, I could see without blurriness. I noticed that her skin was dark, soft and beautiful. When I became more aware of the woman I could see why her light had dazzled me, although I still asked the voice, just to be sure. "What is it I asked?" "It's her aura, Melissa. She is a lady, and her name is Suki, and she loves colour. "The colours mix with her aura to reflect the light from within her soul it said" Although the woman was

beautiful, she was not smiling, she seemed worried. I saw her in the metal box thing that moved, that mummy also had. I didn't know what it was, but I did understand the sounds. They were the sounds of the things that usually took me somewhere. There was a rumbling sound, and a smell, that I never understood, but was always there. Often when we went somewhere in this, Mummy often used the words "Let's get into the car". I don't know if this was what it was, but this lovely lady, Suki was in one. For a long while I just watched her, and although I didn't understand all that she was thinking, I felt scared for her. She was in danger, but she was not aware of it. I saw Suki stop the car, and sat still for a while. I felt she didn't really want to get out, but I could also feel her desire to do good in some way, so she forced herself out of the car. She walked for a while, down a very small quiet area, with not many houses, but with lots of beautiful trees and flowers. These were things I knew very well, in my Special Place, these were everywhere. Although there, they are much more beautiful and brighter. Suddenly a stab of fear entered my whole body. I wanted to leave.
"No you cannot leave, Melissa said the voice". "You must stay, and watch". The woman stopped for a moment. There was a house in front of her. Now I knew why I was in fear. Now I knew why I didn't want to stay. The Hate lived here.
Suki was scared, but she did not know the real danger she was in. I wanted her to stop now, and leave this place. She walked to the door and rang the bell, that I had heard occasionally, when I had been there, with Jessica. No one came to the door. I

was so happy. the lovely lady would have to go home now. I watched her as she headed back to the car, but No! She touched the car door then stopped. "Go back home, I said, go back". Instead, she turned around and headed back to the side of the house. Slowly I saw her walk down the narrow pathway, filled with more beautiful flowers. It was strange, for I knew The Hate had made the flowers, yet how could something so beautiful, come from such hate! The smell was amazing, but nothing could truly cover the burning hate within. Suki came to a small garden The Hate's garden, it was all green and lovely, trying to hide the horrible being close by. There was another door, at the back of the house. I watched as her hands were poised on the handle. She was shaking and looking all around. I prayed to the voice. Please, please do not let it open.

"There are some experiences we choose to submit ourselves to. Suki is one of those" said the voice. "Suki has chosen her own destiny, that now she cannot avoid" "What about my destiny," I said? "At the moment Melissa, it is your destiny to observe" I had to carry on watching. The handle, as I feared, moved down, and slowly the door opened. The lady moved slowly into the house. The stench from The Hate was so overpowering, it made me feel as sick, as much as when Mummy or the other people gave me things that were supposed to make me feel better. The lady was scared; I could feel her heart beating so fast it hurt. The lady slowly moved about the house, not knowing where she was going, but I had been there before, and I knew nothing good ever came from being amongst The Hate.

There did not seem to be anyone around, yet The Hate was "everywhere". This house was old. It was the first time I had seen it, although I knew I had been here before. It was dark, and let very little sunlight in, I remember The Hate, saying once that the house was haunted, whatever that meant. The lady moved through the narrow hallways, breathing heavily, her fear growing, as she came to the end of the hallway, I could feel her desire to leave. Suddenly she noticed a heavy but small dark door almost hidden under the staircase, and was drawn to it. I wanted to cover my face, as she moved closer. I could tell she was deciding whether to go in or leave.

Her hand rested on the round doorknob. I watched her turn it, slowly and push the door open. There was a slight scream or gasp, I'm not sure which. I tried to stop looking, but the voice wouldn't let me. I stared into the room. It was a small space. The lady looked around the room turning around and around so fast, and breathing so heavily she made me breathe in rhythm with her. When she stopped moving, I looked at the walls. I don't know what are on walls in most rooms, but here on these walls, they were covered with faces, of people I knew, but had never really seen before. I had never seen a room with walls such as this. The voice told me that the one face that covered most of the walls was in fact of JESSICA.

Chapter 15.

I didn't understand, but the reaction of Suki told me that this was very wrong. There were pictures of Jessica everywhere. Some with her and The Hate, but mostly they were of her on her own. She looked beautiful in them all. She was my sister, so there was a part of me that could not understand why the lady was so upset and was crying. There was a table in the room, with yet more photographs. These photographs, however, were different. They were pictures of a woman and another child. The voice told me: "Melissa they are of you and Your Mother. I looked intently, was that my Mummy? Was that really me? I wasn't really interested in looking at me though, but I saw that I was in a big chair on wheels. My head was bent backwards as if looking up to the sky, my body looked strange, and I realised that I looked different from the other people in the photos. It made me feel funny, it was not how I imagined I might look. I was much more interested in looking at my Mummy though. Her hair was so long and dark in colour, with golden lights. It was very shiny, and it made me remember it touching me, as she cuddled, fed or talked to me. Now I knew what she looked like. She was my Mummy, "The Love".

I was annoyed while looking, as many of the pictures of my Mummy had dark words written on them. I was still trying to understand writing and had tried to read sometimes, in the Special Place. I moved in closer to look at the words written on my mummy's lovely face. I was upset that someone would even want to cover her. I read but didn't understand the words, except one: Bitch. That was a bad word, as mummy sometimes used it when she was angry. "Slut, Cow, Whore," The voice said these were very bad words too. I could see, also, how upset the Suki was. She knew they were bad words too. She seemed to cry more and more, but covering her mouth in case someone might hear her. Although I was less interested in my own image, I could not help but look at them. "Die, was written on one. Suffer, was written on another". I watched the lady rip off some of the pictures from the wall, and take some off of the table too. She turned quickly and began to leave the small dark room. Again the lady moved slowly along the low gloomy hall. Suki was more upset now and wasn't sure where to go. I could feel her confusion. The lady stopped in a larger room, which was a bit lighter than the other rooms in the house, and I knew I had been there once or twice before. She stopped and looked around. In the corner, a shiny brown piano stood, it took up so much space in the room. I could remember this thing. It had made a nice sound when it was used correctly. Jessica had played with it, so it sounded so bad it made me want to scream. Suki was about to turn away, when I heard a calm dark voice utter: "What the fuck are you doing in my house?" The lady turned around, so fast I thought she would fall over. I could see The Hate was standing there. Suki stuttered. "I've seen everything" she shouted! I know what you are, she shouted again. I've seen the room. "Those disgusting photo's, but I've got them now, and I'm taking them to the police!

I could feel her fear. The poor lady was too kind for the likes of The Hate. "Are you aware Ms Kaur, you little do-gooder bitch, that I can have you arrested for breaking and entering? This is my private home, and you, scummy paki, have entered it, without my consent!" "

It doesn't matter what nasty insults that you say to me" said the lady, "you are obviously sick, and I am going straight to the police, and it will be you they arrest not me!"

The Hate laughed. She wasn't scared, but she knew the lady was. "Do you really think the police are going to pay any attention to those pictures?". "Yes, they will do, when they see you have written all those nasty words on the pictures of Bex and Melissa. "My God, what kind of crazy person are you?"

Julie looked down at the floor, contemplating her next move. I was scared, as The Hate was clever, cleverer than most, and I could tell she knew being horrible to Suki was not the way to get herself out of trouble, she knew that Suki deep down, believed that everyone was good. Suki was wrong of course, but she didn't know it. When Julie at last looked up, she was sobbing, but there were no real tears in her eyes. "I feel ashamed" she eventually said. "I know those pictures look bad, but I was so angry with Rebecca when she fired me.

"You must have had those pictures for ages, I'm not a fool," said Suki. The Hate carried on, "I loved those children, and I would never hurt them. I lost my own child years ago, and yes maybe it's true, I was, and am in love with Jessica, but I would never really hurt anyone in that family. I couldn't help it. I

love Jessica, and I miss her. I can't believe that Rebecca will stop me from seeing her again" She began crying again. The lady looked confused, but I couldn't understand why. She's lying, I found myself shouting, hearing my own voice for the first time, *"those tears aren't real! You cannot believe her!"* Suki looked at the crying hate. *"Have you any idea of the pain you have caused Bex and Michael? "I know. I know"* replied Julie. *"I can't believe what I've done. I'm so ashamed. Please, Mrs Kaur, don't tell the police or Rebecca about this. I'm so sorry"* She carried on sobbing.

"Those disgusting pictures, were you going to hurt Bex and Melissa?". "No! I would never have done that. I know the pictures in the room are extreme, but I loved them all so much, I felt, at last, I would have a family. I took pictures of them all the time only because I loved them. I only wrote those horrible things on the pictures when Rebecca fired me. I know it was wrong, but I was so angry and felt so lost without them!" Suki moved closer to The Hate, and to my horror, I saw her gently put a hand on her shoulder. *"I don't really understand you, or your actions, and I believe you must have some serious problems, but I would like to know, how you lost your own child?"*

"Yes, I will tell you," said The Hate. *"It is a story I have never told anyone else before".*

Chapter 16

I was exhausted and wanted it all to stop, but the voice calmly said: "Melissa, keep watching, and your strength and understanding will increase". Julie sat down, still crying. Suki slowly sat opposite her, after a moment the lady said: "Julie if you want my help I need to know what has made you this way? You obviously have a psychological problem, but I would like to give you the chance to explain to me, where this may have come from?"
I'm willing to listen so I can try to understand, and before I go to the police, as I feel I must? Julie looked up, and I saw for the first-time real tears in her eyes. "Yes, she answered slowly. I will tell you: Back in 1964, I was just 14. My life was simple. I was still at school, and doing really well. Although we were poor, I still had dreams of going to University, as I wanted to become a doctor. My life was uncomplicated, then I met a boy called Peter. He was eighteen, and his dad owned the local bread shop. He was the most handsome boy I'd ever seen. Of course, I had never had a boyfriend before and knew nothing about sex and stuff. I mean we didn't talk about things like that in those days. He was always really nice to me when I would go there to get the bread. He talked to me, and it made me feel really grown up, to have someone older than me actually bother to talk.

I always offered to get the bread, whenever it was needed, and not just because of Peter. I always helped my mum when I could. She had a heart problem, so she found doing daily tasks really difficult. I often did the shopping and cooking and cleaning when needed. My older sister Susan never did anything around the house and was really mean at times to our Mum. Susan had a job, but only gave Mum a small amount, and kept most of it to herself. I knew we were short on money, so one day I went to see Peter's dad Jack Sullivan, and asked if there was a weekend job going. I couldn't believe it when he offered me a job on Saturday and Sunday. Early mornings, starting at 4.am, to help deliver the bread. It was great to be making money, helping the family, and seeing Peter every day. I had been working for Sullivan's bakery for a few weeks when Peter asked me out on a date. I couldn't believe it. I was so excited, as I never thought he would be interested in me. I didn't tell my Mum, because she wouldn't have let me go out with an 18-year-old boy. One day, Peter and I met in a small café in Paddington, west London, near where I lived. It was a bit grotty, but I didn't mind. I was with Peter and I was happy. After dinner, he took me to see Doctor Zhivago, which I'd been talking about for a while, not that I thought for a moment that Peter has listened to me, especially when I would say how romantic a film I had been told it was. I didn't concentrate much about the movie, as I was too busy looking over at Peter. He didn't touch me though, or even put his hand over my shoulder. I thought he was such a gentleman.

After the movie I expected Peter to walk me home, but instead, he asked me to walk with him through Hyde Park, as it was such a beautiful evening. It was getting late, but it sounded so romantic I said yes. We were walking deeper into the park, and I was dreaming that he would kiss me. We had entered a very woody area, when a young man walked up to us, and said, "Hi Pete". I was surprised as you wouldn't expect to meet up with someone so late in the evening that you knew in the park, anyway it all seemed really friendly. His friend asked, "so who's this?" "Oh its Julie, he said in a friendly manner. "Julie this is George" Suddenly they both sort of sniggered. I didn't understand why. Suddenly, Peter just grabbed me and started kissing me. Although I'd wanted him to kiss me, I was embarrassed he was doing it in front of his friend. I pulled away from him. "Hey, he said what's going on? You've wanted this all night, haven't you? George was laughing. "Ha, he laughed, in a singsong style, "Julie doesn't want you, Julie doesn't want you." "No, I stammered. It's just embarrassing in front of your friend". "Ah, look" jeered George "she's all embarrassed, ain't she sweet". George suddenly looked at me and said: "Come on love don't be shy, come and give us a kiss and with that, he grabbed me and kissed me roughly. I tried to pull away, but he was so strong. "You bloody whore exclaimed Peter. "I thought it was me you liked? "I just stammered. "I do I do. "You know what I think, said George, she's just a big fat slutty tease, and needs to be taught a lesson. I've never been so terrified in my life. "Please, I said can I go home now. Peter looked coldly at me and replied, "You're not going anywhere love." Peter suddenly grabbed me and both he and George, dragged me into a hidden area of bushes. I tried to scream, but I was slapped across the face, so many times I just cried, and let them do what they wanted. They both raped me in the park that night, I thought I was going to die. When they had finished. Peter grabbed me around the neck and sneered: "If you tell anyone about this, you and your family are all dead. Do you understand? I couldn't speak but nodded, terrified. They both strolled off laughing together as if nothing had happened. I didn't know what time it was, but I knew I had to get home, or my mother would worry. I was in so much pain, shocked, and I was bleeding. I don't know how I managed to get home. But I did. I managed to slip in the back door, and run upstairs, to the bathroom. By the time my Mother realised I was home, I had scrubbed myself as clean as I could, and headed off to my bed, my head, and my body hurting. My mother walked into my room, that I shared with my younger sister Agnes. My mother touched my arm, but I pretended to be asleep, which was difficult, as I found it difficult to stop the tears streaming from my face. Thankfully my sister was only eleven, and fast asleep. I cried silently the whole night.

Suki suddenly spoke. "Julie, did you get pregnant from the rape? Julie started crying again. "Yes, she sobbed. "Oh God, it was awful. I didn't even know I was pregnant, till my older sister Susan, started questioning me about why I was being sick all the time. I hadn't even considered being pregnant. I didn't know anything." I denied it to Susan at first, but she kept on at me till I told her about the rape. She was really calm. She wasn't very sympathetic and seemed to be making me feel it was my fault for getting myself in that position. Susan had been pregnant in the past, and she told me quite casually that she had had an abortion. I didn't know much at the time, but I did know it was illegal. "Can you imagine the shame you will bring on this family if they know you are pregnant", said Susan. Poor mum will have a heart attack and die, and it will all be, because of you! I just felt awful, terrified and ashamed, but not sure what to do. "Tell me what to do I pleaded to Susan? "Well first she said, we need to find out if you're pregnant, I know, someone who can find out.

The next day, Susan took me out, after she had come back from work, to see an old lady, in a grotty street in Bayswater. The lady called Alice told me to undress and lie down on a dirty sofa, with a sheet on it, that was covered in stains. I remember she pushed my knees apart, and it felt like I was being raped all over again. I started to cry, but she told me to be quiet. "Are you trying to get me arrested you, silly cow. I've got kids upstairs. Shut up or they'll hear you, then we will all go to prison. I was so terrified I didn't utter another word. My sister sat calmly on a chair by the window. She didn't say or do anything. When the lady had finished she wiped her hands on a dirty towel and said brightly. "Yes love you're up the duff, about three months I'm guessing". Just hearing the words filled me with panic. "I don't understand I said starting to cry. I didn't do anything! The old woman just laughed. "Ah yes I get it, she said winking in the direction of my sister, "It's just one of them immaculate conception things I guess. To my horror, both she and my sister laughed. "Well what you gonna do, said the horrible woman, directing the request to my sister and not me. Susan didn't even look at me to ask what I thought. She just answered matter of factly, well she'll have to get rid of it, our life is shitty enough without some little bastard to look after. I felt so panicked, I just wanted to say "NO NO Please! But I didn't say anything. The woman said in an irritated tone: I can't do it tonight, I've got me bingo, but I can fit her in tomorrow. Susan just nodded without looking at me. I'm expecting a bloody big discount after that mess you got Kitty James, into last month. "That wasn't me Alice said indignantly. "It was her own fault, she didn't do what I told her, and if she doesn't listen, then that's her bloody fault, not mine"! "Yeah right, said Susan sarcastically, You'll get £2.00 and be grateful, or else I'll start spreading your rubbish techniques about town, "that'll soon put your little business under. You in jail, and your little brats in an orphanage. You're a bloody thief, and a bitch, Alice said annoyed, but she looked resigned to my sister's blackmail. Bring her here tomorrow at eight pm, after my kids are in bed, and make sure you're here to take her home, once she's done I want her out! "Come on said Susan let's get home. On the way home I begged Susan not to do this to me. "Do this to you said Susan angrily. "I'm doing you a favour, remember, and I'm paying for it as well, which will put paid to those gorgeous shoes I've saved up for. "Don't you worry she said in fake concern? it will all be over soon enough, and we can get on with our lives. "Believe me you should be grateful. I felt so guilty. "Yes I am grateful really, but isn't there another option? Maybe I could keep the baby, and you could say it's yours. "What she exploded, as if I'm gonna say I've had some little bastard just so you can play doll's house. There're no other bloody options, so stop going on about it.

Chapter 17.

I pleaded for silence again, but the voice continued to show me the whole horrific vision.

The next day, went by in a haze. I spent the whole day just looking at the clock, waiting. Susan came home from work as usual. She had her dinner, and as she was eating, she said to our mum: "Julie and I are going to see a friend of mine tonight, for a few hours. We won't be back late. "Oh that sounds nice doesn't it Julie". I nodded unconvincingly, but not enough for my mother to notice. At about seven thirty, Susan said chirpily, come on little sis lets go. We took the bus to Bayswater and headed off to Alice's house. I was shaking the whole way, so much so, in fact, Susan told me to stop in case other people noticed. When we got to Alice's house, Susan Said Ok here she is. I'm off to the pub for an hour, I'll be back to pick her up then. Susan hardly looked at me as she swanned off out the door. Alice looked me up and down. "Well come on then, she barked, you know where the room is don't you? I walked as slowly as Alice would allow, into the horrible stinking room. This time there was a wooden table in the centre of the room, covered in a sheet, instead of the sofa, which I noticed was pushed to one side of the room, against a wall. "Well, we haven't got all day, take your undies off and lie down, you should know the drill by now. I was trembling with fear. Slowly I did as she asked, then got on the hard table. On the side of the table was a smaller table with a metal bowl, covered in a tea towel. I lay in abject terror. Alice lifted my skirt up, told me to open my legs. I did as I was told. Alice went to the bowl, that I was assuming she would use to wash her hands. As the towel came off I could see very little. She fiddled for a bit in the bowl, then produced what looked like plastic, with a squeezy bulb at one end. It was filled with something. She roughly inserted it into me. It was painful, but still not as painful, as what she had done before. I just closed my eyes. The pain she inflicted began to increase, however, enough to cause blood. The pain increased even more, and I started to scream and tried to close my legs. She slapped them open again. "Shut up hissed Alice, I'm nearly done. She handed me a dirty cloth. I looked confused. "To bite down on, your silly cow" I bit down screaming into it. There were horrible sounds of scraping, and when I looked up there was what looked like a knitting needle covered in blood. I think I might have passed out, as I don't remember anything else until I heard Susan shouting at me. "Wake up Julie she said, we have to leave" Slowly I managed to move around the table, and Susan and Alice helped me get off. There seemed to be blood everywhere. "Quick said Alice off you go. I've got this mess to clean up. "Expect a little bleeding in the first few days, then you'll be ok. I could hardly stand, never mind walk, but Susan dragged me along. As we got out of the house, mercifully there was a car outside. Hurry up said the guy at the wheel. "Shut up said Susan "It's you buggers that get us into this trouble in the first place", at that moment I vomited. "Damn cried Susan trying to back away. The man behind the wheel, burst out laughing, as Susan remonstrated with him. She grabbed me roughly and managed to bundle me into the car, and the guy, whose name was I think Dave drove us home. It must have been late, as no one seemed to be up. Susan took me upstairs into her room. "You're sleeping here tonight ok. I nodded. "I think I'm going to die I said". "Oh God, stop being so melodramatic, Susan said, as she helped me to change. She gave me a sanitary towel and said whilst holding up my bloodied and vomit covered clothes. "These are ruined; I'll get rid of them". "You try and sleep. "I'll tell mum you can't go to school as you've been sick. I lay on the bed. I felt so dreadful, and there were stabbing pains in my stomach. I prayed I would sleep, but the pains just got worse and worse. I started moaning, and couldn't stop even when an angry Susan told me too. I don't know what time it was, but I could hear crying. I realised on opening my eyes that it was my mother. She sat beside me holding my hand. I don't remember much else. I must have slipped into unconsciousness. When I awoke, I realised I was in a hospital. A doctor looking stern was standing over me. "Well, you are lucky to be alive young lady. "Someone has made a real mess of you. We've stitched you up, and repaired what we can so you can go home tomorrow, these beds are needed for people who are really ill! "We won't be telling anyone what you have done, young lady. I think nearly losing your life is punishment enough. "There is one thing though that I have to tell you, Julie, He said. "The damage that has been done to you during the... procedure was extensive. I'm sorry but you will never be able to have children! I wished I was dead. Oh God, the shame. I was so distraught but so exhausted I didn't even know how

to react, so I didn't. I realised then, that my mother was sitting on the other side of me, just listening. The doctor gave a short sympathetic smile and left. I turned to my mother and grabbed her hand. "I'm so sorry I sobbed. My mother was expressionless. She held my hand for a few seconds, then sharply pulled them away. She didn't look at me at all. She was ashamed of me. I didn't know it then, but she never did forgive me, and my life living at home would soon be over.
Both Julie and Suki had tears in their eyes. Suki said, "Julie, I'm so sorry these terrible things have happened to you, but you cannot behave in the way you have to this innocent family. I have to let the social services know about this. I can tell there are mitigating circumstances in your case, and I feel you need psychological help to make sense of everything, but you have done something very wrong, and it has to stop now. Julie still crying nodded her head in agreement. "Yes she sobbed I know you are right, and I need to let them know what I did, but please Mrs Kaur, let me be the one to tell them what I have done? "I don't' know said Suki looking confused. "Look said Julie, please will you come with me to the social services, so you can tell them about what has happened to me in the past that caused my crazy behaviour. They will be more sympathetic if you are there. "Please, will you? she pleaded. I could see the lady softening to Julie "Yes I will, but I also have to let Bex and Michael know. The Hate suddenly said in a panicked tone: "Please Suki Please don't tell them, at least not tonight. Let me tell the social services with you tomorrow, and then I will go to see them with you, or on my own to

tell them to their faces what I have done, and apologise? "I'm not sure said Suki, Bex has suffered enough, I don't want her to wait any longer to know she is not in any trouble". Julie carried on crying and looked pleadingly at Suki. "A few more hours, please. "It's only a few more hours. The day is already nearly over. Suki looked intently at Julie, and I could see the compassion in her eyes. "Alright, she said finally. Tomorrow. "Please said Julie, can you come here tomorrow, and we can go together? "No said Suki in a firm tone. "You Come to my home tomorrow. I will keep these photographs till then, and she quickly put the offending photos in her bag. My son is with his Father for a couple of weeks, so I don't have to arrange any pickups for him, so we can just get on with everything, Is that okay with you Julie? Julie nodded like a child. "Ok yes, that would be OK. With that, the nice lady got a piece of paper out of a book, started writing in it, then gave it to Julie. "My address she said. Come about nine thirty am, and with that, she headed for the door. "Goodnight Julie," said the lady, "I will see you tomorrow." Julie suddenly grabbed on to the lady who looked startled, as Julie hugged her. "Thank you she said in tears. "Thank you for everything." "Okay," said the lady as she walked out of the door.

I was exhausted, shocked and very confused "is she telling the truth?" I said to the voice. There was silence for a while, and then the voice answered.
"We will see Melissa. We will see."

Chapter 18

The next few days were spent in a sort of fugue. Michael and I hardly spoke about our fears. We carried on our lives like robots, not daring to think, of what hurdles we may have to overcome. I just spent my time with the girls, dealing with the everyday rituals and normalities, if you could call it that. Michael had told his parents what was going on in our lives, and it made me feel better when they called me at least once every day. Even if it was just for five or ten minutes, it made me feel better. One person who hadn't been in touch was Suki. I was disappointed but understood how busy she must be with her own life. One afternoon, I decided to give her a quick call. I rang the number. It rang and rang, for at least two minutes before I hung up. I decided to call later. As the day progressed I called her a few more times, with no answer. Eventually giving up, I carried on with the day, reminding myself I would call the next day. The next day came, and I began calling, from about eight thirty, hoping to catch her before she might go out. Still no answer. I called a few more times, with the same result. By the afternoon, a slight feeling of unease developed in me. I had Rajesh's phone number. I called again no answer. I felt happier thinking that maybe they were together with Ramon somewhere. I knew though that I also had a mobile phone number for Rajesh, and although I felt uncomfortable using the number, as I didn't want to bother him, I rang the number, almost hoping he wouldn't answer. After about four rings, there was a crackling sound and Rajesh answered the phone.

"Hello, I shouted down the phone. Rajesh sounded like he was in China; the crackling was awful. "Hello, who is this?" "Oh hello I shouted again, it's Bex Schaffer here, I'm so sorry to bother you. "Oh that's OK," said Rajesh, his voice so quiet it was almost a whisper. "I'm calling you Rajesh just to ask if you have seen or heard from Suki recently?" There was a moments silence, and I wasn't sure if we had been cut off. "No said Rajesh finally. "I'm, in Florence with Ramon for a couple of weeks. We haven't heard from her, but I just assumed she was busy, she tends to cram a lot in, when I have Ramon, but come to think of it is unusual for her not to call to chat to Ramon". He carried on: "I think Suki's neighbour Jackie has a spare set of house keys, but I'm sorry I don't have her number? The line was getting even more difficult. "Yes, I replied, what house number is Suki's neighbour's house?" "Number 29" he replied in a sound only just audible. "Damn," said Rajesh, these mobile phones will never really catch on. I could hear him laughing. "Ok, Rajesh I shouted, I will pop over to see her later" I'm not sure if he heard me, as the phone suddenly went dead. I hung up the phone. I remember thinking I wouldn't be buying one of those mobile phones in a hurry if that was the usual reception. It was nearly dinner time, and I knew Michael would be home soon so I would go to Suki's after dinner. Michael came home, at the usual time, and over dinner, I chatted to him about the phone call, and that I would go over to Suki's later. She's probably on some errand of mercy he said cheerfully. "Knowing her you're probably right. We both laughed affectionately at my dear friend. After dinner, Michael said he would deal with the washing up, which in our house meant loading the dishwasher. I grabbed my keys said goodbye and headed off to Suki's home. As I drove up I saw her Toyota Previa parked in the driveway. Brilliant I thought, she's home at last. I parked just outside on the street, and then I saw that there were no lights on in the house. Gosh, I hope she's not in bed. Then I thought it's only eight, so unless she's ill she's not going to be in bed. I walked up to the door and rang the bell and waited. No answer. I rang again and waited. No answer. I bent over and looked through the letterbox. I could see nothing, but there was a smell, and it wasn't fresh baking. I am worried, where is Suki? I have to get inside, so I walked back out to the street and found that Number twenty-nine was two doors down from Suki, and almost identical in look and size. I went up the pathway and rang the doorbell. A very sophisticated lady with snowy white silver hair, and impeccable makeup, and aged about of about sixty came to the door. She looked suspiciously at me. "Can I help you she said in a rather haughty tone. Feeling uncomfortable I said, "hello there my name my name is Bex Schaffer, I'm a friend of Suki Kaur at number thirty-five, and I haven't heard from her for a while and was getting a little worried." "Oh yes, said Jackie, looking even more suspiciously than before. I carried on, speaking faster, "yes I've spoken to Rajesh, Suki's ex-husband and he told me you had a set of spare keys. "I'd like to go and check that she's alright. "Well, she retorted haven't you rang the bell"? "Her car is in the drive, so I'm assuming she is probably at home" I was starting to get you a little annoyed at her attitude. "Yes," I replied as nicely as I could, "I have rung the doorbell, but she hasn't answered, and I'm now worried as I haven't heard from her in nearly a week, so I'd like to go into her house just to check that there is nothing amiss. Jackie looked annoyed. "Well I suppose so, but I'll have to go in there with you, "I can't let all and sundry go traipsing around her house. "No that's okay," I said flatly I understand that, so if it's ok could we go and look now? Jackie sighed as if I'd asked her to climb Everest, at a moment's notice. "I'll go get the keys. "Please stay where you are till I come back, please. With that, she disappeared into her house. I was just thinking she would make a great KGB agent. when she returned she had two sets of keys in hand. She closed her own door, pushed past me and headed off to number thirty-five.

As we reached the door Jackie fiddled around with the key for a few seconds. I believe this door is very temperamental she sniffed. They got a cowboy in to build this vestibule thing. "These Asians are a strange lot. What a waste of money it is, "not even very attractive" I ignored the statement. For a few more seconds she worked on the lock, eventually, I heard that familiar click and the door slowly opened. She walked in first and wiped her feet on the mat. I dutifully wiped my feet also and closed the door behind me.

Jackie walked slowly into the hall……… I hadn't had a chance to walk any further before she suddenly and inexplicably seemed to fall backwards, slamming me against the front door, as I started seeing stars from the shock of the head bashing, I could hear Jackie making the most terrible noises, an almost gagging sound. Regaining my senses, I pushed Jackie to one side. At first, I didn't see anything. What the fuck was happening. Then I glanced up. Can I describe what I saw? For a moment I looked away, But the compulsion to look up was overpowering. The sight that caught my eyes would live with me till the day I died. At first, I was trying to work out whether it was a dummy or a human. I had to look hard, no matter how terrible, I had to know what this was. I could hear Jackie physically vomiting and screaming at the same time. I don't know whether I was calm or in shock, but I looked up to study the horrific sight assailing my eyes.

A body was hanging there. The head lolling to one side didn't even look human. It was blotched and bloated and, almost purple-black in colour. The massive tongue hung out, and around the mouth dried up foam lined the lower mouth area. A massive dark pool covered the glossy marble floor tiles below. I wanted to turn away, but I couldn't. I started to look at the surrounding area, suddenly I could see that wrapped around the person's neck, was a multi-coloured layer of once beautiful fabric now stained with things that I could not imagine. I looked at what were once eyes, now they were black, completely black, and looked as though they were hanging out of their sockets, ready to join the brown congealed stains lying below.

The being looked familiar. What and who was it. The realisation began to sink in. The fabric that had taken the life out of this once living being, was familiar also.

Despite the horror of the face, presented to me, the realisation finally dawned. I fell to the floor, screaming
"NOOOO SUKI NOOOO"!

Chapter 19.

I don't know what possessed me but I suddenly thought of the lack of dignity, for my poor Suki, just hanging there. I ran into the kitchen and rummaged panicked through the kitchen drawers. I found a large pair of scissors, without thinking I just grabbed them and headed back to the hallway. I stood at the bottom of the stairs for a few seconds, terrified. I would have to go close to it, to her! I suddenly drew on all of my strength and ran up the stairs, to the gallery where Suki was hanging. I started trying to cut at the multi-coloured fabric, trying not to look at the swinging Halloween character, that was once Suki. After a few seconds of cutting, a pair of arms wrapped themselves around me. "No, no," said the voice. "Don't touch anything". I looked over my shoulder, and an older man looked straight into my tear stained eyes. "Don't touch anything?" he said firmly, "It's evidence. I've called the police let's get you out of here." "No, I screamed I can't leave her like this. She was so proud and beautiful I can't let strangers find her like this." "It's alright," the man said gently "there is nothing you can do for her now". The man held me tightly and guided me down the stairs, and then despite his age, picked me up and carried me. As we entered a house, which I guessed was Jackie's home, I could hear her in the background screaming hysterically.

The man put me down on the sofa in their living room. He held my cheeks as if I were a child. "Stay here my love, we will wait for the police to come". He left me, and I could hear him trying to comfort

Jackie without success. Was this real? What had happened, to the kindest gentlest person I knew. Eventually, I could hear sirens, but whether they were police or ambulance, I had no idea. Soon the man re-entered the living room with his arms around Jackie's shoulders. She looked as though she were in a trance as he walked her through the room and sat her down on a plush armchair. The man came up to me. "Miss, what is your name? "Bex I said flatly. Bex Schaffer. "Ok, he said my name is Frank Gardiner, and I'm Jackie's husband. "The Police are here and I am going over to Suki's House with them okay." Just hearing her name started me crying again. "Oh God what happened to her" I cried. "Who did this?" "Look, Bex, don't worry I'll be back soon, maybe we can get some answers". I nodded. Jackie and I sat in silence. Jackie looked out of the window, out into the immaculate garden. I sat there reliving what we had both just witnessed. Two strangers caught up in unimaginable horror. After what seemed like an age, Frank reappeared into the lounge. This time he was accompanied by two uniformed policemen. With them were two other people, who I assumed were policemen too. Frank walked up to me and said, "This is Mrs Schaffer. She is one of Mrs Kaur's friends, and it was her, with my wife who discovered the deceased". "The deceased". Just the word set me off again. I was trembling. "Who is the deceased I shouted, Suki, can't be dead, can't you help her?" Even as I said this I knew it was ridiculous, but I just couldn't accept, that this beautiful kind being was not alive. "I'm sorry Mrs Schaffer," said the plainclothes detective. "There is nothing we could do to help your friend." I just cried silently. The reality finally setting in. "Mrs Schaffer, my name is Detective Inspector Jeff Singer, and I will be conducting the investigation into the death of your friend. Would it be possible, if you are up to it, to come into the kitchen, where we can discuss your friendship with Mrs Kaur, and if you have any information that may help us to understand what might have happened." "Yes okay," I said slowly. "Is that okay Frank, said the Detective. "Of course said Frank sympathetically. Frank looked at me. "I used to be a copper, he said, that's how I know these reprobates. A slight smile came from him but I was unable to appreciate it, or respond. Suki was dead! In the kitchen which was mostly yellow and cornflower blue in colour, and very cottage like, unlike the rest of the house, Jeff the detective and I sat in chairs around the large pine table. Jeff took notes, but strangely never looked down to his pad once. He asked me general questions about Suki's age, which I realised I didn't know, marital status, that sort of thing. Our friendship, he asked why I had come to see her, and I explained the reasons for that. Suddenly it dawned on me. "Oh my God, Ramon and Rajesh, they don't know. What will Ramon do without his Mother and Rajesh, he will be devastated" Jeff stayed calm, unlike me, and took down the details that I had told him from my own address book, so he could contact them. No matter how many times I stopped talking to cry again, the Detective was very sympathetic and understanding. "It's all right Mrs Schaffer, I would be worried if you were not upset. "This is a horrific thing to witness, for us coppers, never mind you, who was a close friend of Mrs Kaur". Then the Detective asked me a question that shocked me beyond belief. "Tell me Mrs Schaffer, has Mrs Kaur been exhibiting signs of depression, in the last few months". I was horrified. "Of course not". I was suddenly angry; "Suki is the most together person I know!" "You know Mrs Schaffer," said Jeff, "sometimes people don't always say everything that is going on in their heads" "Are you trying to say she killed herself?" I was indignant and close to exploding. "Suki would never have taken her own life. She would never have left Ramon. He was her life!" The Detective looked intently at me and said slowly. "Well Mrs Schaffer if that is the case, then who do you know who might want to murder Mrs Kaur?

Chapter 20

I felt as if I had been away for a long time. All the new things that I had now seen as well as heard, left me exhausted. Gently, I could feel someone stroking my hair, just like my mummy often did. This time though, it was not Mummy, I was still in my Special Place. I slowly opened my eyes, and before me, was the lovely lady, called Suki. I didn't understand. Why was she here with me? This was the place only I could go. "Hello Melissa," she said gently. I felt so safe in her presence, I smiled. "Melissa I can't stay long, but I just wanted to thank you. I didn't understand what she meant. I know you wanted to help me, and your love and kindness have led me to where I am going now. Please keep listening and watching your Mother and Sister. They are still not safe, but I know, you are aware of that. I felt myself feeling sad. "Don't feel sad?" said the lady. "I am going to be okay. I need to get better first, then I have lots of work to do here. I am going to help others who have passed, in the way I have. I didn't understand what she meant, but she seemed happy, so I didn't feel so sad. I felt her light getting smaller, as she moved away from me. "Goodbye Melissa," she said faintly "Keep Listening" and with that, her light was gone.

Chapter 21

The two uniformed policemen took me home. As we arrived outside, Michael came running out of the house to meet us. As the car door opened Michael almost dragged me out, and into his arms. "Oh, Bex he exclaimed. "I'm so sorry. Michael walked me into the house. He led me to the living room. I sat down on our ratty old sofa. Michael returned to the doorway with the Policemen, and they whispered together for a few minutes before they left. Michael sat down beside me. "I can't believe this he said. "You poor thing, what a terrible thing to see. "Yes," I said slowly. "The police think she committed suicide". Michael turned and looked straight at me, "and you?" He said. "What do you think happened?" "I just don't know," I said tears starting to form again. "I cannot believe, Suki took her own life, but it's also ridiculous to think that she was murdered. I mean everyone loved Suki, she had no enemies, none." "God only knows," said Michael. The police said they will be in touch with us, after the autopsy. "Oh god, an autopsy! Now they were going to cut up my beautiful Suki. Would her indignities never end? I felt sick to my core, but I knew there was nothing I could do except wait. After a fitful sleep. I got up early to be with the girls. I needed to be with them, touch them, hold them.

Two days later I got a call from Sue Harrison the Social Worker. I had almost forgotten my own problems, but her voice reignited my fears. I was dreading what she was going to say. "Bex" she finally said. I have been contacted today, as the investigation into the allegations made against you has ended and I have been given the findings. My heart was in my mouth, and as was usual when my stress levels were high, there was a high-pitched buzzing in my ears. "Bex you have been cleared of every allegation made! "What," I said "Yes," said Sue, almost sounding as choked up like me. "Cleared of everything, in fact, it has been said that this allegation, never held any validity on any level. "Every person we have approached have all said what an amazing mother you are, in fact, Dr Shah, said that you are such an exemplary carer to Melissa. He holds you in the highest esteem and says you are one of the best examples of a mother coping, in a very difficult situation. I didn't hear much of the last bit, as I was crying. Crying with relief, and I'm sure I could hear sniffles from Sue as well. After a few seconds, Sue became more serious in her tone. "Bex, she said, I have to tell you that you must think seriously about what you are going to do next? I didn't understand. "What do you mean, I said? Sue carried on, this was a very serious allegation made against you and could have led to very serious consequences. "Bex, you must think very seriously about taking legal action against Miss Ward, to stop her doing this again. My head was whirring. I was so relieved, yet I understood what Sue was saying, but the last year had been so difficult, and now with Suki's death, I couldn't face any more drama in my life. "Sue," I said, "I won't be taking any action against Julie Ward. I'm sure she won't be getting any care jobs in the near future, and to be honest I will just be glad to be rid of her, once and for all". Sue didn't sound pleased. "Bex," she said, "I understand your position, but I think you should reconsider". "No Sue, I've made my decision, no prosecution." "Okay," said Sue sounding deflated, "is it alright if I call you in a few days after you have had time to think, and talked to Michael?" "Yes," I said, suddenly realising I hadn't even discussed it with Michael. "Yes, Sue," I said "please call me in a few days" "Okay Bex, I will speak to you soon" and with that, I hung up the phone. Later that evening I told Michael, and his mum and dad, about the outcome. The relief was tremendous, although tinged with sadness, the first person I would have called to tell, I no longer could.

A week later I got a telephone call. It was Rajesh. I started to cry as soon as I heard his voice. He sounded broken. "Bex," he said. "I've come home with Ramon". "The police have allowed me to go into Suki's house, as it's no longer considered a crime scene". "Do you know how long before they let…. her go, I said, not knowing, how to respond to this horror. They have said maybe another week, then we can take her home, his voice cracking "Do you mean home here I said?" "No Bex, we will take her back to Pakistan to be buried. It's what her family would want". I found myself feeling emotional. I knew this was the custom, but I felt devastated, as I would not get to say goodbye to her. "Yes," I said trying not to sound upset. "I understand". "Bex," he said, sounding like an awkward young man, rather than the mature grown-up psychiatrist he was. "I was wondering. I'm at the house now, and I am trying to sort out some of her things. I know how much Suki cared for you, and I

was wondering if you could bear being in this house again, that maybe you would like to keep something of Suki's to remember her by? At this stage, we were both crying. "Oh yes, Rajesh thank you. I would be honoured". "When would you like me to come over?" "Is there any chance you could come now, it's just that I want to spend as little time as possible here before I put the house up for sale.
 It was always difficult for me to do things at the last minute, but I answered. "Rajesh, I'm alone with the girls, but can you let me see if I can get someone to babysit, then I can come over for an hour or so, just let me ring around and I will call you back "Okay Bex he said, if you can that would be great, and I would really like to see you too. "Okay," I said, "I'll call back as soon as I can". "I'll speak to you later" he replied and hung up the phone. Now, what was I going to do? Who could I call? I went to my phone book, trying to think off the top of my head who could look after both girls. After flipping through the pages, Jenny Bridge's name came up. She was a trained nurse, and an occasional night carer for Melissa, and was a lovely lady, who had often said if we needed help, outside of her agency duties, I was to give her a call. Well, I thought, now is that time. Being pessimistic, I decided that knowing my luck she would not be home, but I rang anyway. The phone was picked up, almost at the first ring. I was so surprised when a friendly voice said "Hello" "Oh" I stammered as usual, "It's Bex here. Bex Schaffer, you look after my daughter Melissa!" There was laughter, as I knew she could sense my awkwardness on the other end. "Yes Bex, I know you, and how could I forget

Melissa." I felt a bit silly. At times like this, I realised I was still as shy and nervous, as when I was young. "Bex I'm so glad you've called, there's nothing wrong is there?" "No, no I said quickly, and I told her the story. "Of course Bex I'd love to look after the girls. "No problem. I'm not even working tonight, so if you need me for longer that's no problem". Oh, what a nice woman she is I thought. I felt so grateful. "Bex, I'm just gonna let my kids know their live-in-slave will not be cooking tonight, and they're on their own, which will serve them right" She laughed good-naturedly. I'll leave them a note, then I'm on my way" and before I could say any more she put the phone down.

See, I told myself, if you don't ask you don't get. Deep down I knew I'd always had a problem asking for help. While waiting for Jenny, a degree of apprehension hit me, I was going back to That House that terrible place where Suki had perished. The vision came back to haunt my mind, and I hoped I could cope when I got there. Rajesh was going through enough, without me having a nervous breakdown in front of him. Jessica was dashing around the house that day, with the energy of a road runner. Our relationship of late had really improved, and she hardly mentioned Julie. I was so glad, as I never wanted to hear her name again. Jenny arrived about half an hour after our call, and although, Jessica didn't know her that well, she seemed very excited at seeing her, and kept dragging her around trying to show her all her special things, Grover, of course, being the first. "Ahh," said Jenny "I love Gwover he is so sweet" She picked him up and kissed him on one of his eyes, which was starting to wear away, after so much cuddling. Jenny gave Melissa a massive kiss on the lips, which she disapproved of immensely. To be honest, it was hilarious, and we both laughed. "Now, said Jenny off you go now, Bex. "You don't need to call or worry about when you come home. Believe me, after looking after my grown-up brood, these two are heaven". "I will only be a couple of hours," I said, then I picked up my bag, and for a moment, didn't know if I should bring something else. Flowers maybe? No, I thought shut up Bex, just go.

As I drove up to Suki's house, an overwhelming feeling of sadness assailed me. The Toyota was still there, a reminder of that night, although at the moment just breathing was a reminder. I could see a Mercedes outside also, and I assumed it was Rajesh's. I slowly walked up the path, my heart beating fast "Calm down woman. Calm down", I rang the doorbell. About thirty seconds went by before Rajesh came, looking drained, to the door. He hugged me immediately, and there were tears in his eyes. I followed him into the vestibule and stopped. "I'm sorry I said, it's just ..." "It's okay Bex," said Rajesh, "I understand. When you are ready." I took a deep breath. "I'm okay," I said. Rajesh looked at me doubtfully but led the way slowly. As I walked in, at first I didn't look up. I couldn't. I could see all the lovely shafts of light and colour from the chandelier dancing along the walls, and the now clean and sparkling marble floor. Beautiful as it was, it could not disguise the horror that had occurred in this space. Come and have some tea, said Rajesh sensing my intense unease, then we can start. I followed Rajesh into the kitchen that held only slightly warmer memories. While preparing the tea, and trying not to look at those kitchen drawers Rajesh said. "You know Bex I don't understand, how this has happened? I thought things were better you know?" "I'm sorry, I said I don't understand?" "What things?" "You know the depression and stuff." "What!" I said totally floored, "was Suki suffering from depression?" "Didn't you know?" said Rajesh looking surprised. I thought she would have talked to you about it, more than anyone." I felt the tears again, only this time they were tears of hurt. "No Rajesh, I had no idea she had ever been depressed." I was slightly annoyed at myself for feeling put out that Suki had not trusted me enough to tell me. "It's strange," I said, "when I spoke to the police, they asked me if she was depressed……. But I had no idea" "She was taking antidepressants", he added. "She saw her own psychiatrist, but she never really talked to me about it all. She didn't want her ex-husband "analysing" her. I thought they were helping, I mean, she said they were helping, his voice trailing off" We drank our tea in silence. After a while, Rajesh looked up at me. "Bex, I'm sorting out things in Suki's bedroom, shall we go up? "Okay," I said following him, trying not to look. I walked up the stairs behind him, not daring to view right or left. When I took the stairs I practically ran up them.

At the top of the galleried floor. I followed Rajesh into a large bright airy room. There were bold abstract colourful pictures, painted by Suki. Covering the bed was the most beautiful gold quilted bedspread. "I was mesmerised. "Suki made it," said Rajesh, his voice cracking. She was so talented. "Yes, she was," I said, "and in so many ways". We both smiled at each other in a tribute to Suki. On one side of the bed were various clothes, scarves, that I recognised, and could remember Suki wearing. There was also a large, rather old-fashioned jewellery box. Green with gold edging. These are some things I've put aside. I don't really know what to do with them, but I thought there might be something there that you might want? I walked over to the selection of things, and absentmindedly picked up a wrap- around leopard print African style dress. I remembered Suki wearing it. I couldn't believe I would never see her wear it again. Rajesh interrupted my memories: "There are a few bits in the jewellery box, nothing of worth I'm afraid, as you know Suki wasn't really into material things, but I'd like some of it to go to someone who cared. I nodded, not knowing how to answer. "Is it alright if I leave you to it for a bit, there are a few other things I need to sort out" "Okay?" I said already entranced by her lovely things. For a while I just touched her few clothes, trying to remember when, or if I saw her wearing them. Lastly, I opened the large jewellery box. As soon as I opened it I smiled. This was so Suki, bold bright confident, or so I had thought. Most of the items I would never wear myself, but I thought maybe just one piece just to remember. The box was one of those with two different levels. Top area was divided for smaller items, so obviously there wasn't much there, but on the bottom section, a few necklaces were dropped haphazardly inside. As I took out each item and admired it I noticed that

there was an extra section, underneath this tray. I slowly lifted it up and looked in. There were only a couple of items in there strangely though, there was a small black velvet pouch. No label, no jewellery shop name. I picked it up and opened it. Looking inside I couldn't see anything, so I just popped my hand in and felt to the bottom. There was something small in the corner of the pouch, something on a thin chain. I slowly put the chain between my thumb and forefinger and pulled it out. The delicate chain came out of the bag and attached to it when it was revealed, was a rose quartz pendant.
My Rose Quartz pendant!
For a few seconds, I was in shock and disbelief. What, where, and how did my pendant get into Suki's possession. I suddenly felt both confusions, giving way to anger. "My God, had Suki stolen my precious necklace? But why? Suddenly Rajesh appeared in the room. I stood up sharply as if being caught doing something I shouldn't. I had wrapped the pendant in my hand so Rajesh couldn't see it. "Well he said sadly, have you seen anything you might like. I grabbed, without even looking, the scarf lying in front of me. "This I said a little too brightly, I'll take this. It's beautiful! "What about the jewellery," said Rajesh, I'm sure she would have wanted you to have some. "Oh no" I replied starting to head for the door. "I think I need to get home," I said. "The kids are with a babysitter who can't stay too long, so I had better go" "Oh okay" Rajesh sounded slightly hurt, and I felt for him, but my mind was all over the place.
All the time I was thinking,
I thought she was my friend?

Chapter 22

I drove home in increasing anger. Why would Suki steal my necklace? There must be another explanation. It's not even her style of jewellery. She was well off and could afford almost anything she wanted. Why would she take this from me? As I got closer to home, I started to feel more and more confused. This isn't Suki I thought. I realise now she had kept things from me, but this just doesn't feel right. As I turned into my road, I could see blue flashing lights in the distance. As I rounded the bend I could see clearly a police car. It was parked outside my house. "Oh no I said out loud: "No more, please. "No more. I parked behind the police car. I was shaking as I got out. I started running in. "It's got to be Melissa!" I screamed, "it's Melissa!" Michael ran towards me, looking distraught. "Oh God it's Melissa isn't it? Michael seemed hysterical "Bex it's not Melissa. It's Jessica. Jessica's missing! Michael and I ran into the house. There seemed to be policemen and women everywhere. They were into everything. Searching in drawers, cabinets, cupboards." They have to search here first Bex, said Michael, they said it's procedure. Melissa was in her chair, trying to ignore the utter chaos surrounding us. In the distance, I could hear hysterical crying. I moved towards the sounds of fear and panic. They led me to the dining room. The door was closed. I pushed it open. A gust of air hit me, as I realised the patio doors were wide open, letting in the warm air from outside. Jenny Bridge turned immediately in my direction. "Oh no Mrs Schaffer, Bex" screamed Jenny, looking absolutely distraught, "I went inside for a few minutes. Just a few minutes. I'm so sorry" She threw herself at me. I found myself wrapping my arms around her, just to stop her from knocking me down to the ground, with her weight, rather than from any sympathy. At the moment I felt no anger towards her, all I could feel was my own panic! "Someone must have taken her" wailed Jenny. "The back gate was locked, I promise it was locked" I realised then that there was another person in the room. I looked towards them. She was about thirty-five, attractive with shoulder length dark brown shiny hair. She looked very professional, but the stern look on her face didn't endear her to me at all. The woman began to speak, her voice as authoritative as her look. Mrs Schaffer, I'm Detective Chief Inspector Sally Wilson. Please sit down. I managed to prise Jenny from my body. I was covered in sweat, hers and mine. "Please Michael, I said can you bring Melissa in here. Michael rushed off, as myself and Jenny sat down.

"What's happened to my baby I said, looking in both their directions. Jenny carried on crying, but more quietly now. Detective Wilson, told me how, Jenny had said, that "apparently both girls were in the garden with her when she felt that .... there was a pause as She looked at her notes. "Melissa. "Yes, Melissa was not comfortable. "She was upset Bex" Jenny interrupted. "she was in the shade, but she was still unhappy, so I took her inside. "Yes confirmed Wilson, so Mrs Bridge took your daughter inside the house, and put her in a chair, near a fan. "Yes," said Jenny looking like shock was setting in. I waited to make sure Melissa was comfortable then I went back outside, but……. but… Oh God, she wasn't there Bex. "The gate was partly open, so I ran outside and started looking, and calling, but she was gone Bex, she was gone. I looked to Michael, who was wheeling Melissa into the cramped dining room. He knelt down, holding Melissa's hand. He was rubbing his face with his other hand, over and over, as if it was damp. I just stared at the scene before me. "Mr and Mrs Schaffer said Wilson firmly. "I know this is difficult, but please try to concentrate. I looked up at her. Straight into her hazel eyes. "Find my child" I screamed at her. "find my Jessica"! "Mrs Schaffer we have already started to search the surrounding areas. It is more than possible that Jessica opened the gate herself and has wandered off" "The gate was locked said, Jenny.... "I'm sure it was locked? "She wouldn't just leave the garden," I said firmly. "She knows it's dangerous, and if the garden gate was locked, which I'm sure it was, she couldn't have got out on her own it could she! Jenny nodded fiercely in agreement. "Yes she may know, said Wilson, "but children do things they shouldn't sometimes, and from what Mrs Bridge has told us, Jessica can be a little... Wilful, at times" "I shot Jenny a look, and Jenny shrivelled just a bit more. "She didn't leave the garden herself," I said my tone harder. Michael looked at me. "Bex maybe she did, but that's good, isn't it? It means she's not far away, and we will find her soon?" "Yes, Mr Schaffer you're right. It's definitely the most probable, maybe with a neighbour?" "No" I shouted, the fear and anger and despair growing minute by minute within me, she did not leave the garden of her own accord. "She has been taken.... kidnapped. I know she has been taken by Julie Ward! Michael looked horrified, "Bex". Detective Wilson suddenly sat up straight on our dining room chair. "Who is Julie Ward?" And why would she want to kidnap your daughter? I tried to relay the story in as quickly as I could. I didn't want to spend much more time discussing this. I needed the cops to get over to that crazy bitch and get my daughter back. As I rattled off a snapshot of the series of events in our life since that maniac came into it. I noticed scepticism right away from the listening detective. I didn't care. I knew she'd done it, and I wasn't going to waste time. After I'd finished I looked at Wilson and said. "Now you have to get to her house before she hurts my child.

"Mrs Schaffer please give me this woman's details, and we will go to her house, but we have to look at the other possibilities. "There are no other possibilities, I shouted. she's done it! She's taken, my baby! "If you don't go now I will, and I stood up to emphasise my point. "Please Mrs Schaffer, you need to calm down and leave this to us. "Well get on with it," I said firmly. At this moment I realised that the things that had happened to us in the past year had changed me. I would never have spoken to anyone like this before. I didn't care what they thought of me, for once in my life.
I wanted my daughter back <u>now</u>!

Chapter 23

Jenny seemed in deep shock now. She was quiet and still, no more crying, just looking into space. "Can she go home now?" I said to Wilson. "Mrs Bridge said, Wilson. She looked into space with no answer. "MRS BRIDGE" Wilson shouted. This broke the trance. "You can go home now Mrs Bridge; we will be in touch if we need any more information. Jenny looked at me helplessly. "Bex," she said, with more tears in her eyes. I knew deep down none of this was her fault, but I couldn't comfort her, my own agony and anger were too all-consuming. She tried to hug me, but I pulled away from her. She left the room and my home in tears, but I couldn't sum up much pity, it was too exhausting. I could still hear the clatter of drawers being opened, and our things being scattered without care, our private life on display to strangers in uniform. None of it seemed real, except for D.C.I. Wilson. She was real enough, and although I couldn't decipher the looks she was giving me, I was completely sure that it wasn't good! Mrs Schaffer, can you give me any ideas of places that Jessica likes to go to? "The park," said Michael desperately "she loves the park". "Okay, good, Mr Schaffer, we will send officers over there now. Mrs Schaffer, we need a recent picture of Jessica. We may need it if we have to go to the press". "The press. My heart sank. "Where are they searching now?", said, Michael. "I want to help" "It would be better Mr Schaffer if you stayed here". "No I can't," he said gripped with panic. Michael looked at Wilson pleadingly. "Okay said Wilson, maybe you could help, I will arrange for a car to take you there. Michael looked at me. He seemed smaller, a broken man. Michael liked order, now there was none, and there was little he could do, he was lost. "Go on Michael, I said do what you have to, I'll stay here. He almost ran from the house, a fruitless search. Why did I think this, because I was sure? Sure deep down, I knew where my baby was, I pulled Melissa's chair towards me and stroked her cool arm. But, I then had doubts, what if I was wrong? I suddenly thought, If I was, then where was she? Please, God, I thought, don't take her from me. Haven't we been through enough! "Where are they searching now, I said, desperately. "They are searching the gardens and houses in this road, and across at Ashford Fields," she said with resignation. "It's dangerous there, I said with rising panic. "There are ponds and mud pools! Horrible visions encircled my mind. I remembered when a woman with Alzheimer's had wandered off and was missing for three days before they found her body in one of the muddy waters, drowned. How would my little baby cope in a place like that? If she got trapped in the mud, it would drag her under, as quickly as a spider catching a fly. I suddenly felt off balance and clung to the chair to try to stop myself from vomiting. "Mrs Schaffer, I know this is terrible for you, but please try to be calm. If Jessica is out there, I promise, we will find her. "Officers are talking to your neighbours, so hopefully someone will have seen something, it would be very unusual for someone not to notice a very young child on her own". "Mrs Schaffer, can you tell me where you have been this afternoon. I was confused for a second. Why the hell did that matter? "Mrs Bridge mentioned that you were going to see a recently bereaved friend! "Yes, I stuttered, um. My friend Suki was...... found dead last week. Her ex Husband had asked me to go to their house, to choose a memento to remember her by". It was all too much, Suki, and now this! I just sat there and cried. Wilson didn't try to stop me or offer any sympathy, and to be honest I was almost grateful for that. "How did your friend die Mrs Schaffer?" I didn't want to talk about it, to relive it again for a stranger, and I guessed she would have known about Suki anyway" She wasn't sympathetic like Jeff Singer, everything she said sounded like an accusation. Through tears I managed to say, "she ah m..... I don't really know? "I'm sorry she said? I was sure I detected an air of mockery. "We don't really know, if, she may have.... taken her own life. I looked at Wilson her mind ticking, accusing, I could just feel it. "I'm sorry to hear that Mrs Schaffer. "Can you remember the officer who dealt with the case? Don't worry if you can't, we will check ourselves" I didn't know what was going through her mind, except she was adding things up and coming up with odd numbers. "Jeff Singer," I said finally." "Ahh, he's a good man". "Okay, I will contact him for more information". "What has my friend's death got anything to do with Jessica"? "Oh probably nothing at all Mrs Schaffer, it just helps to get a wider picture". "You've been through a lot lately, haven't you! "Yes, Yes I said, It's been a difficult time. I'm sorry for the loss of your friend. I didn't reply, as It didn't sound genuine. "Please, Mrs Schaffer could you please find us a photo of

Jessica. "Yes I said, don't leave Melissa I said firmly. "I will stay here, Wilson replied. I got up unsteadily and left the room. I walked to the living room, where we kept the photo albums. I looked through the most recent ones, which were loose in the book, as they hadn't yet been put into the plastic film to seal them. I looked through them, touching the faces on the pictures as I went. I couldn't believe I was doing this for a police officer to give to the press, rather than giving a photograph to someone who loved Jess and wanted a picture of our beautiful daughter to put in their own scrapbook. I eventually came upon a photograph, not a professional photograph, although there were some of those too. This one was Jessica at Drusilla's animal park, about three months ago. Jessica loved meerkats, so we had gone especially just to see them. I remember it was one of the few places that Melissa was not with us. We had decided that the journey was a bit too long for her, so Julie at the time offered to stay with her whilst we went. It had been a lovely day. We had felt so free, and seeing Jessica's face as we lifted her into the clear plastic dome, so she could see the meerkats playing and fighting in their open area, was priceless. Jess had slept the whole way home clutching a plush meerkat toy, that she had named Biscuit. That was the picture I would give to Wilson. I went back into the dining room and handed the picture of Jessica to her. She took it and looked up to me. "She's a lovely little girl Mrs Schaffer", I promise you we are going to find her. I nodded, not for a moment believing her. "Bex, if there is no sign of Jessica today, it would be a good idea to go to the press.

"You and Michael, doing an appeal to the public. If anyone does have her, after that kind of publicity, it will be much harder for someone to hide her!
"Doesn't that mean then that she will be in more danger, that the kidnapper will panic and hurt her, I choked. Wilson took a deep breath. "I think, Bex that that is a chance we are just going to have to take! It was alright for her to say, it wasn't her child in the clutches of a maniac. "We are sending an officer to support you until Jessica is found. If the press gets involved, he's the one who will advise you. His name is Bill Knight, he's an experienced officer. Wilson explained he was an officer who volunteered to work with families in situations like ours. "How many families has he worked with? "Well," Wilson said looking uncomfortable. "You'll be his first family. Actually. "These volunteers have only been introduced into this area in the last few months. She coughed then, looking embarrassed, as well she might.
"Please, will you go to Julie Ward's house".
"Believe me Mrs Schaffer that is exactly where I am going"! There was a part of me that thought that all of this was a lot of wasted effort. Our child was with that bitch! No one needed her picture. At the moment though I knew I was the only one who thought that. "As soon as I have any information I will get back to you, no matter how insignificant. I'm going to leave you now Mrs Schaffer. Is there anyone we can call to stay with you? "No, I said, not any more. Wilson nodded at me. She went out into the hall and then went through the house informing all the other officers that it was time to leave. I stayed with Melissa in the dining room until

I heard the last policeman leave the house and close the door. We were left alone, just Melissa and me. I wheeled Melissa back to the living room, which seemed not too messy. I picked her up, and together we went through the house. It was horrible. Things, personal things scattered on the bed and floor. My underwear pulled out of the drawer and then just dumped back in. I went to Jessica's room. It was decorated with Looney Toons wallpaper and accessories. She had a Sylvester the cat clock, that had been removed from the wall, and dumped face down onto her Beauty and the beast duvet cover. All the utensils from her Barbie kitchen thrown into the pretend sink. Her clothes rummaged through, and although put back, were still hanging out of the drawers. On the floor her Dalmatian puppy costume, with a plastic head. I picked it up, put it to my nose to smell her innocent smell, and cried hysterically clutching hold of Melissa, unable to stop, till there were no tears left. When I managed to stop crying, I felt a hardening within me. Something I couldn't put into words, couldn't explain. So much had happened, I knew I had to be strong for my girls, I knew they were both in danger, and that somehow, Julie was the cause of it all. My anger exploded. "She's going to die, by my hand or Gods, she is going to die"!

Chapter 24

I felt I was outside, I could feel a cool breeze. Initially, it was relaxing and calming. Suddenly though everything around me turned ice cold. She's here! I knew it, I could feel the evil intent, but where was Jessica? Where was Mummy? I called Mummy, Mummy, please hear me! As my vision improved I could see Jessica. The mist was clearing, and I could see she was in a room that I had never seen before. Its walls were like a beautiful garden, pictures of flowers and animals were everywhere. It was a lovely room, but there was no disguising the dank musty smell that was everywhere. Jessica was fast asleep on a soft bed, with a silky canopy, making her look just like sleeping beauty. I knew this story as mummy often read it to Jessica and me. There were carved animals too, that looked very real. I noticed how deeply Jessica was sleeping and was worried as her breathing almost sounded too deep. I still understood sounds better than seeing, but I felt that I was learning what things were, without actually knowing them, or experiencing them. It made things less frightening to me. Looking around, I didn't think we had been here before, yet there was something familiar, but as yet I didn't know what. Apart from the obvious unpleasant smell, I noticed that there were no windows. None at all. This was strange, and I couldn't think of anywhere that had no windows. Looking around the room I could see there were many things in there, that I knew Jessica would like. Toy dolls, stuffed animals. A playhouse that was too small to play so must have been for the very small dolls. I couldn't see where you could get out of the room, so I tried to look around and focus. I eventually saw what I first thought was a pretty but large picture. Looking closer I could tell it was a door, as I could see the handle. There were lots of locks at least three I think, I'm still not good at counting. Why were there so many locks? I didn't understand. I did realise soon enough that the locks were to keep Jessica in, and not let her out! Suddenly I felt, rather than heard the essence of The Hate, I heard stomping footsteps on stairs, getting closer and closer. I tried to call out to Jessica but she could not hear me. She was still in the deepest of sleeps. I heard the noises as the locks were turned. On the final turn, she walked in. I wanted to stop her going near my Jessica. I wanted to stand in her way, but I knew I could only observe. She slid over to Jessica and knelt down next to her. Stroking her hair, she spoke softly. My lovely girl. Just sleep. I am sorry, I had to make you sleep, you were making too much noise, but I understand. You weren't expecting me to come to get you. You should have been more grateful though, especially after all the trouble I've been too. It's okay though my angel I forgive you. Now just sleep. The Hate headed for the door looking back one final time before closing the door and locking all the locks.

"Can I help her" I called out?
 "Time will tell Melissa".

Chapter 25

 I didn't see Michael for about five hours. When he came back I didn't ask him anything. I already knew the answer. Michael and I hardly slept in the next twelve hours. We didn't leave the living room. If we slept it was only for a few minutes, and only out of exhaustion. Time went so slowly, we hardly spoke. Just saying Jessica's name reduced us to tears. The pain of not knowing was unbearable. At about 2am, when Michael had nodded off uncomfortably in an armchair, I looked out of the window. The street was illuminated with the light of a full moon. I grabbed my cardigan and walked outside. It was chilly, but it was refreshing, and I felt I could breathe. I sat at the bottom of the wheelchair ramp, thinking that I would go to Julie's house. I restrained myself though. The police are going to her house I thought. They will find Jessica there, but it was 2am. Surely they had already been there, and if so, why wasn't Jessica back with us? Was she dead? Had that woman killed her? My brain felt it would implode. I suddenly wished I was a smoker. Isn't that what people do under stress I thought. Just sit and smoke, and try to ease their mind. I envied those people. I had nothing to ease my mind. I stared for a while at the clear sky, moon and stars. "what has she done with you baby? Where are you?

 I waited till eight in the morning before I called the station. The policewoman on reception assured me there were continuous enquiries, and that as soon as Detective Wilson was free she would call us. My desire to go to Julie Ward's house was all consuming. I needed to confront her. To get my girl back. It took all of Michaels persuasive gifts to stop me. How I hated that woman. I was consumed. She occupied my every thought. No matter what I was doing, nothing could drown out her face, her hate. My hate.

At about nine, Wilson rang the doorbell, she was not alone, she was accompanied, by a young officer, no more than twenty-five I guessed. Before she entered the house I said "Have you got Jessica? "Where is she? "No said Wilson simply. I almost collapsed. Michael held me and guided me into the living room. "What happened I demanded before they sat down. We went to see Miss ward, she said in a perfunctory manner. We took a statement from her, that she gave readily, and she let us search her house. "And" I shouted. "Jessica is there I know she is!" "Mrs Schaffer, we searched Miss Wards home, and I can assure you, that Jessica is not there".
"Then she must have taken her somewhere," I said, my mind and stomach churning. "No, Mrs Schaffer she is not there, and she did not take her, you are mistaken". I grabbed hold of Michael, "she is there Michael" I said, "she took Jessica I know she did". I realised how insane I sounded, but what was I to do? Just accept what was being said to me. I knew the truth, at least I think I did. I broke down in Michaels' arms. "Where is she Michael, I cried, where is she?" With great swells of tears, Michael cried too. "I don't know Bex, I just don't know".
"Bex said Wilson finally, this is the officer I spoke to you about yesterday. I had no memory of what she had said yesterday. I looked at her confused. "This is detective Bill Knight". Looking uncomfortable the young man introduced himself as

Police Detective Bill Knight. "I've come to spend some time with you, and offer my support". He looked like he'd just got out of police training college. What fucking support could he give us? I didn't have the energy to make polite conversation, and it was Michael who was left to make pleasantries. Melissa was now having minor spasms in her chair. She wasn't happy. I knew she sensed something was wrong, how could she not. I could see it in her face. Her body language, there was panic there, just like me. The policeman looked at Melissa with the usual pity and sympathy. "Um…. I was wondering he said, maybe I could organise some care for Melissa while all this is going on, it must be difficult to cope in the circumstances". I shot him a look that implied - idiot. I hoped he read the sign, it wasn't meant to be subtle. "Mr... what's your name?" I said "It's ah…. Bill……. Bill Knight". "Well Mr Knight, my youngest daughter has been kidnapped, do you really think I would be parted for one second from my other child. Tell me, detective, does that sound like a sensible option to you, considering"? "Bex please," said Michael looking embarrassed. "I'm sorry, Bex is stressed she hasn't slept, well, neither of us have slept". "Please don't apologise for me Michael". "if this is the best you can offer can you please piss off," "is that polite enough for you Michael?" The officer seemed less upset than Michael. "Mrs Schaffer I totally understand your position. I'm a complete stranger coming into your life, at the worst possible time. If you want me to leave I will, and I will admit I am not highly experienced in this field, and I would imagine I

have already made mistakes, and for that I'm sorry. I'm just here to help you, not just emotionally, but practically. I can call the police station if you need me too. I will get hold of Detective Wilson when you need me too. I can even make tea!" There was silence as Knight and I looked at each other. I could see he was trying his best. All the while Wilson watched me, her hackles rising. I could see I wasn't her favourite person, but then for once I wasn't looking to make friends in all this, I just wanted my daughter back, and I was beginning to feel that Wilson, would not be the person to do that, and that made me terrified. "Please, can I make some tea" Knight suggested. "Yes please that would be kind of you," said Michael. He got up to go to the kitchen, and as he tried to move out of the living room he bumped into the door frame. He rubbed his head, then carried on through into the kitchen. "I think that guys in the wrong job". Michael was as upset as me but I was beyond caring about anyone else. Suddenly the doorbell rang.
We both jumped up.

Chapter 26

I rushed to the door. There was another officer I didn't know standing in front of me. "Who are you," I said irritated. "Mrs Schaffer, I'm Detective Stevens can I come in?" I led him to the living room. He sat down, next to Wilson. "Sorry, I'm late Ma'am, home emergency. She shot him an evil look. "Well you're here now she said obviously furious. "Mrs Schaffer we have been to see Miss Ward". "yes," I said, "you already told me" "Yes" she replied, and as I said earlier, "Miss Ward was very accommodating" My head was spinning. "Mrs Schaffer we would like to talk to you about the abuse allegations made against you"! "What" I cried. "Really?" "It was Julie Ward that made those allegations, and I was cleared of everything. I should have done what was suggested by my social worker, and pressed charges against her, instead of letting her get away with it!". "Is that really the reason why you didn't press charges?" "what the hell are you saying?" said Michael, suddenly, very angry. "I'm not saying anything. I'm just asking a simple question". "Of course that's the reason," I said, confused, what other reason could there be? "Could it be, Mrs Schaffer that taking the matter further would have incurred more investigation into the accuracy of the allegations"? I really couldn't believe it. Julie Ward was on form again I thought. Letting these stupid cops believe she's not only innocent but that I'm still guilty of child abuse. I started to laugh, the laugh of the damned. Julie really was cleverer and more devious than any policeman. Already they were on her side and believed her evil lies. Wilson though suddenly changed tack.

"Mr and Mrs Schaffer, it is time we went to the press. "We cannot waste any more time. Please, will you agree?" We both nodded. It seemed at this point we had no choice. I realised that I had to look at the possibility that Julie had not taken Jessica. I had wanted to believe it was Julie, as the alternative to that was just as unthinkable. Thinking Julie had taken her was the easiest option for my mind to process.

"I will call the press office now," said Wilson getting up and disappearing into the kitchen, where Knight had also disappeared to twenty minutes ago. Within two hours a BBC van had parked outside, and our house was again filled with people. These people seemed much kinder than Wilson, and her gang. We sat in our living room in a daze as lights were set up, and a microphone was attached to both of us. The interviewer was very gentle. She said her name was Mandy Sawyer, and she said if at any time we wanted them to stop filming they would and if we didn't like a question we did not have to answer it. In the end, not many questions were asked of us. As the red light went on, Mandy asked us just a little bit about Jessica. It was surreal, but we answered the questions as best we could. Michael broke down, but strangely I didn't. I wanted people to know about our daughter. I wanted to get things cleared out. I wanted them to understand and help us. The interview ended as quickly as it had started. I could hardly remember what we had said, but I knew there were tears on my cheeks. Mandy said they would edit what they had, to fit in with the news time slot. She kissed us goodbye, and I wished she would stay, as she seemed the only one who showed any genuine sympathy. Afterwards, Michael, myself, Wilson and Stevens sipped tea, finally made by Knight, and sat in silence. "After this, all comes out," said Wilson eventually, "I have to warn you both, that the press will be everywhere. Please, I'm asking you do not talk to them. They will twist everything you say to get television ratings or sell papers" Yes, I remember thinking, they will anything for ratings, so what are you doing this to me for?

Chapter 27

Wilson and Stevens left us after the tea. She had asked us whether we wanted her to be with us when the appeal was aired. No, I had replied. She was the last person I wanted by my side at that time. As the evening news time approached, we sat together, Michael and me, holding each other on the sofa, and Bill looking slightly nervous sitting on the armchair. Melissa in the middle, hopefully not knowing anything. As the credits ran, the main news at the time, was the horrible and unforgivable massacre of school children by a lone gunman in Dunblaine, Scotland. We watched stunned, as the story unfolded. The news item was understandably long. It was horrible and made me realise the evil that lurked almost undetected in our world. Suddenly Jessica's face filled the screen, on seeing her Michael began to cry, and I had a rock-hard lump in my throat. The newsreader's voiceover announced in dramatic tone: two and half year-old Jessica Schaffer, from Ashford Kent. Is missing, possibly kidnapped from her own back garden, her parents have made an emotional appeal for her safe return to them. The screen was filled with us. I couldn't remember anything we had said, and it was like hearing it for the first time. Michael and I both looked a mess. I realised I sounded like some kind of robot. I hope they realised that I was like that because I didn't want to break down. I listened as I said to the camera, "please, to the person that has our Jessica please please return her. She will be missing her Mummy and Daddy, and her older sister. You will not get in trouble, please tell us where she is, so we can bring her home". The camera seemed to hover on me. I looked cold, stressed, and shocked, at least I thought that was how I looked. Suddenly another picture appeared of Melissa, myself and Jessica. Where did they get that I thought? As the report ended I said out loud. "where did that picture come from? Michael looked at me, and I knew. "Why Michael, why give them a picture of us all, "I don't want Melissa in all of this! "Wilson said it would help to have a family picture! "So then why aren't you in it, my anger rising with every breath? "Well, she really just wanted you guys. "I don't understand? "Well Bex, Wilson thought there would be more sympathy for us if Melissa were in the picture. "What" I bellowed, as I stood up. "You damn idiot Michael, how could you let them use Melissa's disability to get the sympathy vote. Our child has been stolen, isn't that enough? How much more sympathy do you need!" Knight looked embarrassed to be a part of this argument. I stormed out of the room, but where could I go. We were going to become prisoners in our own home. Our privacy shot to hell.

Within minutes of the television broadcast, the phone started ringing. It was the press, from every paper, every television station, there were even calls from abroad. I was scared. Scared of their questions: "Why were you not with your children when Jessica was taken? "Is it true that your friend committed suicide because you were having an affair with her husband? "Does Michael know? And on and on. Scared to give answers. Mindful of what Wilson had said. Why was this about me? I couldn't fathom. Bill had eventually disconnected the phone.

"They'll be here in force tomorrow, he said. Don't worry I will come before 7 am, so I'm here when this all kicks off". "Bill," I said, "how is any of this going to help us find Jessica? All they seem interested in is lies and finding some kind of scandal". "Bex I know it's awful, but it might be the only way to find her. "There seems to be no sighting of her as yet. We just need one lead, that could change everything". "I'm sorry, I wasn't very nice to you, Bill," I said. "Listen Bex don't apologise, however, I can help you I will if that means you give me a slap every now and then, well that's alright" I looked at him and smiled, tears in my eyes.

Wilson and Knight weren't kidding, by eight in the morning there were, it seemed dozens of press outside our house. If we went anywhere near the window, a crescendo of clicks and flashes assailed our ears and eyes. At first, they rang the doorbell incessantly until Bill said they would be arrested for harassment if they carried on doing it. Thankfully that stopped most of them, but not all of them. Occasionally one of them would shout some ridiculous puerile question through the letterbox, they seemed far more interested in our private lives than in helping to find Jessica. This was all truly a nightmare. Time moved so slowly. The third day of Jessica's disappearance, and we were no closer to finding her. No evidence. No sign of where, or worse, with whom she had gone with. It was like she was a ghost, just disappeared. Late that afternoon the doorbell went, again, I got up. "No Bex, I'll go said, Bill. He opened the door. I could hear the loud voices and shouted questions from the press, but I could also hear familiar voices. "It's Mum and Dad said Michael jumping from his chair, and running to the hall. "Bex", cried Michael, come out. I almost ran to the front door. "Oh Bex, Jack cried. I almost collapsed into their arms. Thank God you're here cried Michael thank God! After the emotions had calmed down Jack and Angie joined us on the sofa, Bill going off to making more tea and coffee. I had not spent a lot of the time with Michaels parents, but they were always lovely to me and had welcomed me into the family, but I was nervous about them staying with us, especially in this situation, and the fractious relationship between myself and Michael. About an hour or so after Jack and Angie arrived the doorbell went again, and again Bill went to open it. It was Wilson and she wasn't alone. She came into the kitchen where we were all just sitting around the table.

"Have you found Jessica? "No, Mrs Schaffer. We would like your permission to search your house". "I'm sorry I don't understand; you've already searched our house". "Yes, but we would like to do a more thorough search". I was so angry, I wanted to say no, but I knew it would put us in a bad light if we did, so I breathed in and gave her permission. "When do you want to do it? "Now, Mrs Schaffer". I looked at Michael and we nodded, resigned to it. The house was full again with policemen and women. It was a warm evening, so we all decided to get out of the house and into the garden. We sat on garden chairs, as my home was violated again. "I don't understand this," said Jack, "if they have already searched your house, why do they need to do it again"? "I wish I knew" I replied. One thing I was sure of though was that whatever it was it wasn't good. After what seemed an age, we watched them as they left the house, with some of our possessions in bags. "What the hell do you want that for?" said Michael angrily, as my laptop was taken. They were in the house for nearly two hours. They left carnage behind, even worse than the first time, so together we all started the process of clearing up, including Bill who I liked more and more. I couldn't tell exactly what was taken, but it seemed to be things like computers, our private address book, and random letters. We were all too exhausted to search in depth as to what was taken, especially as we were innocent, we had nothing to hide.

It was a baptism of fire for Jack and Angie. Jack raged as we tried to clear the thoughtless mess. "I cannot believe you can be treated this way it's disgusting". Most of the rant was directed at Bill. It seemed every piece of anger we directed at the police was always directed at Bill Knight. Where was this leading us I thought. Was I not behaving in the way I was supposed to? Was there a formula for grief and loss, if there was I hadn't read the manual. Later on in the evening, I was alone with Bill in the kitchen, as Jack and Angie, were playing catch-up with Michael, which I had no energy to be involved in. "Bill I said nervously, what's happening. Is this normal, for the police to behave in this way towards a family in our situation. Bill sipped on his tea, not meeting my eyes. To be honest Bex, in a case like this, in many instances it is someone who is close to the child, who hurts them. I do not for one minute believe this to be true in this case, but without any other evidence to go on......." "We are the prime suspects right"? Or is it me, who is the prime suspect"? "I know, Wilson's tactics are a little, harsh, but if she doesn't look at every line of enquiry, then she wouldn't be doing her job properly. It might not seem it, but she will find Jessica, and if that means making your life uncomfortable, that's what she'll do! I laughed, with the agony of it all. "Bill, I'm scared". "I know you are, but you're a strong woman, Bex. Stay strong and you'll get through this, we will find Jessica, and soon this will all seem like a horrible dream". "I hope you're right Bill". Somehow I didn't believe it. Angie made some food, and I tried to settle into what would probably be another restless and long night.

There was a banging on the door. I was confused, what were the press doing now. I looked at the clock. It was six in the morning, too early even for them. I could hear Jack's raised voice downstairs, Michael was wide awake now, we looked at each other, fear rising. Suddenly I heard heavy footsteps coming up the stairs. My heart was beating a mile a minute. Two people entered our bedroom, with Wilson at the rear. "What the fuck is going on" cried, Michael. I was terrified, rooted to the spot. "Mrs Schaffer" Wilson directed her cold look towards me. "What do you want I said in quiet fear. "We would like you to come to the police station, for questioning, concerning the disappearance of Jessica Schaffer. "What I said" utterly confused and terrified. "Please get dressed, Mrs Schaffer" I turned towards Michael, wanting him to help me but knowing he couldn't. Michael was screaming at her, so much so Wilson threatened him with arrest if he carried on. "It's Okay Michael," I said trying to calm him. "I will go, I'll be okay, Michael stays calm". I quickly got dressed, in the jeans and top, I had been wearing the day before, they were still lying on the back of the chair. As I left the bedroom, one of the officers held onto my arm. "Let her go you bastards, she hasn't done anything" I turned back and looked frantically at Michael. "What's happening, I started sobbing as I was led out of my house, like a criminal. There was a few press outside, and their cameras snapped, as I was dumped unceremoniously into the back of a police car. Michael had run out of the house behind me. "I'm coming he screamed at me, through the car window. "I'll get help, Bex. I promise!" His voice sounded muffled, but all I could do was watch him in terrified despair, as the car drove off with me in it, lost and alone.

Chapter 28

I stayed close to Jessica. I could now hear and see her. Not all the time, but a lot of the time. The Hate spent a lot of time with Jessica in the special room. She was always trying to keep Jessica happy. She would play with her, disappear for a while, then return with a toy or food that Jessica liked. Jessica was not happy though. "I want my Mamma". "Where is my Mamma? "But Jess, I'm your Mummy now, you don't need her. She doesn't love you like I love you. She doesn't want you back. She is happy with Melissa now. Jessica would cry when she said this. "It's not true she would cry. "No, it's not true Jessica! I would call back. "Mummy loves Jessica. Sometimes The Hate would get angry, in the way that I always knew she could.

I don't know what day or time this was, but The Hate had brought Jessica fruit, which I remembered she loved, but Jessica was unhappy and tired, so she refused to eat it. The Hate shouted, picked up some of the fruit and tried to force it into Jessica's mouth. She almost slapped the red fruit onto her face. Jessica was panicking, and her breathing was so heavy, and as the fruit was forced down, Jessica made a terrible choking, gagging sound, and spit up all the fruit. I was scared, as The Hate was so angry, everything The Hate felt on the inside, was now showing on the outside. She raised her hand to hit Jessica, then stopped. She lowered her hand. Jessica was screaming hysterically, and I wanted to scream too but couldn't. "I know you're tired she said grinding her teeth, I'm going upstairs, but I will be back later, and you better start behaving, or there's going to be trouble. She stormed out of the room, and I listened as the door slammed and all of the locks clicked. Jessica just sat and cried and cried, and I realised I was crying too. I could feel my face was wet, like in the bath, yet different. I couldn't help. I just watched. I just said, It's ok Jessica, I know you can't hear me but I'm here. I love you and I'm trying to help. After a few moments, Jessica's chest stopped heaving, and her crying became less. She seemed to be calming down. Oh, Jessica, I said. It's going to be all right I promise, I don't know how but I'm going to get you out of here. I realised I was crying again.

"Issa, Issa, Jess wanna go home"

For a moment I was stunned. Was Jessica saying my name?

"Issa, I miss mama" *I couldn't understand, but I repeated.* "Jessica" "Yes Issa, me wanna go home!" *Could she hear me? No one but the voice could hear me.* "Jessica please listen," *I said, try not to make Auntie Julie angry, and soon you will come home".*

"Jessica why don't you go to the sink and wash your face, it is all red". *Jessica giggled.* "I'm all red". *She giggled again.* "Jessica, can you hear me?" *I felt fear and other feelings that I wasn't even aware of.*

There was quiet, and I realised I must have made a mistake. Then suddenly: "Of course Jess hears Issa"

My sister could hear me. I felt so happy. I didn't understand how, but it didn't matter, she could hear me.

I soon realised that Jessica couldn't always hear me, but I found when I concentrated hard, she could. Maybe I can help her I thought. I've got to help her.

*I was resting, when the voice came to me.
"Hello Melissa," it said.
"My sister can hear me," I said joyously. "yes, of course, she can. Love can cross all borders. You know Melissa now you are needed by your family more than ever. Only you can change the outcome" I didn't understand every word it said, but I knew I had to help. How can I help them? "Follow me, Melissa". I suddenly felt the strangest feeling. I was moving fast, not like in my wheelchair, but like the flying feeling, when mummy spun me in my play chair. I remember her doing it once and suddenly feeling terrible. "Oh no," mummy said, "she's going to be sick, she doesn't like the swing". Well I don't know what sick is, but I felt it again, only it wasn't as bad as in the swinging chair. Suddenly things slowed down and the sick feeling went away.
We were in a big room with lots of people. They seemed very busy and were talking fast, to each other and talking into a plastic thing. I seemed to be hovering over the people. I knew they couldn't see me. But now my eyes were fixed on one man. He was looking at something and concentrating as I do sometimes. I just watched him for a while, but I had no idea who he was, or why I was there. "His name is Sam," said the voice. "Do I know him?" I said "No Melissa, you don't know him, but you need to get your Mummy to know him, he will help you to get Jessica home" "How do I do that?" "Just*

concentrate," said the voice, " you know how to concentrate". I felt the voice leave. I didn't know what to do. Concentrate on what? I didn't know, so I did what I always do, I just listened and watched. "Cutlack," said a voice that frightened me. Sam stood up and followed the voice. He went into a small room, where another man, with lots of lines on his face, not like Sam at all, was standing. "Cutlack" he shouted again. Who's dealing with the Jessica Schaffer case? "Ah um," said Sam, "Matt Smith, but he's off with flu" "Flu Screeched the man. "We haven't got time for flu, by the time he gets his lazy arse back here, a body will be found, and the story will go to the Sun or Mirror. "Well to be honest Guv no matter what, I think the story will go to them anyway. It always does. "My God" bellowed the man, his face getting redder and redder, "whatever happened to ambition around here?" "Well Dave, working for the Ashford Chronicle, kinda knocks it out of you. you know what I mean?" "Jesus said the man, don't you want the opportunity to cover something other than the Ashford Women's Guild cake competition?" "Well yes, of course, said, Sam. "So Cutlack, what are you sitting here for, Bex Schaffer has been taken into custody for questioning. I need you to get over there, and get us a story before the tabloids do". "But Guv, there will be hundreds of reporters there, all wanting the same thing, and none of them getting it". "Matt said he sat all day outside the family's house, and no one comes out". "And that's it, is it"? "So you just give up. "Look Cutlack, the readership numbers of this rag is in a shit state. If we can't up it soon, you won't have a job to cover at all". "okay" said Sam, "when do you want me to start". "now for Christ's sake. "Now"! "But sir, I'm writing the piece about the cat rescued by the fire brigade". "The man gave Sam a look of something that I just couldn't describe. "Get your lazy arse to that Police station, and don't come back till you get me a story". "Okay," said Sam not sounding happy, or convinced of his own abilities. "Listen to me Cutlack, just to let you know, there are going to be changes around here, and people are going to have to be let go........ Don't let it be you!" I watched as Sam slowly, went back to his screen, and turned it off, then he walked out of the big room. I was unable to understand in any way, how this man was going to help my Mummy or Jessica.

Chapter 29

I sat alone in a small room, looking around, and taking in the ugly aertex walls, badly painted, a pale blue. No windows, just a stark table, with a tape recorder on it. It felt cold, but that was ok because my whole being was on fire. Terrible fear mixed with fury at the injustice of it all. What was I doing here, I should be waiting at home, and these damn idiots should be finding my Jessica. Tears filled my eyes, but I wiped them away. "Why should I show them I'm scared. I didn't want to give them the satisfaction.
Suddenly the door opened, and I almost jumped out of my skin. Wilson and Stevens entered the room. I shot her a hateful look. Damn bitch I thought, I'm not letting you get to me. They both sat down. "Bex said Wilson, "It's Mrs Schaffer to you, only my friends call me Bex". "Ok, she replied, a little amused, Mrs Schaffer, we have brought you in for questioning, concerning the disappearance of your daughter Jessica. Would you like us to appoint a solicitor for you? For a moment I thought about it. I didn't know what evidence Wilson thought she had on me, but I didn't think she would pull me in unless she thought she had some kind of a case. "Yes, I replied I would like a solicitor. Wilson looked shocked, she obviously hadn't expected me to say this, and to be honest neither had I. "you know Mrs Schaffer she replied, trying to brush off the surprise, waiting for a solicitor to be appointed can take a while to organise, wouldn't you like to get this over with now, rather than have to spend time in the cells waiting. I shivered with fear,

thinking that they were going to lock me up, but I had to play Wilson at their own game. "I want a solicitor now!" I said trying to sound calm. I wanted out of this place, but I didn't want to get myself in a hole, that Wilson had dug for me, then not to be able to get out. I felt if I was stuck here with her trying to pin something on me, then I might never get Jessica back. It suddenly felt clear to me that the only one to get Jessica safely back home again was me. "Ok said Wilson. She left the room and returned with a uniformed officer. Constable Jenson will take you to the cells while we sort a duty solicitor for you. I stood up unsteadily and followed the officer. I had left the house with nothing, except what I was standing in. They took my rings, the pendant necklace that I had been wearing since finding it at Suki's house. They let me keep my wedding ring though. Everything was done in a perfunctory way. I was led by the officer, to what seemed the back of the police station, and to a long corridor with about six cells. Officer Jenson opened the cell door and waved me into the cell. "Would you like a cup of tea, love, he said in a friendly manner. "Yes, I replied, yes, please. "Okay," he said "sugar or no sugar?" ."Sugar, yes please" Jenson closed the door, and there was a clanking of keys as he locked the door. I sat on the cold horrid excuse for a bed and shook inwardly. What the hell had I gotten myself into? Hours seem to have passed. Suddenly the door opened and a woman looking like she was in her late 20s to early 30's walked in. She smiled at me. "Hello there Mrs Schaffer, my name is Megan Weiss, I've been appointed as your solicitor, while you're here. She sat down next to me. "I don't know exactly What they have on you as yet Mrs Schaffer, but I don't think it's much, otherwise they would have arrested you by now. "Okay," I said, confused, "I don't understand, I've never been in this situation in my life before". "You must be scared, I know, but the best information I can give you when you are questioned is to say as little as possible. Wilson is good at fooling people in an interview room. She will try to tie you up in knots. If you feel confused just say, No comment. Don't answer without thinking, that's what she wants you to do. She will make you feel guilty, even if you're innocent" "but I am innocent" I replied, tears falling, "I haven't done anything wrong". "Well that's good" she replied putting her hand on my shoulder, "then listen to me, and we will get you out of here as soon as possible".

Megan called the officer. He walked with us back into the same interview room as before. Megan sat by the simple table, and I sat beside her to her right. She turned to me, winked and smiled. The door opened and Wilson and Stevens came in again. Wilson looked irritated, she had been caught short, with my asking for a solicitor, and she didn't like it. They both sat down opposite us. "Hello, again Mrs Schaffer and Miss Weiss". Megan nodded, and Wilson forced a thin smile. "We will be recording this interview," said Stevens. "Gosh," I said, "I didn't know you could even talk". Wilson shot me an irritated look. Stevens turned on the tape recorder, said the date and time, and then Wilson read what was called the caution. I had heard this statement a million times on television shows,

never once believing that a police officer would ever say them to me:
"You do not have to say anything. But it may harm your defence if you do not mention when questioned something which you later rely on in Court. Anything you do say may be given in evidence."
"Now Mrs Schaffer, looking like a lion eyeing up her prey, we have brought you here today, just to have an informal discussion with you, about your missing daughter Jessica, and some other examples of information, that has become available to us.
 Is it true that a former employee of yours accused you of child abuse? I looked at Megan. She shrugged, "Yes I," said trying to be calm, "but this former employee had a grudge against me because I fired her, which is why she made those allegations, just to get back at me". "Is there a reason that you didn't take legal action against this employee after you had been cleared through lack of evidence of said child abuse" Megan interrupted Wilson. "My client was cleared of these charges because there was no validity to them, not through lack of evidence". "Oh yes," said Wilson, "I'm sorry". "Detective inspector", I said, "I have already told you these things before in my home, I don't know why you feel the need to ask me again!" Megan looked at me as if to say. Stop talking, so I shut up. "Can I ask you, Mrs Schaffer, where were you on the day that Melissa went missing". "I've told you this before too. "I was at my deceased friend's house that afternoon. Her ex-husband had asked me to come over, as he was clearing the house, before selling it, and wanted to know if I would like a

small memento to remember her by". "And did you take a small memento, Mrs Schaffer". Suddenly I felt guilty, but I knew I hadn't done anything wrong, except take back what was mine. Megan sensed my unease. "I don't really see what that has to do with anything," she said. "Well it's just that," said Wilson "we were wondering what your relationship was with Mr Kaur!" I laughed with derision. "If you think I was having an affair with Suki's ex-husband you are wrong, and if you've spoken to him I'm sure he has confirmed that". "Yes" nodded Wilson "he has indeed". "There is one thing though". She took out a page from the file, a copy of something, and put it in front of me. "Please, could you read this Mrs Schaffer, and then please confirm if you wrote it". Megan snatched the paper, read it then handed it to me. "You don't need to say anything about this". I felt scared and took the letter from her.
I read the note, and as I did I felt shocked.

Raj, I am going insane at the moment without you. When are you going to tell Suki about us? You're divorced, so you are not doing anything wrong. I am going to tell Michael soon, that we are going to be together. I can't bear him near me. The only touch I want is yours. Please don't ignore me, as it makes me upset. I love you. I want to be with you. I will be with you. Please contact soon, Bex xxxx

I looked at Megan, horrified. "I didn't write this! "I promise I didn't write this! "Have you spoken to Rajesh, I said to Wilson, "he will tell you this is ridiculous. "Did he tell you he had received it? "We have spoken to Mr Kaur, and he has confirmed he never received it, that doesn't, of course, mean that you didn't write it". I threw my hands up. "This is a joke I said. "I can guess who wrote this rubbish, but I can assure you it was not me!" "Ah said Wilson, are we still now talking of Julie Ward, the Woman whom you have continually, since the day of Jessica's disappearance, verbally attacked and accused, not only of Jessica's kidnap but now this? I'd fallen into her trap, and she was loving it. "I believe Julie Ward has my child, and I know that she must have written this.... this rubbish", I said throwing the paperwork at her stupid face. "Ok said Wilson, please don't get upset, and be careful who you accuse, as Miss Ward is already on the brink of putting forward charges of harassment, and defamation of character". I put my hands to my face. I wasn't crying, I was just angry, no not angry. Murderous. I wanted to kill Wilson, and then kill Julie Ward!

"What else do you have Detective Wilson", said Megan, trying to restore some form of order, "this is becoming tiresome". "A letter that the so-called receiver never actually received". "Anyone with access to Mrs Schaffer's handwriting could have written this letter". "Yes," I said "anyone!" "We also have your laptop in our possession" Wilson added. "We have checked the browsing history, and there is something that disturbs me. I made no answer, I couldn't imagine what was coming next. "There are certain searches on your computer, that are not the normal searches of a regular suburban housewife". "Oh God get on with it," said Megan, "are you trying to play barrister and detective, we are not in court! "Yes," said Wilson looking a little embarrassed, at her own arrogance. Wilson took more printed pages from the file. "Mrs Schaffer, this was a search done on your laptop, the night before the death of Mrs Kaur, I would like you to read it" She pushed them in front of me. I began reading them. They were searches about hanging…

The best way to hang yourself.
How to commit suicide by strangulation?
What are the best materials to use to hang yourself?

I couldn't stop myself, it was all too much. I just sobbed. I knew now how Suki had died, and it was at Julie Ward's hands, but how had this search been done on my computer? How could Julie ever have had access to my house and computer, after she had already left us? Suddenly my blood ran cold. The keys! I thought, she must have had a copy of our house keys cut! It made me feel horrified, that that woman had got back into our home, probably whilst we were all still in the house. Her clever conniving evil knew no bounds. She was scared of nothing, feared no one, as long as she could achieve her wicked goals. The sudden realisation was of course that Suki had not only been murdered but could have only been killed by Julie's hand. It was all too much. As the shock built I now found that I was finding it difficult to breathe. I looked in panic at Megan. "Mrs Schaffer please will you calm down so we can finish this interview". I tried to ask what was happening, but I couldn't talk, and I couldn't breathe. "She's having a panic attack," said Megan, "stop the tape!" I fell to the floor, and with panic rising, my lack of breath became all-consuming. I can't remember what happened, till a bag was produced and I was ordered to breathe into it. A man was there that I didn't recognise, he was helping me though. "Breath Mrs Schaffer," he said gently" Just breath". My breathing calmed, and the terror subsided until I started thinking of Suki's murder, and the attack started again. I don't know how long it took before my breathing returned to normal, but as the bag was eventually removed from my mouth, I saw the look on Wilson's face, that said loud and clear. She's faking It!

I was taken to another room, where I was given some tea and a couple of plain biscuits. Megan entered the room. "Hello, Mrs Schaffer are you feeling better"? I nodded, but how could I feel better, I had just found out that my dear friend, had suffered that horrific death, by a woman that I had brought into her life, and I couldn't convince anyone, and my daughter was still missing, with the same woman responsible, and no one would believe me, no one. "I think we should carry on the interview tomorrow," said Megan. "No I said, I need to get this over today. Please, Megan, I'm alright, I want to carry on". "Okay Bex, if you're sure, I'll let Wilson know" and she disappeared from the room. After what seemed an age Megan returned "Still okay to carry on she said in an uncertain tone. "Yes," I replied, "I'm ready". Megan walked with me back to the interview, it was as though they had sat there in judgement, the whole time I had been away, but I knew that wasn't the case. "Please sit down," said Wilson, "are you feeling better?" I didn't answer her, she didn't care, so I felt there was no need to play the game. "Are you ready to continue Mrs Schaffer she said?" "Yes, Detective Wilson I'm ready". The recorder was switched on again. "Mrs Schaffer, at the end of our last interview, we showed you some searches on your browsing history, do you need me to show you the copies of these again?" "No" I replied, I would never forget, what those copies said, ever! "All of this so-called evidence is without any foundation, and "none of this is proof of anything," said Megan. "Anyone with access to this computer could have done these searches, and it was not my client". "Well, Mrs Schaffer, what have you to say about these searches. I looked straight at Wilson with all the hate I could muster. "I didn't do any of this, I am being set up". "Set up by whom, Mrs Schaffer". I did not reply to her question, I just reiterated, "I'm innocent". There was quiet in the room. "Mrs Schaffer, how long have you been friends with Mrs Jennifer Bridge?" "I'm not friends with Jenny, she's one of Melissa's night carer's". "I see, so she's not a friend, yet you left her alone with your two children". "One would think you would be wary of leaving your children with a virtual stranger, especially if what you said about Julie Ward was in any way true! I stuttered "Well she wasn't a stranger, she's a trained children's nurse, and I wanted to go to my friend's house to help Rajesh". "I see," she said tapping her pen irritatingly on the desk.

"Have you ever lost your temper with Jessica?" I looked confused, as I looked at Megan. "The question is ridiculous," said Megan. "Jessica is a toddler, and anyone would find it hard to believe that any mother has not lost their temper with their toddler, wouldn't you agree!" "Ok then, have you ever lost your temper enough with Jessica so that you shook her? "NO" I shouted, "of course not, I have never laid a hand on either of my children". "Look, Mrs Schaffer, I am not accusing you of anything, I am just trying to get the facts, and clarify things".

"Your life must be very difficult at times, mostly on your own, dealing with two young children, and one with such severe disabilities, it would be quite understandable, if things just got too much". "No, I have never 'shook' Jessica as you say, I have never touched my girls in an aggressive way. I love them and I would never hurt either of them. Anyway, Jessica went missing when Jenny was looking after them. If I had done something, she would have to have known". I couldn't believe this was happening. It was obvious Wilson believed I had in some way hurt Jessica. It was difficult to process this whole situation, I just put my head in my hands. "I'm sorry to upset you Mrs Schaffer, but you must understand, we have to ask these questions". I just shot her a hateful look. "We are coming near to the end of our questioning, but there is one more question I would like to ask you". "What's that," I said wiping the last of the tears from my eyes. "Is it true that on the evening of seventh of May 1995, you said to Mrs Jennifer Bridge, that you wished your daughter Melissa was dead!" "What!" I couldn't believe it, and I couldn't speak, for once, however, there was a grain of truth in what Wilson said. I remember we had had a week of dreadful times with Melissa. She was suffering so much, and nothing we did seemed to help. She had pneumonia again, and the antibiotics weren't working. She was suffering so much. She could hardly breathe. I remember that night sitting with Jenny, listening to Melissa's agonising attempts at catching her breath. I can't bear it, I had said to Jenny. How long will this go on for, how long will she suffer like this? I don't want it to go on any more. If I could I would take it away, there is no point in her living like this. I wish God would take her, so she can be at peace. Don't say that, Jenny had replied. She'll get through this. Will she, I had sobbed, I don't think I can take much more. Of course, I was in despair. I didn't mean it. I couldn't believe that Jenny would tell them what I had said, in what was a dreadful situation. She must have known I didn't mean it, how could she tell them, so they could use it against me? "Mrs Schaffer, can you please answer the question, did you say to Mrs Bridge, that you wished your daughter Melissa was dead". My head was down, I felt despair and anger, all at the same time. I lifted up my head, glanced at Megan, then looked straight into Wilsons eyes. "NO COMMENT". I looked at Wilson, wanting to tell her that Julie Ward had my girl, but I thought, what's the point, She didn't believe me. No one believed me, and I wasn't sure that they ever would. There was silence for a minute. Wilson eventually sighed. "All right Mrs Schaffer, I think we have finished our chat for today. I'm sure we will talk again, but for the moment you are free to go". I looked at Megan, "Can I go" I asked her. "Yes Bex, you can go. I got up as fast as I could. Megan walked out into the hallway with me. "Bex, if you need me just call" she handed me her card. "Thank you I said". "You did well in there Bex, you spoke too much, but mostly you held your ground, you did well" She smiled shook my hand and started walking away. Suddenly she turned. "I think your husband is waiting for you". "Thanks" I whispered back. Wilson came out of the room and gave me a look, that I couldn't read. As Wilson walked past me she said. "One thing Mrs Schaffer, has Jessica got a passport? I was surprised by the question. "er, yes, I replied simply. "Mmmm," she said, her brain whirring. "We haven't found one in the house! The fluid filling my ears deafened me with the pressure, and I steadied myself on the wall with my hands. She's going to take her out of the country, I thought, and no one is going to do a damn thing about it! If someone was determined enough they would get Jess out of the country... Wilson slowly walked out of sight. Another interview door opened, and a woman looking extremely upset emerged, as I looked closely I realised it was Jenny. What had they said to her I thought, how frightened was she, that she had felt the need to say something that incriminated me, in Jessica's disappearance? Were they trying to implicate Jenny as well as me in this case? Maybe they thought we were in it together, and that Jenny was just covering for me. It was all unthinkable, but I knew what they were capable of. As I walked into the reception, Michael and Jack were waiting for me. Just seeing them I burst into tears. "Michael it was awful just awful". "I know baby it's going to be alright I promise. He hugged me. "Bex my love," said Jack. "There are dozens of reporters outside. We have no protection from the police so we will have to make a run for it, to the car". I felt sick. I hadn't eaten for hours and just felt extremely weak. They both held me on either side, and we headed for the door. I could hear them loud and clear before we set foot outside. As we exited we were being pushed from all sides, Michael and Jack trying to protect me. They were like a pack of wild animals. I just ran with them, not knowing in what direction. "Bex" someone screamed, "Did you murder Jessica?" "Bex, why did you do it?" "Bex, where is Jessica's body?" The inhumanity was astonishing. We eventually reached Michael's car, and it took all their strength to open the door, push me in, then get themselves in. I put my face in my lap, trying to drown out the sights and sounds. Michael was swearing as he tried to get out of the car park. They seemed happy to be knocked down, rather than move, we were moving at such a slow snail pace. Just so as not to hit them, I just wanted to scream. Leave me alone, you fucking bastards. Eventually, we began moving faster and then the car screeched away. On arriving at home, there were a few reporters, but not enough to stop us getting into the house, quickly and safely. When we arrived home, it took us all a while to recover from the awfulness of which we had just been a part of. As I cuddled Melissa, I was still shaking from our experience in and out of the police station, and shuddering, as I thought of that awful conversation with Jenny Bridge. Angie hugged me and told me to go and have a bath and try to calm myself. It sounded a good idea, I just wanted to be alone.

I went into the family bathroom, where I had bathed my two girls, so many times. I filled the water with cheap bubble bath and got in. It was too hot, but I felt the need for the physical pain, almost as if to match the mental pain and exhaustion I felt. I sunk down, into the bubbles, never wanting to emerge again. I held my nose, and put my head under the water. There were silence and a feeling of immense calm. I felt I needed to come up, but held on to my nose, not wanting to carry on with this madness. I started to splutter, as I released my hand from my nose, and the hot water rushed into my mouth and nose. I wanted to hold on. Hold on till it was all over, suddenly I felt a strong hand pull me from the water. I choked and spluttered, feeling sick, having inhaled so much water, I hung over the bath, coughing, and trying to release the soapy water from my lungs I looked around me, expecting to see Michael, but to my surprise and confusion, I was completely alone. I still looked around, but I was most definitely the only one in the room. I felt afraid, and guilty too. I sunk down under the bubbles again, covering my arms which were cold. What had just happened? Had I imagined it? I didn't know, but I knew one thing. I hadn't dreamt it!

When I eventually came downstairs, Angie had cooked another meal that no one would eat. Even when I thought I was hungry, as I did now, as soon as the food was put before me, I would feel nausea rising, and I had to push it away. After a while of pushing the pasta around my plate for a while, I apologised. Angie seemed to understand. "It helps me having something to do she said". It was getting late, but I sat with Melissa for a while, with idle chatter going on around me. It was comforting for a while, to pretend things were normal. I realised I had fallen asleep when Michael nudged me. "Go to bed Bex, you look exhausted. Michael took Melissa, but before he did, I kissed her gently. I needed to sleep. I got into bed still in my robe, and feeling very cold brought the covers up to my neck. I knew in my heart that Julie had murdered Suki, but why? I had no idea. They hardly knew each other. The pain was becoming too much, I felt completely alone, and still feared it was me, whatever the outcome, who would be accused of Jessica's disappearance. I felt I was going crazy, I put the duvet into my mouth to stifle my cries of fear and despair. When I eventually woke up again, it was dark. I looked beside me, where Michael lay snoring, for a while I just watched him. It was amazing how sleep could disguise the pain within. I got out of bed, slipped on some leggings and a t-shirt. Melissa's baby monitor was on, and I could hear her gentle breathing, interrupted by a little hiccup or snore. I realised there was no carer tonight, or probably for any other night, from now on, in fact, we had almost now given up on them. I suspected, that some of them secretly believed I had something to do with Jessica's disappearance. I crept downstairs, I went to the kitchen, put on the kettle and waited. I made myself some coffee, and sat in the darkness, just thinking, as, that was all there seemed to be time for nowadays. I sat for a while embracing my coffee as it got colder and colder. I stood up and looked out of the window. All the reporters were gone, yet across the road was a black ford escort. I doubted it was the press at this time of night, it was probably the police. They were sure I was guilty, and it looked like they were in it for the long haul, till they could find, any scrap of evidence to convict me. I sighed, resigned, yet my desire to be outside, and to feel some air in my lungs was overwhelming.

I grabbed my cardigan, slipped on my trainers and went towards the back door, and into the back garden. I stood outside for a while breathing in the musty air. I desperately wanted to walk, as I hadn't been anywhere since this whole thing started. I walked toward the back gate, the same back gate where Jessica had been taken from. When I looked at the lock, I realised that she could have reached it to unlock it, although why she would have wanted to was a mystery, unless of course, someone had been on the other side, encouraging her to open it or they had their own key. I unlocked the door and headed outside. I looked around me. It was a boring middle-class estate. All the houses were the same, building by numbers. We had been here two years and didn't know many of our neighbours, and the ones we did, we were only on nodding terms too. Ours was a corner plot, that had been the show house originally. I pretended at the time that having the biggest house on the estate, held no interest to me, I was lying, however, as I couldn't help but feel a little smug. I was disgusted at my own shallow thoughts, I couldn't believe I had attached such importance, to something so utterly trivial. We lived in a faceless place, with other faceless people, in a boring town, living a boring life. It was ironic that now I wished I was back to being one of those boring, ordinary people. I suddenly toyed with the idea of driving to Julie Ward's house, but I knew I'd be in trouble. I was being watched and probably followed, and wouldn't get away with it. I knew it would make Wilson's, and Julie Ward's day if I did. I knew if Wilson could get me charged with something, even if only harassment, I knew she would. I started wandering away from my house, to the one and only green area, where there were housed a few wooden benches, and some newly planted trees, that would probably take years to grow. No swings or roundabouts. They didn't want to encourage the children to play outside! I remembered how the neighbours, that we didn't know had made a fuss when we needed to install a ramp for Melissa's wheelchair, perhaps it was making it far too obvious that there was someone disabled on the street. It ruined the facade. The street where some thought they were better than others. They, who thought they were going up the ladder of success, sitting in our faceless detached boxes. Let's not ruin the image. The ramp made them feel guilty when all they wanted to feel was superior. They didn't want to feel that it could happen to them also, that money didn't buy protection.

It was a humid night, and incredibly still. The sky was slightly cloudy, and looked a little spooky in the night sky, as clouds swirled across the milky moon. I came closer to the green area, as I approached though, I got a shock, as I suddenly realised, a man was sitting on one of the wooden benches. I was slightly afraid and wanted to turn back, but I had come to a point where I had no real

fear, as things I believed couldn't get any worse. To be honest I was more annoyed than afraid. It was late, why was someone outside at this time of night. I understood the irony, so I carried on walking closer and closer to the figure on the bench, as I was almost upon him, I noticed the piercing but the small glow from a cigarette. "Hello, the man said, looking as surprised as me. I couldn't find my own voice but sat down next to him anyway. I half turned towards him. "Hello, I managed to say. "What are doing out here so late the man asked me? "I don't know I stuttered as always when I was nervous. "I couldn't sleep; besides I could ask the same question of you? "Ah he replied flicking ash from his cigarette, an addiction I'm afraid, as you can see, not allowed to smoke inside. "I take it you live here, the man said. I was relieved, as it seemed as if he hadn't recognised me. "Yes," I said number seventeen on the corner, not realising that saying this, gave my identity away. "Ah" was all the man said. He didn't offer any information, as to his own whereabouts on the estate. "Would you like a cigarette? You look like you need one" "Well I shouldn't really... I mean... I don't any more".
I started to remember at school when my mother was dying. I missed so many lessons, yet still pretending to be the good girl, to keep mum happy. It was only when I sat at the back of the gym block, bunking off, where I would meet other students trying to be cool, and smoke with them, feeling a strong sense of release from everything that was going wrong in my life. I felt it from the very first puff. "Come on," said the man "it'll only kill you" and he chuckled. I turned towards him and looked

at him for the first time in the misty light. He was younger than he sounded. His hair was a dark brown. He had a floppy fringe, and as we spoke more I noticed how many times he pushed it away from his face, almost in anxiety rather than need. He was about thirty-ish I would have guessed. Heavy set eyebrows, with piercing eyes, that I couldn't tell the colour of, which made me a little uncomfortable. Slowly I went for the packet, and with two fingers pulled out the evil weed, and put it to my lips. He then snapped his lighter and held it towards me. As I inhaled I was worried for a moment that I might embarrass myself and cough, especially as I hadn't had a cigarette since god knows when? My first inhale was light, as I didn't want to choke. It felt good, but the second-deep inhale was amazing, and strangely for the first time I felt a small sense of release. I exhaled long and low. "Wow," said the man you definitely needed that". He put his hand out "My name is Sam" He smiled, as I shook his hand. Even though the air was cool, his hand felt warm and strong. I held on a little too long. "Sam," I said. "Really" "Yes he said looking at me in bewilderment, and not a little amusement. I don't usually make up names for myself when I meet new people. I felt my face redden, and I was so relieved it was dark so he wouldn't see. "Oh, I'm sorry it's just that Sam was my Mother's name". "Has your Mother passed away?" Sam said showing concern. "Yes, she died when I was eighteen of cancer. "I'm sorry, that must have been tough. "Yes, I said, thinking of her, it's nice to say her name" To lighten the mood, I said, "I'm Rebecca, but everyone calls me Bex". "Do you live near?" I said? "Yep," he said looking away, pretty near. He didn't elaborate further. "Okay," I said bemused. We sat in silence for a while, as I couldn't think of any more to say. "Are you the mother of Jessica Schaffer?" he said suddenly. I was so disappointed. Damn, he does know me. I didn't answer. "You know it's hard not to recognise you from the papers and the news," he said. "Yes," I mumbled, "and from living in the same street". "Oh yes," he added, "that too". "It must be difficult to live in this street now mustn't it," I said apologetically. "Who cares about the other people in this street. You're the one who is going through hell on earth", you shouldn't care what other people think. I know I said, not sounding in the least convincing, despite this his words made me feel touched and emotional. He must have seen the glint of tears in my eyes. "I'm so sorry he said I didn't mean to upset you, but I don't know how you're coping." "I don't know either," I said wiping my tears. "Are you any closer to... "Well, you know? "Depends what you mean I said. As I said it I almost hit myself. Another person to tell your madness to. "Sorry said, Sam. "I don't understand? "Forget it, I shook it away. "It's late and I'm crazy. "Look said Sam, you don't know me from Adam, but sometimes it's better to talk to a stranger. "That's what one of the reporters said to me recently I replied bitterly. Sam suddenly looked away. "I'm sorry," he said "oh no don't say sorry, at least, I know you mean it, and are not just after some story for the paper" Sam didn't respond, he just shifted in his seat. He looked uncomfortable, so I guessed I had said too much. "I'd better go, I said "NO," said

Sam so loudly it echoed across the street. For a moment I felt worried and hoped the police in their car hadn't heard him. "Sorry I didn't mean to shout, it's just it's nice talking to you. "yes it's nice talking to you too. "I don't want to be nosey but are you any closer... "NO, I said. No closer. The police think I did it! "What said Sam, but that is ridiculous. "Thank you for the vote of confidence, I said, wishing the police thought the same way. "What evidence do they have Bex"? "Nothing really I said looking out into the blackness, just a few lies and rumours, trouble is I think they believe them, which means of course they have, I think given up looking, not that they would admit to that though. "Bex do you have any suspicions or anything? Strange question I thought, can this guy read my mind. For a moment I stayed silent. How could I tell this stranger my real fears and beliefs, especially as I was the only one who did believe them? "We've been through a lot you know, I said. "Yes I can't even imagine", "I mean before Jessica...you know. "Yes I've heard about your other daughter, I'm sorry I don't remember her name. "Melissa," I said. "Her name is Melissa". "That's a beautiful name," said Sam, smiling at me. He was definitely handsome. His teeth were only slightly yellowed from the cigarettes, and his smile was sweet, yet I detected a little sadness about him. He looked like a guy with something on his mind. "We used to have a carer for Melissa and Jessica, but she turned out to be a head case so I let her go. She had become obsessed with Jessica" "but surely Bex, she must be the main suspect in this"? I laughed in frustration. "Yes Sam you'd think so wouldn't you, but she is a very clever woman, I think it was actually her that made the police first to begin to really suspect me. She did things...... I decided not to divulge any more. I had said enough. I couldn't believe I was talking to this complete stranger, yet it helped to try to unburden myself. It felt easier with a stranger, I felt I might not be judged so harshly, although why I thought this I had no idea. In the dark on that park bench, it didn't even feel real, it wasn't like I was talking to a real person, who might have an agenda of some kind, just a kindly neighbour, who would listen, then walk away, back to their own life. I don't know how much I had said, but after I finished we both sat in silence. I had not looked at him whilst I was talking, Now I turned to face him and realised he was looking at me. "Bex" he said in a strong yet gentle tone. "Let me help you!

Chapter 30

Sam asked me to give him the address of Julie Ward. "you mustn't go anywhere near her, she is dangerous, also if the police are watching me, in fact, they are watching from the car around the corner, just waiting for me to slip up, if they catch you snooping you'll be in trouble with them, and I can't let you do that." "Bex, look all I'm going to do is watch her. Why would police be watching me? You said it yourself, they don't even think she's a suspect, do they? Also "I'm not going in all guns blazing, I mean I don't know her, and besides, even you have said Bex, that you could be wrong. "Yes I suppose, but you shouldn't get involved. "You don't know me, Sam maybe I'm the head case? "I doubt it said Sam kindly, and anyway I'm a big boy, and I can look after myself, and make my own decisions can't I?

"Yes I know, but don't you have a job or something to go to? Sam slightly stretched his neck, both right and left, so I heard the crack. It made me shudder. I hated things like that. I'm self-employed, which in English actually means that I'm unemployed", he said not looking at me, so I guess I'm free. I didn't know if this Sam could be trusted, but there was something about him, that seemed to be, genuine, and I guess I needed a friend after Suki, I had been so lonely. There was no one to talk to, someone who was on my side. Could such a strange chance meeting with Sam, be the answer to my prayers, a new friend. Someone to help me to get my little girl back! I had to make my moves now. I had to do it for me, but I also had to do it for Jessica.

Sam and I exchanged phone numbers, but of course, he couldn't call me at home. It was now I wished I did have one of those silly mobile phones, even though the reception was so bad. "If you are going to watch Julie I said, please don't let her see you. "I don't know if she has Jessica, or if she has, where she is keeping her. "Please don't worry said Sam interrupting. "I'm just going to watch her, that's all. If she is hiding Jessica somewhere, I will find her. "Ok I said, it felt so good to have a friend. I'll try to get to a public phone somewhere to contact you, but I might not be able to. "Don't worry Bex I'll find you said, Sam. I stood up and walked slowly back home, leaving Sam on the bench, I walked a few steps then turned around. I waved lightly at Sam, and he waved back. I went back in through the back garden, and back to bed. I didn't sleep of course. I was thinking of Jessica and Sam until the Sun came up.

Wilson called early the next morning. Michael spoke to her, as I could now no longer bear to see or hear her. When they had finished their conversation Michael said, "Bex, Wilson wants us to do another appeal for Jessica's return, but this time, with all the press there. "We can write our own statement, and they can ask us a few questions, but we don't have to answer them. "What, I said, you mean, and then they will make us both look guilty when we don't answer. "She's probably trying to make us both look guilty now! "I don't think that's true Bex, I don't think we have a choice, we need to do this. I looked at Michael feeling exhausted. "Ok Michael, if that's what you want. I was too tired to argue anymore, even after the way I was treated by Wilson, he still thinks she will get Jessica back. Bill told us that the appeal would take place at our local village hall. He was calm and encouraging as always, but I was under no illusions about him. Ultimately he was a copper, and their job was to find and convict someone if they couldn't do it through hard police graft, it looked like it was going to be me, that was the culprit, of whatever deed they thought I had done. Bill was nice, but he was a part of them. He wanted information, and he thought I had it. Wilson came to the house on the day of the appeal. The press was swarming outside. The whole thing made me feel sick. We headed towards the front door. "Michael tried to hold my hand, but I felt smothered by him and pulled away. His look of hurt was tangible. "Wilson had observed the scene. "please hold hands she said. It shows solidarity. Without blinking I took Michael's hand and headed for the unmarked police car outside. There were only a few reporters outside as we got into the car, which was unusual. "Where are all the press I said surprised? "They are already on their way to the meeting hall, she said matter of factly. "No surprise I thought with a shiver. As we turned up at the meeting hall, only a few miles from our house, I could hear the rising sound of voices reaching to a crescendo as the car drew near, thankfully the car carried on past them and drove to the back of the hall. A caretaker was waiting to open the gate to let us through. We pulled up at the back door. I had been to this meeting hall, a few times for birthday parties that Jessica had attended. How ironic, we were now here to plead for the person who had abducted Jessica to bring her home. We went into the back of the meeting hall. There was a small changing room, where we sat and waited for the vultures to settle, as they had been let into the hall. Wilson prepped us again, without much empathy as to what to say. I found it hard to listen to this woman. How could one woman be so, cold to another woman in this situation, although I knew she did have a job to do, even if that meant suspecting me. I sometimes felt whatever she did now wouldn't be right in my eyes. I disliked her, how could I not, after the things she had accused me of. I didn't listen to much of what she was saying, as I couldn't hear. My ears were blocked so much, with anxiety, that I had to keep swallowing to clear them.

As we stood up and headed to the main hall, Michael held my hand again. His was clammy and sweating, so much, I wanted to pull away again, but I knew it was wrong and cruel to do so. The door was opened and we walked in slowly. We were instantly blinded by what seemed like thousands of light bulbs. The clicking, the noise, it was unbearable. There was a long table. Michael and I were guided to the middle of the table, and Wilson sat to my right, and other officers, I think, filled up the extra chairs. Wilson spoke first. She was puffed up like a peacock. Our misery must be the highlight of her career I thought, as I watched her. I felt a thousand eyes on me, accusingly. There were things alluded to in the press, where I felt they also, suspected my guilt. "I wasn't grief stricken enough for them, I wasn't sympathetic enough for them. Was I having an affair with My dead friend's husband? Was everything just an act? I remember thinking if I was acting, yet was not upset enough for them, then it showed I wasn't much of an actress. As we walked in I could see the accusations in their eyes, real or imagined I didn't know. I opened the A4 piece of paper with our written statement on it. I read it out loud. "Our beautiful daughter Jessica has been missing for nearly five days now. We have recently discovered that her passport, which was in our house, is now missing. Light bulbs flashed, blinding me for a few seconds. "Although the police are looking out for her at airports, train stations, we implore you to keep vigilant, as to her whereabouts. Please as we have said in the past, please, we are begging that to whoever has our daughter, please return her to us, as the agony for us... her family is unbearable. Please bring her home soon. I stared down at the paper, tears in my eyes. I finally looked up, the bulbs and camera's flashing like a lightning strike. Wilson asked the line of press to begin their questions, so many came at once, at first we couldn't understand what they were asking? Wilson asked for calm, then again questions were thrown at us, but less randomly. "Bex" do you have any idea who may have taken your daughter? I didn't answer immediately, but looked at Wilson, just for a split second. I knew I couldn't say what I wanted to say, what was on the tip of my tongue. "Please go to Julie Ward's house, I wanted to scream. "She has my Jessica; she has my girl! In the space of my silence, flashes went off in my face. I was dazzled. I saw rainbows in front of my eyes. I tried to concentrate. Wilson strangely touched my arm gently. I leaned close to the microphone in front of me. "I don't know who took

Jessica? "I just want to beg the person who has taken her, to please bring her home to us. She is our baby please bring her back. My throat was so dry I could hardly swallow. "Bex, what else do you want to say to the person who took Jessica? "I stuttered, please I want them to know they are not in trouble, just bring her back please, safely to her mum and dad. We love her. We miss her. My voice cracked. This was a nightmare. I could not believe it was me saying these things about our own child. "Michael was crying, but also realised I could not speak any more. Michael took over. "Jessica is our youngest and our eldest daughter Melissa misses her sister very much. We all miss her. "What's Jessica like they asked as more lights flashed. "She's beautiful. Said Michael slowly. "She's got a strong will though, and she lets us know what she wants, she loves her toys, especially ....Grover" he said trying to not break down. I looked towards Wilson. She understood. That is all for today, she said. Thank you, ladies and gentlemen. As we stood up the lights and noise heightened again, as we moved away more, questions were thrown randomly at us, almost rhetorical questions as if they didn't seem to expect an answer. "Do you think she's still alive Bex? "Are there problems in your marriage "Bex". "Do you think she knows her abductor, Bex? "Bex". "Bex" "Bex".

Chapter 31

I was listening to Mummy and Sam. I couldn't see them. I was tired from concentrating. I would speak to Sam when he was alone. He didn't show me if he could hear me, so I didn't know if it was helping, at times Sam was difficult to try to connect with. When he was at home, he would drink a lot of brown liquid from a large bottle. It would make his head very messed up, so it was difficult to get through to him. He had bad nightmares at night and sometimes would scream out in terror. I tried so hard to reach him, but he was a sad person most of the time, unlike mummy, who was sad, but only when bad things happened. Sam didn't need bad things to happen. The voice would tell me that Sam had had a very bad childhood. He wasn't like me surrounded by the love of a mummy. He had been hurt badly as a child, but the voice wouldn't tell me in what way, he would just say, that a person who should have looked after him, hurt him very badly, and because he had kept it a secret, the pain would eat away at him, causing him terrible pain. He couldn't trust anyone and sometimes wanted to hurt himself. The voice told me, helping mummy would help him, although he would not find peace until he let go of all the pain and hurt. Can I help, I said. The voice told me I couldn't help Sam, He himself needed to ask for help, and I was just too young to do that. I was glad though that I had got him to talk to Mummy. It must have worked. I didn't want Sam to be sad, maybe helping my Mummy would help him get better.

After I had rested I watched Sam go to the big place again, with all the same people, talking and talking. "Cutlack", screamed the man with the lined face. "What news have you got for me about the Schaffer case?" Sam looked really tired. He was drinking something that he obviously didn't like, as each time he drank it, he pulled a face like I do when I don't want something done to me.

"I've got nothing much Guv he said. "Did you go to the press conference today? "Yes Guv, of course, I did. I knew Sam wasn't telling the truth, as I knew he was not there with Mummy. "So Cutlack, what else do you have? Nothing Guv, at least not at the moment. "What do you mean nothing? "As I said Guv I went to the house, rang the bell. No one answered. I went to talk to a few neighbours, but most of them didn't seem to know the family very well, and most of them complained about us reporters hanging around all day, blocking the streets with our cars. They weren't friendly, so I hung around, to see if I could catch anyone who might come outside. "And did they then, he said angrily. "No Guv no one came out. I stayed till 11 pm when the lights in the house went off. I hung around a bit longer, then I left. "I've decided though to go back today and speak to more people, just to see if any of the other reporters have seen or heard anything. I'll also see if I can get any information from a couple of copper friends I've got. "Ok said the man well get on with it. "God knows what I'm paying you for? Drinking coffee and talking to your mates it seems, well piss off and get on with it! Let me know when you get anything? "I will," said Sam. He walked out of the room and threw the horrible

tasting stuff in a box. I didn't understand why Sam didn't say he had talked to mummy, to the man. He didn't do many of the other things he said he'd done either. He wasn't like the other men and women who were outside mummy's house, trying to find out things. He wanted to help mummy. I could tell he didn't care about doing what the old man demanded he does. I watched Sam get in the car, and start it moving. Where are you going, Sam? He didn't answer. I watched him drive whilst listening to music, which I loved. I loved listening to singing, especially Mummy. Here in the Special Place, it sounds different, it makes me calm when I am upset, it helps me sleep too sometimes. I love those sounds. After a while, I knew where he was going. He was going to The Hate's house. He stopped his car a few houses away from The Hate's door, and on the other side of the street. I could hear Sam thinking, I'm going to get you, bitch, he said, trying to hurt a child. I am going to make sure you don't get away with it. Sometimes I wasn't sure if it was The Hate he was talking about. He carried so much anger, but not as The Hate did. He was kind and gentle. It made me feel bad seeing him so sad and alone. Sam lowered himself in his seat. I'm not sure why, but he just sat there for...... so, so long. I became tired. Can I go to sleep? I said to the voice. Yes, Melissa sleep now, Sam is there watching, all is calm.

Chapter 32

We were all completely drained after the appeal. It seemed to intensify our fears. I didn't feel better for having done it. I felt dirty somehow. It seemed an exercise purely for the press and those who wanted to be voyeurs in our agony. After the appeal, there seemed to be even more press outside. I felt like a caged animal, pacing the house, terrified of even going out to the back garden in case I was spotted, which I always was. They were everywhere, the same shouted questions over and over again. "Any news Bex? "Please talk to us "Bex. I couldn't understand how they thought using familiarities would fool me into talking to them. The papers were filled with the story. Our beautiful Jessica's face plastered over every newspaper, fodder for a hundred gossiping conversations, over coffee and a Kit-Kat. Tabloid stories, from people we didn't even know, talking of the "double tragedy" in our lives. A severely disabled child, then the abduction of our so-called "Normal child". I wonder if they would have cared so much if it were Melissa who had been abducted? But then who would want to do that they intimated? Life was a living nightmare. Five days of agony. Would any of this ever end? There were times I wished I weren't alive. I would hold Melissa for hours, terrified of the future, and if Jessica were alive, or lying, cold and alone in a ditch somewhere.

Melissa could tell. She could feel the atmosphere. Sometimes I would talk to Melissa, telling her my fears, and despite the fact that she was also just a baby, I saw and felt an understanding in her. One evening I was holding her, a tear trickled down her porcelain cheek. She very rarely cried with tears. I knew that she knew. The evening after the appeal, when everyone was pretending to be asleep, and the house was in darkness, I had decided on not going out in the dark, as some of the reporters were staying long into the night, of course, the same police car was in its usual place, so I wasn't going to risk it. It was about one-am I was alone. Michael had decided to sleep in Melissa's room. Since this, all started, and the carers stopped coming, and sadly a couple of them, had gone to the press, telling them personal things about our daily life, which was mostly conjecture, as most of them only came at night, so we could sleep. There was no one to trust anymore, except Sam. Old school friends talked to the press also, and of course, the press found out about the death of my mother. Once that came out, I was painted as a troubled young woman dogged by tragedy and death. At times in black and white, it didn't seem too far from the truth.

I was often comforted by the dark. The silence. Not having to make conversation, when all you wanted to do was rock back and forth in a corner, trying to block the pain. I looked out of my bedroom window, looking at nothing in particular. Suddenly I saw a wave. I backed away. Damn, I've been seen. I went back to the window and slightly moved the curtain to see. I saw him standing there still waving. I moved the curtain all the way back. It was Sam. I ran to get my cardigan and tripped over as I was putting my trainers on, slamming my head on the back door. I was more worried that I would wake someone up, rather than the pain on my forehead. I tried to calm myself before I set foot outside. As I eased myself outside the door, I looked around, just in case. I ran to the back gate and slowly opened it. Sam motioned me with hands to come over. He started leading me to the benches where we had first met. When we got to the green, I felt breathless, but I didn't know why. We didn't talk at first. Sam handed me a cigarette like a furtive drugs dealer. I took it, and without words, he lit mine then his own, and for a few seconds, we just sat together inhaling the dangerous nectar, as if it were oxygen to breathe. "Bex I've spent all day outside Ward's house, and I'm telling you something is definitely not right? I felt my heart beat fast. It wasn't hot, but I was sweating. "What is it Sam please tell me what? Sam took another couple of deep drags of his cigarette before answering. "I know this is not going to sound like the most incriminating stuff out there, but Bex, I'm sure she's got someone in the house, and I think it might be a child! "Was it Jessica I had to stop myself screaming! "well I didn't actually see anyone. I felt myself deflate like a burst balloon. "What do you mean then Sam? Sam seemed to be trying to work out how he was going to word his answer. "Well, Ward came out of her house a few times while I was there The first time, she just went off to get a paper. Then later in the day, she went out into her car. I followed her, she went to the local supermarket. "Did she see you, Sam, I said panicked? "No I'm sure she didn't, anyway, I followed her back, and parked, not too close. She had one of those old-fashioned style string shopping bags. "Ok, I said, not quite getting the relevance. "You know what I mean? "Yes, Sam but what does that tell us? I was starting to feel annoyed at his somewhat dramatic rendition of the story. "Bex it wasn't the bag, but what was in it? "There was the usual, you know milk and stuff, but there were other things that didn't add up. I resisted the rising urge to scream at him. "There was, yes I told you milk. "Yes, you told me! "There was yoghurt, but it was that yoghurt that was in really small pots. The kind people buy for their kids. Then there was that cheese in triangles. I felt myself explode. "fromage frais", and Dairylea, triangles, "they are both Jessica's favourites. I didn't know how to cope with my emotions at that moment. At first, the relief was intense, "Jessica was alive, then right behind that thought, was the hate and fury. "That fucking woman I'm going to call Wilson. "NO said Sam, No not yet! "What do you mean Sam? "Bex if you think that the police will go over there over an allegation of buying kids yoghurt and some cheese, you're wrong. "They're gonna think you're... mad! "Yes but Jess must be there, they will find her won't they? "Well Bex, remember they searched the house before and they couldn't find her could they. "My thought is that Jessica is there, but she has a secret place, either in the house or garden, that the police haven't found yet. "But can't we just tell the police this? "We can't just sit here! "Look Bex you know I could have got it wrong, its not proof, also even if we go to the police, if they don't search right away, and I can promise you they won't, it will give this Julie a chance to move Jessica, and that could put her in much more danger, if Ward is scared she's gonna get caught. My mind was racing, was this real. Julie Ward had

Jessica, I wanted to get her back now. "What are we going to do Sam?
"Let me think Bex, I'm not used to being in a situation like this!" "and I am, I said, irritated! He started trying to get another cigarette out of the packet but dropped it on the floor. He looked as wired like me. He managed to light another cigarette. He was looking up to the sky as if looking for some divine intervention, and not finding it. "Sam I shouted at him, not caring if anyone on the estate heard. "What do we do Sam? He looked at me, actually scared. "Bex I've got to get into that house!

Chapter 33

I was roused from my sleep from someone singing. It wasn't as good as mummy's singing, but I liked hearing it. At first, I could only hear, then as I tried to concentrate, I was getting better at this, I saw a lady. She was pretty with whitish, hair, she was walking around a house I didn't recognise, but it was light and nice. There were little dogs and cats. Not real ones, but pretend ones. We have real ones around when I'm in the Special Place, but there, they are so funny. They make funny noises and chase each other among the grass. They swim in the river, and I like to watch. This was different though. These were not moving, and I think we're just there to look good. The lady was picking them up, wiping them with a cloth. Putting them down again and still singing, there was almost something familiar about her voice. I followed her into the room where you make tea and food. She put the drinks maker on and tapped her foot waiting for it to get hot. She poured water into a cup and sat at the table. On it, there was a paper. Jessica and Mummy's face were in it. She started reading it shaking her head as she did. I was getting bored now, as I wanted to go to the garden now and play with the animals, but I felt I was supposed to stay with this lady. Suddenly the lady dropped her cup, it smashed, and the liquid went everywhere, but strangely she didn't react as I or mummy would have. She just kept looking at the paper. She got up, then sat down. She was acting so strangely. She went into a box and pulled out something. I watched her, she took the thing to the paper and started putting marks on it, at a part of the words that I couldn't read.

Then she went back to the room where the dogs and cats were. She picked up the thing people use to talk to people who weren't there, and I could see she was crying. I heard her say "please Michelle, can I talk to David? After a while, the lady still crying was talking. "Oh God David, I think that our Samantha's dead! She was quiet for a moment, as she seemed to be listening to the voice talking to her. I've just read the paper, David, and you know that little girl who's been abducted, little Jessica, well her mother is called Rebecca Schaffer, but that is her married name. Her maiden name is Burns, and her Mother's name was Samantha!

Chapter 34

I paced around the house all night. Making coffee then not drinking it. Looking out of the window constantly, but with no real reason to do so. There was nothing to see, except the slow stages of daylight emerging. As daylight dawned, the sky was grey, changing to dark menacing clouds, a sure forecast of bad weather. At about eight the reporters started arriving. No thought for the neighbours as music boomed out of radio's and c.d.'s. I could hear Michael was up. He was chattering to Melissa. We all did this so much. I think in our minds we all believed that Melissa answered us back. Maybe she did. I always hoped so. "Bex", Michael sounded concerned. I ran up the stairs. Melissa was having a full-blown seizure. She often had petit mals, but this was big. I ran to the drawer, to get out the Diazepam liquid. I filled the syringe to 10mls as quickly as possible, she was spasming so much I found it difficult, to access the gastrostomy tab, so I could give the medication. I didn't want to pull it and hurt her. After a few unsuccessful attempts, and with Michaels panic rising, I managed to release her gastrostomy tab. I inserted the diazepam as slowly as I could, given the circumstances. "Put her on her side Michael I said as calmly as possible. She was dribbling profusely, so as the diazepam took effect, and she was spasming less, I wiped her mouth, put a couple of tissues underneath her chin, and Michael and I talked lovingly to her. Michael stroked her arm, and I stroked her golden hair, as slowly the movements calmed down, till eventually, they came to a stop. "God that was a big one said

Michael, with a look of concern and relief on his face. "Yes, I know. We looked at each other and laughed in relief that it had stopped. She hasn't had a major seizure in a long while, poor baby. "Should we take her to the hospital? "No Michael, not yet anyway, let's just see how she does in the next hour. The Diazepam had done its work but had also left Melissa unconscious.

With all the commotion, Jack and Angie were standing at the bedroom door, both with hands to their mouths in horror. To us this was "normal", we didn't realise sometimes, what a shock it must be for others to witness it. Angie had tears in her eyes, and Jack looked shell-shocked. "It's ok I said, in an upbeat fashion. she has these occasionally. She'll be ok, out for the count for a few hours, but hopefully, that's it. "What can we do to help? "how about breakfast? I don't know about Michael, but I'm starving. Angie smiled, glad to be useful and ran downstairs. Jack still stood there looking concerned. "What happens now? "Well she can't be left at all today until she's conscience again, so Michael and I will take turns watching her. "But Bex, how do you cope when Michaels not there? "I just do, I said nonchalantly, I carry her around the house. I call her my little pack of spuds. Jack gave a nervous smile. "You guys go downstairs said, Michael. I will stay with Melissa for a while, then I'll dress her and bring her downstairs. "Ok, I said touching Michael's arm. "Can I sit with her too? said Jack. His love and concern for his granddaughter was touching. "Ok I said, I'll go and help Angie with breakfast. As I walked out of the

room, Jack turned to me, almost in a whisper, he said. "Is she really going to be all right?"
"Of course," I said positively.
 As I left the room I said under my breath.
"This time".

Chapter 35

I watched Sam when I could. I was busy now and was beginning to see more people, and things. I felt a pulling towards him, as though needing me to see what he was doing. I expected to see him outside The Hate's home, but he wasn't. He was in a big building. It had lots of different rooms. Some had other people in, and others did not. Some rooms had glass lights on the ceilings, shiny wooden walls which I had seen before in some building, within my Special Place, but never here before. Others though had lots of what I thought were books, or something similar. I watched Sam looking on a television screen, and tapping the board in front of it. He was searching and searching, but for what, I didn't know yet. As I looked closer, I could see that he had a piece of paper. I tried to make sense of the letters, as I had been told to, here in the Special Place. I understood that what was written on the piece of paper said:

Julie Meredith Ward.
Date of Birth: Second February 1950.

I realised he was looking at things written about The Hate. I had to concentrate so hard, my head was hurting. Sam was reading more things on the screen. It was the same as the writing that he had beside him, after a while, Sam went outside of the room he was in and got some liquid in a cup. He didn't pull a face this time though. A lady started talking to him. I could tell that although she didn't know him, she obviously liked him. Sam answered her back but, not really in a friendly way. I don't think that Sam meant to be unkind, but I could tell that his mind was filled with worry. I think because of this, the lady walked away from him, looking a little sad.

Sam, didn't stay long in the hallway, he eventually went back into the room, and back to the screen. He carried on looking. Suddenly he jumped off his chair and it fell over, crashing to the floor. Other people that were in the room all looked at him. Sam didn't notice. He seemed to have trouble breathing. A man came up to him and said, "are you all right Sir? "To be honest, I don't think I am. Is there anything I can do then, said the friendly man? "No said, Sam, I'm ok, just got a shock, sorry about the chair. "That's all right Sir, it's amazing how just looking up Births and Deaths can cause interesting reactions in people. The man smiled and left. Sam sat down again, and the other people in the room got back to what they were doing. Sam now though looked almost scared. I knew I had to concentrate hard. I moved in closer, as Sam was still looking at the screen, trying to concentrate almost as much as me. I saw at the top of the screen were these words in black,

DEATH.
Registration district: Canterbury
Subdistrict: Canterbury. District: Herne Bay
Administrative area: Kent
Date and place of death: Dead on arrival on 2nd July 1985, at Canterbury General Hospital Kent.
Name and Surname: Julie Meredith Ward.

I didn't understand, really, but I could see now why Sam was so upset. I knew that Julie wasn't dead. It didn't make any sense. I had met people who said they were dead, and that was why they were in the Special Place, but, I'm in the Special Place I would say, does that mean I am dead? "No, they would say, you just choose to come here sometimes. So I thought, if Julie had been dead, she would have been here with me! I was glad she wasn't dead because I didn't want her here. Not her!

Sam spoke to the nice man again. "Please can I order a copy of this certificate for today. "well not today young man, but I can order a copy for you? "When do you need it by? "Tomorrow at the latest please, It's really urgent "Ok the man said but that will have to be delivered Special delivery, which will cost you more. "I don't care, about the cost, Sam replied, but I need it tomorrow. "No problem, you've ordered before four-pm, so you will definitely get it tomorrow.

"Thank you," said Sam. Sam was upset in a way I didn't understand, I watched him as he went into a small room. He was looking around, opening the few doors in the room, as if checking to see if someone else was there. He went into his pocket and brought out some white powder in a bag. I watched him, as he sniffed the powder into his nose. Immediately it was impossible for me to read him. His mind went crazy, so many things were happening. What's he doing? I said to the voice. He's hurting himself again Melissa, and there is nothing you can do. Sam has found a way of coping, but it is the wrong way. Can't we help him I said? No said the voice, it is, I'm afraid up to Sam

to find help. He can only do this when he is ready and is he ready yet I said feeling sad. No Melissa not yet I'm afraid. For a little while Sam stayed in the small room, he was so confused, it made me feel confused. It was a horrible feeling, and I didn't understand why he would want to do this to himself. When he left the room and the big building, he threw himself down on one of the many stairs, outside of the building. He put that cigarette to his mouth. It lit up. He also had a small bottle of the brown liquid. I couldn't believe he would take anything more that would hurt his head, but he did. He drank it down quickly, and after a short time, I could feel Sam feeling better. His mind was whizzing so fast; I could hardly keep up with it. For a while, his breathing was very fast. It still was, but he seemed calmer but no less upset. I spoke to the voice. "I don't understand what any of this means? why does the writing say that The Hate is dead?

"*Everything will become clear in due time Melissa, but Sam needs to move fast. Jessica could still be in danger. Only he can help her now.*"

Chapter 36.

For the rest of the day, Melissa kept us busy, but nothing could take away the gnawing pain within me. I knew now for sure that Julie had Jessica, but where was she, in that dark horrible house? For once I wished I had one of those mobiles that Rajesh had, just so I could go somewhere and call Sam. I wanted to call Wilson so badly, it just ate me up that I shouldn't, at least not yet. I knew Sam couldn't risk calling me at home. I had decided though that if Sam doesn't see me tonight after everyone is in bed I'm going to Julie's to get my daughter!
Trying to keep calm was almost impossible. That day Bill came later than normal to be with us. There was something on his mind I could tell. "Can I talk to you both he said, looking glum. Michael and I sat down, a little worried. "What is it Bill, said Michael? "I've been told that I have to go back to my normal duties after today. He looked guilty. "Did Wilson say that I asked? "Yes he said finally, I don't think Detective Wilson thinks too much of family liaison officers. Michael smiled. "Is that what you are, we never knew did we Bex". "No not really I said feeling sad. "We will miss you I said, and meaning it. "I'll miss you too said Bill, and for what it's worth, I have never for a moment believed any of you have anything to do with Jessica's disappearance. I stood up and hugged him. "Thank you, Bill, that means a lot to me. "You know one day, he said, it will be normal to have someone like me around, when something terrible like this happens to a family. "Oh god really, said Michael

good-naturedly, trying to lighten the mood. "Yes smiled Bill, well maybe not exactly like me. "Just to let you know, said Michael, you make a great cup of tea! "Thanks nodded Bill". "Thank you for everything I said, and for believing in us. "It's ok said Bill sadly, and I do believe in you. We hugged again. "Shall I make us a goodbye cup of tea, he said. "Well why not I said, as he disappeared one last time into the kitchen.

Melissa was unconscious for two hours before the first flicker from her. I knew she would be very tired for the next forty-eight hours, not just because of the Diazepam, but the after-effects of such a grand mal seizure. I knew adrenaline was pumping within me, but with nowhere for it to go, I felt sick to my stomach. I noticed and felt itchy red welts appearing on my arms and chest. "Bex your eyes are all swollen said Angie" looking alarmed. "Oh I said, suddenly feeling it, just a stress reaction, I'll go and get some antihistamines. I always had them on standby, in pill and liquid form, just in case. As I took the tablet, I thought about the time, when Melissa had an "allergic reaction" to sunlight. I knew now that hadn't been caused by sunlight. I couldn't even begin to think what she had done to Melissa, to induce that reaction. I didn't dare contemplate as I swallowed the pill, I saw myself in the mirror, bright red, swollen, deformed. "Oh no I thought I'm a mess. It was a Saturday, and that I reasoned was why there were fewer reporters outside, which was a relief to us, even vultures needed a day off. I was sure the neighbours were pleased too, hoping that the press was losing interest in us. Maybe they were, but I doubted it.

The doorbell went. I decided to get it. Wilson was at the door. What was it, I said to myself about vultures. I invited her in. She said she had come to see us to discuss the police's ongoing enquiries. I didn't know why she was wasting her, and our time pretending she cared. "Are you any closer to finding our daughter I goaded? "We are pursuing various leads in this regard. "Really, I said, and what are those then I said sarcastically. I couldn't believe we had a detective in our home, and yet it was me and Sam who knew where Jessica was. "Well she said, mind spinning again, we are still going through all the CCTV, that we have recovered, and various other leads. "In fact, there may have been a sighting, that hasn't been 100% verified yet. "What sighting, Michael and I said in unison. I sat bolt upright in my chair. "Well Mr and Mrs Schaffer, she looked extremely uncomfortable, I didn't really want to impart this knowledge to you until we were sure. "well what is it said Michael, sounding panicked and excited at the same time. "Please tell us? "A local Tesco in Canterbury' Kent's CCTV shows a person with a young child. "Is it Jessica?" cried Michael... "Yes, Mr Schaffer we think it is. "Who is she with. When was this? "The sighting was recorded on the day of Jessica's disappearance, at 7.59pm. "The person with her is wearing a black hoodie and jeans, they were also wearing a baseball cap, pulled low over their face, so it's impossible to get a good description. "Oh God," said Michael. Both Angie and Jack stood listening, holding each other. "Mr Schaffer, although we couldn't get a description, there is one detail, that we are absolutely certain of ..... "And,"

said Michael, looking as if he was about to explode. Wilson looked at us both, her face reddening, yet she spoke in a calm tone. "It was a Woman!
Ha, I thought they have got her. The desire to tell Wilson everything was all-consuming, but I held back, as I had no idea what page she was on, it even crossed my mind that maybe she thought it was me, and I'm sure for too long, Wilson harboured the serious belief that it was me. This was, of course, the reason, that delayed her in looking further in the beginning, for Jessica's abductor. I could have been wrong, but I wasn't willing to open up to her yet. "What information can you glean then of this woman from the CCTV, I enquired, a little too calmly, yet my anger for this Woman rising. Michael looked at me in a strange way. I don't think he could understand why I wasn't in the state that he was in.

My heart went out to him. My own husband. Jessica's Daddy, and I couldn't trust him with this knowledge. It was between me and a stranger. A secret I wasn't ready yet to tell. "We think she is about 5 foot 6-7inches. Well, I knew then it wasn't me. I was only 5-foot 2inches, even I couldn't fake 5 inches. I could tell how uncomfortable Wilson was. She knew it wasn't me, and it stuck in her craw, like a ten-inch hunting knife. She thought this was all going to be sorted quickly: Distraught Mother of severely handicapped child, finally snaps with the pressure, attacking her youngest child who demanded her attention once too often! It all got too much, and she accidentally kills her daughter. To cover up her crime she buries her somewhere, then tries covering it up as a kidnap. Yes, indeed, but,

Mrs Rebecca Schaffer obviously didn't realise what she was dealing with, when the all-powerful, Detective Sally Wilson dripping with ambition, came on the scene! Ten-year sentence for Mother, and a quick top promotion for the professional investigative officer involved, who solved the heinous crime. Nicely done madam. All done and dusted!
 I could see the notions of the top job, falling like confetti around her. She had thought it was me from day one. No serious investigation happened at the beginning, as she was so cocksure her instincts were spot on. The look on her face now, almost made me feel sorry for her, but not that much!
"Well, what else can you tell us said Michael exasperated. "The CCTV shows a woman with dark hair, but we saw that as the woman adjusts her baseball cap, it is clear, she is wearing a wig, and we think at the time the woman had dark blonde hair. Whether it's like that today we do not know.
"So where is our Jessica, she could have taken her anywhere by now. "No Mr Schaffer we do not believe that to be the case, as it would have been impossible to leave the country, with all the police security we had in place. "But it was day three before you had a thought she might be taken out of the country. She could be long gone. Michael had his head in his hands. "She's not left the country I said softly. "What do mean Bex? All eyes were on me. I looked up...... I just know that's all. I would know if anything bad had happened to her. I could see the disappointment on Michaels' face. He thought I had more. I did of course, and after tonight everyone would know.

Chapter 37.

Sam spent the whole day near The Hate's house. He drank lots of the brown liquid and just watched. What was he going to do? I didn't know, but I was scared. Sam was angry, and it frightened me. Occasionally The Hate would come out of the house. When she did she always looked around, as if she thought someone was watching her, and of course, she was right. After it got dark he left The Hate and drove to Mummy's house. He stayed outside waiting. When the lights all went off in our house, Mummy came out, dressed in dark colours as black as the night. Sam didn't get out of the car but waved at mummy to come close. She got in the car. "What do you know Sam? Tell me" "Bex, Julie Ward isn't Julie Ward" "what Sam? What are you talking about?" "Bex, I've spent the day at The Register of Births and Deaths in London. I looked up her birth certificate, then I checked the deaths register. Julie Meredith Ward died in a car accident in 1985. Julie Ward has been dead for nearly ten years! "What, but, Sam that's not possible, how can that be? It must be another Julie Ward, I mean it's not exactly an unusual name. You must have it wrong!
"Well Bex it's always possible, but every bit of information you gave me from contacting the care agency is the same. "what does it mean Sam? I said shocked. "Bex it means that Julie ward is an imposter, who has stolen the identity of a dead Woman! "Who the hell is she then I said shocked. "I've no idea Bex, but you don't steal someone's identity unless you have something pretty big to

hide. We sat in silence for a few moments, trying to absorb this new shock. "What do we do now Sam? "while I was in London, I went to a library to look up Ward's house, or whatever her name was. house. Just to see if I could find plans for the layout. It's a very old building. The house dates back to the 1700's. It's had at least 3 alterations over the years. It used to be an old smugglers alehouse, where they would use it as a front, for hiding their loot. There was a cellar somewhere under the house, that runs nearly the whole length of it, where the entrance is I'm not really sure, but I know it's there. "So what do we do Sam? "I want to go alone, Bex. It's dangerous. "Sam you are not going to Julie's house alone. Jessica is my child and I'm going to get her. "Come on Sam lets go"!

It was raining heavily as Mummy and Sam got close on foot to The Hate's house. "Please Bex, let me go into the house first. I'll let you know when to follow me I promise. Mummy looked at Sam with tears in her eyes. "I'm scared". "I know; so am I.

 "Sam, Mummy said, why are you doing this for me? Sam at first didn't answer. He just looked out of the window. Let's just say that I knew a kid once, who was in trouble, and he begged for help, but no one ever came. Oh no, said mummy and what happened to the little boy? I'm not sure really, I think he killed himself when he was a teenager. Oh, how dreadful said, Mummy. Yes, it was said Sam, but to be honest I think after all the pain it was a release for him. I wish someone could have saved him said, Mummy. Yes, maybe if he'd had someone to love him he might have survived. Is that really the reason you are helping me Sam, said Mummy?

"I don't know Bex? maybe I'm also just a little bit in love with you. I suddenly felt a little uncomfortable. Mummy, put her hand on Sam's arm and he turned around to face her. Mummy touched Sam's hair and brushed it away from his face. They kissed. It was gentle, like the way she kissed me, and yet somehow completely different. Sam looked into mummy's eyes. "I'm going to get Jessica, and he got out of the car. Sam didn't shield himself from the rain. I always hated the rain. It was cold, and I couldn't wipe it off my face without mummy.
Sam went down the same part of the house that I remembered Suki went through, and I could feel his fear was a lot greater than Suki's was, maybe that was because he knew how bad The Hate was. Suki was just a kind Woman trying to help Mummy. Sam wanted the brown liquid and the white powder really badly, and I was glad that he didn't have it. He needed his mind clear tonight. Sam felt the same handle on the back door. This time it was closed tight, and Sam couldn't open it. He walked down against the house, just looking, and getting wetter by the minute. Sam carried on around to the other side of the house. There was a window that looked slightly opened. He pulled it slightly. The window opened a little more, and then a little more. Sam looked around then tried to fit his body through the gap he had made. I forced myself to go to the inside of the house, before him, as I realised I couldn't avoid where Sam was heading. I watched him as he managed to get his body inside. There was a sink with cups and things in it. He tried not to touch them, but there was a slight clatter as he knocked one glass into another. For a few moments

he didn't move. Just waited to see if anyone had heard him. I couldn't hear anything, but I knew if Sam got into the house I would need to lead him to the room where Jessica was.

The house was so dark, even in the day, so at night it was hard to see anything. My sight was getting better and better, and I realised I could see clearer than Sam. I stood in front of him, as his feet touched the cold stone floor. I was suddenly aware that Sam seemed to be looking right at me. He looked confused. "Sam I said, surprised, can you hear me? Sam didn't answer, but he put his hand forward as if he could see something. "It's your aura, Melissa, the voice said. Sam can see it, use it to guide him. I felt happy that such a good, yet troubled soul could see my light. I started moving slowly, so Sam could see me, through this house filled with hate greed and death.

I led him to a room where there were machines. These were I think items that you use to clean clothes. My Mummy had one, and I always remember the lovely smell when mummy or Daddy dressed me. It always smelled like flowers, like in the Special Place, only not as strong. There was a carpet in the middle of the floor. It didn't cover the whole room, but I knew that underneath the large carpet, was the entrance to the room, that Jessica was locked in. There were long silver steps against the wall. Behind the steps was a heavy curtain. I tried to hover my light around the carpet, but Sam seemed unsure and started looking around the room, looking into the machines and around the back of them. I kept my light against the thick dark carpet. Suddenly Sam looked at the steps. He moved them away, whilst trying not to make any noise. He looked scared as he started to pull back the curtain. Behind it though was just a wall. Sam looked disappointed. He then left the room, and I felt panicked. "Come back Sam, Come back! He eventually came back and stood on the carpet on the floor. He went to move away from it, but as he did there was a creaking sound. Sam looked down. He looked for a little while before he touched the corner of the carpet. Slowly he pulled the carpet away, exposing the boards shaped into a door hiding underneath. Sam looked around, his heart beating very fast. There was a round metal ring inside the wood. Sam went to lift it and held it in his hands. He slowly pulled it. At first, nothing happened. Then he pulled a little harder. The hidden door lifted to expose the darkness beneath. Michael shone a light into the blackness, and he could see the stairs winding down to the prison below. Slowly Sam started walking down the stairs. He kept putting his arms to the side as if there was something to steady him, but there was nothing. He walked. It was difficult to see even with the light, so I moved in front of Sam, down the horrible wobbly stairs, showing him enough light to guide him. Sam slowly followed me down, and each terrible step, caused him to breath faster and without regular rhythm, the beats, getting faster and faster, as we reached the bottom of the steps, suddenly he saw it. The metal door with so many locks on it. He opened his mouth as if to speak but nothing came out. His fear was so intense; I could feel him shaking. "Jessica he said quietly. There was no answer. He knocked on the door gently. Jessica, are you there, it's a friend of Mummy's, still no answer. Sam began trying to look for a key, something to open the door. There was nothing. Sam suddenly seemed stronger, and he was angry. Very angry. He ran back up the stairs without me to guide him. He tripped a few times, but he just kept on. He knew Jessica was behind that prison door, and I could feel his fear, that Jessica may be dead. He ran back into the room where he first came in and started looking through the drawers as if searching. He had some metal things and started running back down the stairs, with no more fear of the noise he was making, or the dark, but he should have been afraid. The Hate was awake and knew he was there.

Sam was using his strength to work with the locks. There was a sudden click, and the lock snapped open. He did this with more of the locks, but still, the door seemed closed. He sat on the bottom stairs and started kicking with all his strength. "Help him, Said the voice. I concentrated further, with every kick of his weight on the door. Suddenly the door cracked an inch, but Sam didn't stop, he kicked and kicked again. The door burst open. Sam ran into the room. For a moment he tried to look around, after the darkness, he was momentarily blinded by the strong lights in the room. He couldn't focus. Then he saw her. The beautiful sleeping figure of my little sister. My Jessica. "Jessica he cried and ran to her. "Jessica he said again. Please wake up, but she didn't, she couldn't. The Hate had given her things to keep her asleep and quiet. I think for a minute Sam thought Jessica was dead. He checked her as if trying to tell. Mummy had to give me, things to make me sleep like that, but they were to help me stop shaking when bad things happened to my body. But Mummy did this to help me, The Hate did it to keep Jessica quiet. Jessica now hated The Hate as much as I did. Sam scooped up Jessica, relieved as he knew she was alive and ran up the stairs. "Be careful I called to Sam, she knows you're here. He kept running. He ran towards the door at the back that was locked. As he tried to open it there was a terrible force, that I couldn't protect him from, as he was hit from behind. He tried to stay upright, but The Hate was in charge. He tried not to drop Jessica as he slid to the floor. I watched in horror as The Hate just stood there, Jessica trapped underneath Sam's body. She started laughing. It was the laugh of pure evil. I had been told in the Special Place that there were people on earth who were born of the devil, and would eventually return to him, once evil on earth was achieved. I didn't understand it all, but I knew The Hate was very bad. The Hate went down on her knees. She stroked Sam's hair. Oh dear oh dear, she said. Now, look what you've done! I didn't want her to touch him. Was he dead? I didn't know.

Suddenly I heard a voice: "You Fuck! Let my baby go. The Hate started to turn her head around. Mummy had a stick made of metal and gold and black. I watched, as mummy swung the stick, which struck The Hate on the side of her head. Red liquid was pouring. The Hate seemed confused. She didn't really react. She touched her head, wiping the liquid, and looking at it. I thought she was going to hurt Mummy, but after looking at it, she looked with such hate at mummy, then she fell to the floor falling on top of Sam and Jessica. Mummy started

kicking her with such might, and a strength not given to her by me. She kicked and pulled The Hate's hair until she was moved away from Sam and Jessica. Mummy gently pulled Sam off Jessica and picked her up in her arms. She was crying, holding Jess as she shouted at Sam. "Sam are you ok? "Sam talk to me, please!
There was nothing.
Mummy cried more, holding Jessica close to her. As mummy turned Sam groaned. "Bex" he moaned. Mummy laughed with relief whilst still crying. "Oh my God Sam, I thought you were dead! She touched him gently. "Just stay there, Sam I'm going to get help. "I don't think I could move if you asked me to, he croaked. Mummy touched him again before running to the plastic thing and spoke to someone. I need an ambulance and police and get DCI Wilson over here please too. Mummy gave The Hate's address. After she had done this, still carrying Jessica she went back to where Sam was still lying. She sat down beside him. "It's ok Sam it's ok they're coming. All the while Mummy kept her eyes on The Hate lying on the floor covered in red horrible sticky smelly stuff. "Is she dead said Sam pointing at her. "I fucking hope so said Mummy angrily. At that moment Jessica stirred and looked up at our mummy. "Mamma, where have you been? Mummy just cried and cradled Jessica. "I'm so sorry baby, it took Mummy so long to get to you, but I'm here now and we are going home soon. "Mamma I'm tired she said sleepily. "It's ok baby just sleep, we have all the time in the world to talk!
Sam looked at Mummy with such love. "Shit Bex, I thought I was supposed to be the hero, what am I

gonna tell the paper? Mummy suddenly looked strangely at him. "Paper, what are you talking about Sam? "What paper? "Oh, I'm sorry Bex. "Forgive me please, I didn't mean to deceive you. The look on mummy's face told me she wasn't just angry with Sam, she was hurt. I could feel the sadness in her heart. Mummy moved away from Sam to the other side of the room and leaned against the wall, rocking Jessica, whilst looking away from him, tears streaming down her face. Strange sounds filled the air, although it was frightening, I knew it meant Mummy and Jessica were safe. I realised they didn't need me, and as I felt very tired. I went to sleep but felt happy at last. Jessica was safe.

Chapter 38.

Jessica and I were taken to the hospital, to be examined. I knew I was ok, but I didn't know what had been done if anything to Jessica. She was in and out of consciousness. She desperately tried to stay awake, but both the doctors and I told her to sleep. "Everything is all right I said, not quite believing my beautiful girl was with me. I would never let her go again. After a blood test the doctors discovered, she had traces of diazepam in her system The bitch I thought. You drugged my baby, god I hope you're dead because if you're not, I'm going to kill you! "There's no permanent damage physically, Mrs Schaffer, said a lovely doctor. Psychologically though who knows? There was a lump in my throat, and I shuddered at what damage that cow had done to my little girl. Whilst Jessica and I were waiting, the door to the room opened. It was Michael. He almost screamed when he saw Jessica. He ran towards us crying. "Is she ok, "Is she okay? "Yes, Yes, Michael she's Okay. "She's going to be all right! Jack and Angie were at the door cradling Melissa. "she's safe I cried in their direction. "Yes they both cried, holding each other, she's safe. We all just hugged each other. Jessica opened her beautiful brown eyes. "Daddy" she cried. "missed you. Again, we all started crying again. We were a family. No one could break us. Julie could never hurt us again.

Jessica was kept in hospital for a day, just to check on her. Michael and I never left her side, and Jack and Angie stayed with Melissa, till we came home. On coming home, there were even more reporters outside our home, and it took four officers to shield us from them, and help us get into the house. Wilson had come to visit us at the hospital, but at the time, she was one of the last people I had wanted to see. "Mrs Schaffer you shouldn't have taken the law into your own hands, any information you had you should have let us know, and we would have dealt with it. "Like you dealt with Julie Ward"! "My daughter was in that animal's house for a week, drugged, and in a locked cellar, and you never found her! "You said you searched, but you didn't do it, or you didn't do it thoroughly enough, if I'd left finding Jessica up to you, my daughter would be dead now! I really had no time for her. "You wouldn't have believed me about Julie Ward, she murdered Suki Kaur, but you didn't care about that did you"? You just wanted to pin this on me, from the beginning. "That's not true Mrs Schaffer, she protested, looking as guilty as she truly was. We will look into Mrs Kaur's death again. If she is guilty, and we have evidence, or Ward admits killing her, she will be charged, but you have to understand Mrs Schaffer, at the beginning of an investigation of this nature, everyone is a suspect! No! I shouted, not everyone was a suspect, just me! I threw my hand out dismissively. "Is Julie ward dead yet I said? Wilson looked disapprovingly at me. Miss Ward is alive but is in a critical condition. "Good" interjected Michael. "I hope she croaks!" "Well, Mr and Mrs Schaffer, she said trying to restore her authority on the situation, I hope for your sake, Miss Ward Doesn't die, as things could get a little difficult for you if she does. I looked at her defiantly. "You used excessive force, Mrs

Schaffer, you nearly killed her. "Are you trying to say that I will be charged with something, whether she does or doesn't die? "It's always possible, Mrs Schaffer, of course, but.... ", whatever happens, she sniffed, the matter will have to be assessed, but under the circumstances, that you found yourself in though, I don't really see the likelihood of any formal charges. Oh god, I thought, when have I heard that before.

When Wilson discussed Sam, the atmosphere changed and became distinctly frosty between Michael and me. He moved further away from me. I hadn't really explained about Sam, how we had met. Why I didn't tell him, and what had happened. How we had been the ones' involved in this, without telling Michael anything.

"We have word, on Mr Cutlack, continued Wilson. His condition is stable. He has a fractured skull, but he will recover. "Are you aware Mrs Schaffer how dangerous it was to get involved with the press? My bravado had left me somewhat. I felt very guilty. "I didn't know he was a reporter when I first met him. "He told me he was a neighbour, he said he just wanted to help, and to be fair he did. "That was very naive of you, Bex she said, "you are aware of course that the likelihood of all your interactions with Mr Cutlack, will be in every paper in the country. It will the biggest story his local rag has had in centuries. I felt myself redden, not helped by Michael's death stare in my direction. How could I blame him? I had betrayed my husband. We hadn't had an affair, but the secrecy itself was a betrayal. I was attracted to Sam; I couldn't deny it. I still was, in fact, but now I was angry too. What an idiotic naive fool I was, and I knew Wilson thought the same. I just trusted a total stranger and a damn reporter too. He must have laughed all the way to the editor's desk. Well, I thought, after this, he'll be the head reporter for the Sun or the Mirror. "Well good luck to him! I knew I had no right, but I also felt betrayed. Back at home. Despite Jessica's surprise at the reporters all camped outside the house, she seemed relatively undamaged by her experience. Michael and I occasionally broached the subject with her, but she would just say: "I was scared at first, but Issa came and said its ok, so I was ok. We didn't understand, although I remember looking at Melissa and wondering "Could she"? but at the moment it didn't matter. The hardest thing was stopping Jessica going outside, to talk to the press. We managed this, but could not seem to stop her peeping out of the window, and poking out her tongue at the press, with bulbs popping. She thought it was hilarious, In the end, we did a short television interview, thanking the public, for all their support, and asking us to be left alone for a while. I wasn't allowed to talk to them yet, about my involvement in her rescue, although they already knew, as it was all over the newspapers. It was obvious the press had it in for the police, especially Wilson, which was hypocritical, as I believed them to be just as culpable as her! The constant blurb was about whether Wilson would resign. This time it was her house they were hanging around. Whenever she came out, things were shouted at her: When are you going to resign detective Wilson. Do you admit you bungled this case, by accusing an innocent Mother, of the murder of her daughter? When the press asked us the same question, we always answered "No comment". I didn't like Wilson, she was a damn idiot, but there was no way I was going to conspire with the press to bring her down. I think she'd done that well enough on her own. Michael and I waited and waited for Sam's story to hit the headlines, but it didn't. There was nothing from his paper or any other. I saw in one of the tabloids, pictures of him leaving the hospital in a wheelchair. My heart ached as I saw him looking so frail, yet still so handsome, accompanied by two older people whom I assumed to be his parents. There were no comments from Sam however on any level. He had protected our secret. He refused to talk. I would be forever grateful, not that it made my relationship with Michael any easier. No matter what was going on, Sam was always the elephant in the room.

Julie Ward stayed in a critical condition for nearly a week, before she began to recover, and was charged whilst still in the hospital with kidnapping, and false imprisonment. There were pictures of Julie all over the newspapers, with awful headlines: "Nanny from Hell." "The real Hand that rocks the cradle."

One thing that surprised me was that Sam had not told the police about his belief that Julie Ward was an imposter, using someone's name, although knowing Wilson, he could have told her, and she had done nothing, and not believed him. I wasn't sure if I believed it either. I didn't want to think about her any more. I'd wasted so much time on that Woman!

Chapter 39

Two weeks after Jessica had come home. Things hadn't calmed down, as far as the press was concerned. The story and all the things that the press didn't know was continually written about. They hated being in the dark, and as yet no one was talking. The stories were becoming more and more elaborate. A reporter even pretended to get into Julie wards hospital room, by wearing a doctor's coat and stethoscope. Thankfully the Policeman on the door smelt a rat, and the phoney doctor was arrested.

One morning the phone rang. I absentmindedly answered it, then regretted it instantly, thinking it must be a reporter. "Bex". Immediately I knew, it was Sam. "What do you want I said? "Bex look, I know you don't want to talk to me and I understand, that, but there is a lady who has got in touch with me, about the identity of Julie. "so I said annoyed, why would that interest me? "Bex her name is Jill Saunders. "Well, that name means nothing to me! "Saunders is her married name he said his voice cracking. Her maiden name is Jill Burns! I felt myself shake. I tried to brave it out. "So what? "Burns is a very common name, is she trying to pretend we are related because it won't work Sam. "I'm not the same fool I once was! "Bex look I know you're mad at me, but I honestly I cared for you, and I would never tell anyone about what happened between us. "Nothing happened between us, I barked defensively. "I know, I know he said, trying to be calming. I just want to help you to know the full picture, about who Julie ward really is. I want you to know before the press does, then It will be up to you if you want to tell the Police or the press. I promise Bex, it will never come from me. "So who is this Woman then I said.

"Bex', This woman is not trying to pretend to be a relative. "She really is, as much as I can tell, your Mother's younger sister, and not just that, she knows the real Julie ward! I was holding on to the wall, feeling my ears fill with fluid. How could my beautiful wonderful mother have any connection to that evil witch! "I don't know what you're trying to achieve here Sam, Julie ward cannot have a connection to me or my mother, please leave me alone, I don't want to hear any more. Despite saying this I couldn't bring myself to put the receiver down. "Be I know I don't deserve any forgiveness from you, but believe me I have no interest in writing any story about you.... us. You have to meet this Woman. "There are things you have to know.

I didn't get it, why was Sam trying to hurt me. Please, Bex, see this Jill, she is your aunt, I promise you, that, but there is something else, and you have to know the truth!

"I need to think Sam. Give me her number. I wrote it down, my hands shaking. I didn't say goodbye I just put the phone down. I sensed a presence. Michael was standing, leaning on the door. His features were like stone. He was waiting for the explanation. So I told him, about me and Sam, not everything of course, who would it serve to tell him Sam and I had kissed. It certainly wouldn't help our marriage, recover, if I even wanted that, and to be honest, as I talked to Michael I still wasn't sure of my feelings for Sam, and whether they were strong enough to rock my once stable marriage, to a good man, and a great Father. Michael didn't say much as I talked, but the hurt was palpable, and I truly hated myself. After I had talked. Michael said gently, are you in love with this Sam Cutlack. I wanted to be honest, there had been enough lies. "I really don't know Michael I said. He got up to leave the room, but as he did he turned around, "are you going to call this Woman? "Yes I said, slowly, probably, I mean even if she's lying I want to hear what she has to say. "I know Mum did have a sister called Jill, but it's easy enough to get that kind of information. Michael sighed." I don't know how I feel about this Bex. I mean we are going through hell, and you are carrying on with another Man. "It wasn't like that Michael, I needed help, and I felt no one, including you, would listen or believe me, when I said I thought it was Julie who took Jessica. You all thought it was just me out for revenge, but it never was. Michael listened and seemed to believe me. It doesn't make it ok, I said, no way does it, but we didn't sleep together I promise you. I looked directly into his eyes to show him I wasn't lying. I couldn't tell when he returned my gaze, whether he believed me or not?

About another hour later the phone went again, Angie answered it. She chatted for a few seconds then came over to me, saying brightly "Bex sweetie, a Jill Saunders is on the phone. For a moment I was furious. Sam's given her my number. I said to Michael, "I told him I would call her! I was just setting up Melissa's liquid feed. "Bex I will finish this said Michael, you go take your call. I got up and picked up the phone and went into the kitchen.

"Hello I said tersely, this is Bex Schaffer. "Oh, Bex said the gentle voice with a London accent. I'm so sorry to call you. I know you wanted to make the decision to call me, but I really need to talk to you, not just about your Mum, but this woman calling herself Julie ward. I was silent for a moment, feeling my left eye twitch with anxiety. "Look said Jill, I know you have been through something awful, but there are things you just have to know. Please, please see me, Rebecca, please? I had been a fool in the past and didn't want to get caught again, but this woman sounded genuine enough for me to meet her, why was I so trusting I thought, everyone I thought I could trust had deceived me, and here I was doing it again. I found myself saying, "Ok, but, it's difficult to meet. The press are outside my house all the time. I know I'm watched, we all are, then I suddenly remembered! There is a late-night cafe, in Canterbury. "Maybe we could meet there I suggested. "Yes, that sounds great. "Tonight please Bex. Did I really want to know any of this? Yes, I think I did, so I gave Jill the address, and fixed a time, then I hung up the phone, and put the phone back on to the charger.

"You're not going alone Michael said sternly, she could be anyone. She could be a friend of Julie's. You never know. To be honest I was grateful not to be doing things on my own for once. "Yes Michael, please come with me. We both smiled at each other. The first genuine smile that passed between us for a long time.

Chapter 40.

Canterbury at night was always pretty, but more importantly, it was easier to park. The car park we chose just at the entrance to the pedestrian-only main street, was virtually empty. We parked and started walking towards the small but lovely cafe, around the back areas of the town. Nestled in and around the area, where there were a lot of new age shops. Crystals, books about Reiki, reincarnation and the afterlife adorned the window displays of the now mostly closed shops.

Maria's was a cafe run by a couple, selling homemade cakes, with low sugar with no additives, and amazing sandwiches and paninis, using only natural ingredients, I remember thinking how Suki would have loved this place. I was so sad we had never met here, having coffee, or a natural homemade cordial, and nattering about nothing in particular, then off, to go girlie shopping. It was a fantasy of course. People like us didn't have time to do those sorts of things. There was a lump in my throat, as I thought of what could have been. We were scheduled to meet at eight, but it was about eight fifteen before we entered Maria's. For the time of night, it was quite busy, with people chatting, drinking coffee, and generally having a relaxed evening. My eyes scanned over the people. What, or who was I looking for, I had no idea. Suddenly I saw her! A woman, about forty. She had long hair, which she swished about a little. She was a bottle blond, but it suited her features. There was a familiarity about her that I couldn't deny. It almost made me feel a little unsteady. She was so like my

Mother, suddenly Our eyes locked and we knew. Michael looked directly at me. "Is that her. "Yes I think so, but as I was saying it I was heading off in her direction. He followed behind. She was sitting at a two-person table. She stood up, and there were tears in her eyes. I wasn't willing to give in to this as of yet, I mean, Mum's family had disowned her, for being pregnant with me. I wasn't going to play happy families yet, but the resemblance was uncanny. "Bex she said spluttering, you are so like Samantha. There was an awkward silence before Michael held out his hand. "Hello I'm Bex's husband Michael" She returned his handshake warmly. "Oh I'm so glad to meet you, but I'm so sorry I didn't know Bex was coming, with someone else, although it's a very good idea, I mean you never know do you. "If I had known I would have got a bigger table she flustered. "It's ok said Michael kindly, I'll see if I can get an extra chair, from one of the waitresses. "Sit down Bex, now what does everyone want? Jill was nursing an empty cup. "Oh well thank you, Michael, I will have another peppermint tea, please. "Ok and what about you Bex? "skinny cappuccino please I said, still looking intently at Jill. Michael went off to get the drinks, and I sat down next to her. The table was so small I felt a little uncomfortable being in such close proximity to her, with our shoulders touching. She started telling me a little about herself, in a rambling way, she had started our conversation, she told me about how she lived in Kensington London and had lived there with her husband David for about twenty years. "I've always been a Londoner. I could never leave, although if David and I had kid's, things might have been different. But we never did so....... "Oh, so you never had children then? "No, she replied, sounding disappointed. We tried through the years, and the doctors said there was nothing wrong, but I guess sometimes these things just aren't meant to happen. Michael appeared carrying a tray, with our order, and behind him, a waitress carried a chair, and she put the empty chair next to me for Michael. "Thank you very much, Michael said gratefully. "Your welcome said the waitress, and quickly rushed off, as more people came through the front door. Michael just managed to squidge in next to me. Lucky we are married I thought. We checked our drinks for sugar etc., and whilst stirring my cappuccino I said, "so tell me what you think I ought to know. Jill exhaled deeply. She fished a folder out of her large yellow and black, messenger bag. Inside the folder were many pictures. Just looking over at them sparked my interest. As the first few were passed over, I could immediately see and recognise my Mother, so young, beautiful and carefree. Jill pointed out herself and showed me the picture of my Grandmother, who I had never met. "Who's that girl, said Michael pointing to a child younger than Mummy, but older than Jill. She had stringy fair hair, but the pictures were in black and white so I couldn't tell completely. She hardly ever seemed to look directly at the camera, in fact, she ruined a few pictures, where everyone else was smiling, but she wasn't. She looked like she didn't want to be there, and the photographs certainly proved this. Strangely even, with pictures taken in a different setting, Christmas, Birthday, day out, she looked miserable in every one. "Yes I said who is she? Jill swallowed hard. "It's my older Sister Barbara. "She doesn't look very happy does she, said Michael in an amused tone. "No, she doesn't agree Jill, unless she had a man on her arm she was never happy. Barbara was different from the rest of us? "Really I said, in what way? "Well, Jill said taking a deep breath. To be honest she was trouble, right from being a young child. She was always getting into trouble in school. She bullied other kids, our Mother was mortified, as she was such a gentle soul, she never did understand her, so she just pretended it wasn't happening. As she got older, and into her teens, she started mixing with the wrong types of people. She drank a lot, and we think she was taking drugs of some kind. When mum was ill, her medication used to go missing, god knows what Barbara did with them? "She was very promiscuous for the time, I mean it was the 1950's, and she would sleep with just about anyone, and then say she was in love, and if the man didn't feel the same, which they usually didn't, all hell would break loose. "She would harass them, by going to their homes, calling their wives, if they were married, and they often were, and then if that didn't work, she would then accuse them of all sorts of horrible things. "She broke up a few marriages, I can tell you! Funny thing was though, that if they did want to stay with her, suddenly she didn't want them anymore. "Thrill of the chase or something like that. Of course in those days, if you had sex on the first date, the man usually dumped you, and that's what happened to Barbara, over and over again. She used to steal as well. It wasn't unusual for Barbara to turn up at the house accompanied by a policeman because she had stolen from a store or something. Strangely she always managed to charm her way out of it.

"It must have been difficult for you all said Michael sympathetically. "Yes it was, although I, was just embarrassed by her, most of the family wanted nothing to do with her, except Samantha of course. She always tried to help Barbara, and get her out of the scrapes she got herself in. "There was a five-year age difference between them, so Samantha was always the supportive big sister. "Of course with the way Barbara behaved it was inevitable that she would eventually get pregnant, even then she caused trouble, saying she had been raped by these two local lads. It was all lies of course. Poor things nearly got done for it too, thankfully Samantha found out she was lying and managed to get her to withdraw the charges. "Did she get an abortion I said my interest spiked. "In those days' abortion was illegal, and Barbara was having none of it anyway. "so she had the baby then? "Yes, a little girl. "I'm sorry I don't understand I said suddenly feeling angry. You rejected my mum when she got pregnant! "No, No that's not true, interjected Jill, though I guess I can understand why she might say that to you. "So what is true then, I said my eyes boring into her. "Well after Barbara had little Kimi, we thought she would calm down, but things got much worse. It seemed to make Barbara more... I'm sorry, I can't think of the right words, "crazy", sorry that's the best word I can come up with. She used to leave Kimi with Mum, but most often it was Samantha, who looked after her, she loved her so much. Barbara was out again caterwauling, as our

Mum would say. She was drinking a lot and was off with men again, but now she had such a terrible reputation, she only got men who used her and knocked her about. About this time, Samantha had decided she wanted to be a teacher, so was going to study at university full time, and would not be able to look after Kimi, who was about thirteen months old. Barbara was incensed at this. Mum was very ill, at the time with heart problems, and the stress was so bad for her health, but also she wasn't fit enough to look after Kimi, so Barbara, had to be at home more, whilst Samantha was at college. Trouble was she still went out, but this time, leaving poor Kimi on her own. She sometimes brought men into the house, she would have sex in our living room, I mean it was a small house, it was horrible, I used to sleep with cotton wool in my ears and the pillow over my head. Mum couldn't take the stress, anymore, so she said she'd have to move out. "Then it happened!: "What happened" said Michael leaning in.

"One evening there was a terrible scream. It was Samantha. She found Kimi..... "she wasn't breathing. "We called the ambulance, but it was too late, Kimi was dead. "Samantha was beside herself, and she was so angry, she said Barbara had murdered her, "now we knew Barbara was trouble, but murder No, we couldn't believe that. None of us believed her. Barbara seemed inconsolable, at Kimi's death, but Samantha wouldn't stop the accusations against her. It really fractured the family. Nothing was ever the same again. "So what did the professionals say about Kimi's death? "Well, there wasn't even an inquest, or autopsy or anything like that. It was just decided that Kim had died of a sleeping syndrome, where a baby just dies in their sleep, I think It's called Cot Death today isn't it? "So nothing happened to Barbara, but Samantha wouldn't let it go through. After Mum died from heart failure a few months later, Samantha decided to leave London, to go to a college in Kent. We didn't know where though, exactly, and I'm sure she never told us? When she left I really believed she would come back, but I never knew what had happened, and I never saw her again. Jill sniffed back tears and wiped her nose on her sleeve. "We never knew that Samantha had given birth to a baby. "So what happened to Barbara? "Well things carried on in the same way really, "Barbara carried on, sleeping around, causing mayhem, and getting pregnant again. This time, she didn't have any help, except me, but I was done with her. I wasn't going to get involved. She had the baby, another girl. Her name was Florence. I moved out of Mums house to stay with my auntie Jean. I didn't want to live with Barbara any more, especially now she had another baby. I went to visit her and Flo a couple of times, but all she ever wanted was money, fags, drink, or for me to look after the baby. When Flo was about five months old she also died. "This time was different though. "The doctor who went to witness the death noticed that there were marks on Flo's neck. He reported it to the police. There was an autopsy, this time. It was awful just dreadful. Florence had been beaten. She had broken bones, her spine was severed, then she was strangled to death. The poor wee mite. death must have been a release. Jill cried long and hard. I held her whilst some of the other patrons craned their necks to see the drama. Once she had calmed down, she carried on. "Did she go to prison? Barbara I mean, I said in shock. "Not really, they found her guilty of manslaughter due to insanity. A psychiatrist said she had a psychotic personality disorder, "God we didn't even know in those days what that was, I still don't. She was sent to Rampton, high-security hospital. I went to visit her a couple of times. She was completely gone. I don't know if it was the drugs they were giving her, or if she was just mad.

"I tried everything to contact Samantha, but I never found her. The tears welled up again. Then I read what had happened to your family, and I saw Samantha's name. I couldn't believe she was dead. She was still young. "But I don't understand, said Michael, where does Julie Ward come into all of this? Deep down I think I knew the answer to that question, but I kept quiet and let Jill carry on with her terrible story. "Barbara had been in Rampton for about a year. They must have thought she wasn't a great threat to anyone, as they occasionally took some of the residents out to town. One day Barbara went on one of these outings. They went to a market. Whilst looking around the stalls, Barbara, ran away, and they have never found her. There wasn't a lot of publicity when she escaped. It was embarrassing for the authorities, and also the public would have been furious had they known about the outings for a child killer. I've spent the last eight or nine years looking for her. I knew how sneaky she was, but I never found her or knew what had happened to her, well not until after your daughter was found, and pictures of Julie ward were all over the papers, I knew then. She stopped and began crying again. "Oh, Rebecca I'm so sorry. Julie Ward Is our Barbara, your aunt!

We all sat in silence. "You mean Julie, was actually Bex's Mum's sister? I think he knew. He just couldn't believe it. "Why would she want to hurt her own family? Jill Shifted in her chair. "One thing I can tell you about Barbara is that to her everything bad in her life was always "someone else's fault". "She twisted everything in her life. "Everything was a lie. "When Flo died she tried to blame one of her boyfriends, said she was terrified of him, and he had said he would kill her if she told anyone. "Thankfully for him, on the night the baby died, he was locked up in a police cell, as he had been fighting in a pub, and beaten up someone. "She didn't know the truth from a lie anymore.

"We need to tell the police, I said looking at Michael, and Jill you need to come with us to verify everything. "Yes, of course, said Jill using her napkin, to brush away invisible crumbs. "I just wish I'd found her before she went about trying to destroy your life. "I'm sorry. "That nice reporter Mr Cutlack said she had taken on the identity of a lady who had died. "It just doesn't bear thinking about. "She was out for revenge for some perceived wrongdoing on Samantha's part I assume. "If only we had believed Samantha, all those years ago, none of this would have happened! "It's not your fault, said Michael, having brushed off the comment about "that nice Mr Cutlack". "Who would believe there was such an evil within your own family? "Yes, it's haunted me. "I missed your mother so much over these years. She was the only

one who would understand, and of course, she really knew how wicked Barbara was before we ever did. I looked around the cafe and realised it was nearly empty, and the waitresses were tidying in a way that tells you to get out. I checked my watch, it was ten pm. Two hours of such horrific revelations. Letting a murderer into my house, my home. With my innocent babies at her mercy. We all agreed to meet at the Ashford police station at nine.am the next morning. I would leave a message at the station, for Wilson, saying we were coming. We offered to put Jill up for the night, but she declined to say she was staying in a local hotel, not far from us. Michael and I drove home in virtual silence. I think both of us were aware of how much danger Jessica had really been in at the hands of a psychotic woman. Even I had never for a moment thought that she would hurt Jessica. I realised now how wrong I had been, and it would have only been a matter of time before Barbara got bored with her as she did with her own poor babies. We were obviously relieved she was in custody, even if at this time that meant her being at the William Harvey Hospital, which was within spitting distance of our home. It made me shudder.
When we arrived home. The house was quiet. We checked on Jessica and Melissa. The baby monitor flashing on. We both went to bed mentally exhausted. If only this was the end I thought. But there was a trial and all the increased publicity that would go with it. Now of course armed with this new horrible information. Things would get even worse.

Chapter 41.

As soon as day dawned, despite the tiredness, both Michael and I were awake. Sleep wasn't the calm release it always used to be. It was now filled with darkness and storms. Being close to evil filled my dreams. All naiveté was gone with the realisation, that such wickedness could invade your heart and soul, never to be released or repaired. Deep down there was a part of me that believed I would never recover. She was a part of me. My Mother knew. She tried to protect me, but it was never meant to be. I knew that now. Michael and I held hands, whilst still lying in bed. No words. We needed to be touching, bringing some light to our new darkness. At about seven I got up and called the station. I told the answering officer, that I would be coming into the station at nine. The officer knowing my name said he would send a police car to pick us up. I was grateful. The press was already gathering outside. It was always difficult to get by them, but having the police take us always made things easier. "God," I thought, they will have a field day when they realise that the kidnapper is, in fact, a serial killer, who has already escaped an insane asylum for murdering her own children. It didn't bear thinking about. Our lives would never be normal again!
At about eight we were all sitting in the living room. waiting. We hadn't told Michael's parents anything much yet. It would be enough of an ordeal going through it all again, and realising that last night wasn't just a bad dream, but the real, horrible truth! Suddenly the doorbell rang. "I'll get rid of them said Jack striding out to give the reporters a

piece of his mind. The door opened and closed, and Jack walked back into the room, he wasn't alone. Wilson was with him. "What are you doing here I said? "we wanted to come down to the station! I've never seen Wilson look at me like this before. She actually looked afraid. All the hairs on the back of my neck stood up. "What" I cried. "What is it? "I'm so sorry, Mrs Schaffer, Julie Ward has escaped!

I just remember screaming "No". I fell to the floor, unconsciousness enveloped me!

Chapter 42

The Hate was free.
She laughed. She was more wicked than even I had thought. She believed she was so clever, and really she was right. She was becoming less human than when she lived with us. She was an energy, rather like me, when I was in my Special Place.
"what can I do"? I said to the voice.
"Melissa, her hate and desire for revenge are very strong. She is no longer human in the earthly sense. She has transcended all borders, and become an earthly energy of hate and destruction. There is very little that can be done. Only death will release her from earthly bonds, and take her to the darkest realms, where she will have to face and pay for her wickedness on the earthly plain."
I watched her go deep into the forest, living like an animal, but without a soul, without love. Existing only to destroy others. To destroy Mummy. Every breath was revenge, just waiting. She talked to herself, unaware that we could hear her. Unaware that we knew, she lived only for destruction. How could she exact revenge on my Mummy? She sat eating and singing. This time the songs were sad and frightening:
"Oh Melissa, a little girl, oh so sweet. She cannot move she cannot bleat. The monster comes to cull the lamb, to slit her throat, a bloody treat. Poor mummy tries to save her soul, but her ultimate death is the monsters goal."
She survived well in the forest. She killed animals and ate them, without thought. The innocence she took, where would it end?

I cried for Jessica, and I cried for Mummy. Maybe they would find her. Lock her up forever, till death claimed her. I prayed to the voice this would happen, but I didn't know, and the voice didn't say.

Chapter 43

A doctor came to see me after I fainted. I didn't need or want one. He was kind, however, and prescribed sleeping tablets and anti-anxiety medication. I took the prescription, knowing that I would never use it. I needed my wits about me now, In every way. We were being hunted, and I needed to be alert. Wilson told us that she couldn't leave the country as her passport had been taken on arrest. That gave me a grain of comfort. She mustn't get away I said. Jill was at the police station and was giving them the statement that would probably rock the country. She was given twenty-four-hour protection, which I hoped was enough, although I didn't believe that Barbara had any idea that she had told us anything, or that we even knew her. I couldn't believe we were a part of all this. A police officer moved in as protection, which I appreciated, and as we were used to strangers in the house, it didn't matter. Plain clothed officers were everywhere. We didn't even know where they were? We only felt comforted to a degree though. We knew what Barbara was capable of, well I think we did. It seemed it was another waiting game for us. Waiting for the police to capture her. After two days living in the no-mans land, Jack and Angie came to tell us that they had decided to go back to Portugal. We were both disappointed, but couldn't really blame them. They had done all they could do. It was up to us now to get on with it. "Bex, "Michael, they said. "We want you to come back with us? "What we said in unison. "Yes said Jack, we have been talking, and we think the best thing would be for all of you to come back home with us. "You will be safer with us in Portugal more than anywhere else. At first, it sounded crazy, especially as we had never taken Melissa out of the country before. "Melissa would be fine said, Angie. We have already spoken to the doctors here and in Portugal. The care for the disabled is good in Portugal. We can get carers in much the same way as you do here, if that's what you want, also the hospital isn't too far away if we need it. "Wow said, Michael, you two have been busy. "Yes we have, they both laughed nervously, "but what about Wilson I said ", we can't go without her say so. "Well said, Jack... "You've already spoken to her haven't you, said Michael smiling. "Yes we have, said Jack, smiling like a cheeky teenager, "and she says there is nothing to keep you here in the UK at the moment, not until the trial.... whenever that may be! "I don't know, I said nervously. "Can you imagine?" said, Michael, NO PRESS! We would have some freedom until Barbara is caught and put in jail. Jessica came into the room, holding the policeman's hand. "We are married. "you're what, we said, all laughing at the breaking of the seriousness. "Apparently, said a bright red officer, she says we are married. "Oh my, said Michael you are starting early aren't you. "I didn't dare argue said the officer. "she's scary when she's mad! We all laughed, although a part of me, shivered as I thought for just a second. I hope it's not genetic? Then I brushed it away, as the ridiculous notion that it was.

"Yes", I said out loud to all who would listen. "Yes, I want to go to Portugal. "Poual" said Jessica. "Yes,

Jessica we are going to go for a while and live with Nanny and Granddad" in Portugal. "Yay Yay said, Jessica. Seaside! "Yes, Jessica we will go to the seaside every day. Tears were welling up in all our eyes. Michael and I hugged. I felt for the first time that we were going somewhere where we would be safe, even for a few months. I called Wilson, to see how she really felt about the situation. I wouldn't say that her and I would ever be friends, but the animosity between us had calmed, and we had reached an even truce. "I actually think it is a good idea, Bex, there is little you can do until we have found Ward... sorry I mean Burns. Just hearing my maiden name gave me a shock, especially in the context of my now connection with Barbara... My Aunt. Wilson felt it too. "Sorry, she said. "No, no it's ok. It is her real name. "How long before the press gets hold of it? Well, I would like to say they won't, before the trial, but I know that is unlikely. "No matter how we try, there is always some rookie officer, who tries to act big, who will feel important by telling the press. "I hate to admit it, but that's the likelihood. I was impressed by her honesty, and it warmed me to her more. "Mrs Schaffer she said quietly. "I am sorry for the mistakes that we...... I mean I have made in this case. "It's ok I said. We are all human. "We make mistakes. I forgive you. "Thank you she said, and I thought briefly I could detect a slight sniffle. "Bex, she cleared her throat, I will contact you regularly with updates, and obviously whatever the time if it's ok with you, if we catch her, I will call you immediately. Thank you, Sally, I said awkwardly. I don't think I had called her by her first name before. "Yes, well good luck, and I will be in touch soon. "Oh, and by the way, you'll need to leave the country quietly, so we will take you to the airport late in the evening when you've sorted things out, so you won't be followed. "I must warn you though, it won't take long till the press finds out, and some of them may even go out to Portugal, but it won't be many, so things might not be as bad there. Thank you again," I said, bye for now. I clicked the phone off.

Chapter 44

It took us a week to sort out things for Jessica to travel abroad. Barbara had obviously stolen her passport, and because of what was happening in our lives we hadn't thought to get a new one. It took the intervention of Detective Wilson, to get the passport office to understand, the situation, and process a new passport. Melissa's first passport was a slightly easier affair, despite the difficulties in getting a decent picture. We contacted a consultant, at the hospital recommended by Angie and Jack, who was an expert in brain injuries, and who was happy to take on Melissa as a patient, when we needed to. Jessica was so excited, in fact, we all were, I think there was a part of us that thought maybe we would never return to England. Michael's work had been so understanding and said it might be possible to get him a transfer to Portugal, even though Michael didn't yet speak good Portuguese. Despite the offer though, Michael decided that he wanted to have some more time with his family, and perhaps at a later date, start his own accountancy business. He put in his notice, which was really scary, but exciting at the same time. We were still on high alert though, as Barbara had still not been apprehended, but we still felt it was only a matter of time, as the whole country was looking for her. Her picture was all over the papers. The CCTV of her and Jessica in the supermarket was regularly shown on television. We booked tickets under different names, helped by Wilson, and started to prepare for our trip. On August 11th, it was Melissa's sixth Birthday.

Obviously, it was a low-key affair, with a few balloons, cake, that Melissa couldn't eat, and a happy birthday sing-along. When Melissa had been born six years previously, we couldn't have dared to hope that she would see in this birthday, so for that, we were grateful. At about ten in the evening the day after Melissa's Birthday, we were hustled to Gatwick, to get a flight to Portugal. As we all boarded the plane and started our journey, I felt a deep sense of calm. At last, I thought a new beginning. Sadly, for us, it was really the beginning of the end.

Chapter 45

Portugal was beautiful, but very hot when we arrived. We weren't used to it, except Jessica, who was as happy as a pig in mud. She looked reborn, even Melissa's breathing difficulties, seemed to improve, with a new regular dose of vitamin D. We got up early, ate fresh food, with lots of fruit and vegetables from the local market. Having a life built around the outdoors was so liberating for us. There was laughter in Jack and Angie's home. We had no idea how long we were going to stay, but Michael's parents seemed to love us all being together and said although they loved their life in Portugal before, having us there made everything complete. Jessica became a little beach baby, and just loved the water, either sea or the pool. Melissa loved the sun too. Her head would always face towards it. We had to shade her pale delicate skin and bought her the cutest pink high protection sunglasses. She looked so cool. There was an improvement in her general health right across the board. Fewer small seizures, which were so regular back home. The peace that we were experiencing was good for my relationship with Michael. Things weren't perfect, it was still a work in progress. I found myself thinking about Sam, less and less, and realised that I had fallen into the trap of believing that the grass was greener, at least that was what I told myself. It was hard for any relationship to survive what we had been through, but we were trying.
Three weeks after our arrival, our peace was to be shattered. The phone rang at about eight in the evening. We had just finished dinner. Jack took the

call. He came in looking sombre. "It's Detective Wilson, she needs to speak to both of you. "I'll talk to her said Michael taking the phone from Jack, and leaving the room. "Maybe they've captured her I said hopefully. "Maybe, said Jack, not sounding too convinced. Muffled sounds by Michael couldn't be deciphered, but Angie winked at me hopefully. I smiled back. When Michael came into the room, I knew by the look on his face, it wasn't the news that we had so hoped for. "Tell us, Michael. What did Wilson say? He sat down on the armchair and put his hands through his hair. "Bex, Jill committed suicide today! "NO... That couldn't be right. I stood up. "She would never have done that I screamed. "She left a note, apparently, he said, using his calming hand to cool me down. "It said she was sorry, but she couldn't live with herself, after what she had allowed to happen to us. "That's ridiculous I said tears streaming. "It was never her fault ever! "I know said, Michael. We know that. "That poor Woman said, Angie. What suffering she must have gone through, god rest her soul. "No, I said there is no way she committed suicide. She didn't. That fucking bitch killed her. "I know she did! I just collapsed. Michael held me as I wept. "We should go back I cried. "No Bex, Wilson says we should stay where we are. We don't want to stir up any more publicity. "Surely, we can't just stay here in the sun knowing..... I just cried and cried. "There's nothing we can do Bex, "Let David and their family deal with this in private. "But I'm her family I wailed. "I know babe he said holding me, but you know our presence wouldn't help anyone. "Jesus, I thought will we ever be allowed some peace.

We sent flowers for the funeral and a letter to David. We spoke briefly on the phone, the night before. He sounded drugged, and I couldn't blame him. She was his life. "I don't know what I will do without her, he cried. "I know. "I know, was all I could say. Another death because of Barbara, even if she hadn't done it herself, she was to blame. I remember on the day of the funeral, I prayed properly for the first time, to a god, any god who would listen. I'd never been brought up to be religious, and at first, it felt silly talking to nothing, but after a time I found it somewhat comforting. Sometimes I would just talk to god about anything and everything. I didn't really care if anyone could hear me. It felt good, and I felt less stressed.
We bought a lantern, to commemorate Jill's life, lit it and sent it flying. Jessica thought it was lovely. It was, but I cried, over the senseless loss of a good Woman, my aunt.

Chapter 46.

Life at home was calmer now. I spent less time in my Special Place. I didn't really know where we were, but I liked it. It was always warm. Inside and out. Jessica was always wet, which was annoying at times, as she often splashed me, but she was happy. We were outside more, and I could feel the lovely warm breeze on my skin, which was good. I didn't feel The Hate as much as before, but I knew she was getting closer, but I didn't know in what way. One day the voice asked me to be more aware, and start watching things again. He took me away to a very big place. When I looked out of the window, I could see really large metal birds. Some flying. Some on the ground. There were so many senses and sounds. I was led to an area where lots of people were waiting. The voice said they were going to get on the big birds and fly. I was bored after a while watching them, as for a while nothing happened. There were children running around having fun. It was obviously something people liked to do. Suddenly all at once the people all stood and started towards a desk, where there were people in the same clothes, looking at the papers, that they had with them. They were all smiling. Then they would give them back their papers, and the people headed off down a long indoor pathway. I got closer to one of the ladies. People were still going by, then a lady gave her papers to another friendly lady. Suddenly darkness enveloped me, and all the warmth I knew had disappeared. "Well hello there. "Tell me, Miss Burns, how long will you be in Portugal? "Oh, she replied, just a couple of weeks,

I'm off to see my family. "Well, have a lovely time won't you, Miss Burns. "Yes I definitely will, she replied, and please just call me Barbara!

Chapter 47

The few weeks after Jill's death, were subdued, until we had a call from Wilson telling us that the news had got out about the real Julie Ward and that she was a woman who had died in a car crash in 1985, and Barbara had taken her identity. I think David was the catalyst for all this getting out to the press. Personally, I couldn't blame him. He was an angry man. The truth about Barbara Burns conviction and sentence to a hospital for the criminally insane was front page news, as we had always known it would be.

Suddenly we were not living as much of the private life, that we had enjoyed for such a short time. The police were under increasing pressure, for as yet not recapturing Barbara, the serial killer. Debate raged that Jill Saunders' death had maybe not been an accident, and to be fair I agreed with them, and hoped they would open the case again, although how Barbara could have done it, I couldn't understand, but then, who understands the mind of a psychotic monster. The family connection was obviously the main topic. Calls started coming in. How they got our number I will never know. They called at all times. We had to disconnect the phone at night, but there was always the fear that we would miss an important call. Apparently, pictures of us in Portugal started appearing in the British tabloids. We would go to the beach, and there was always a photographer in the crowd snapping pictures. It was also difficult for the locals, as suddenly the press was descending on the little village, asking questions about us. The press was also filling in the locals on the ghoulish facts and fiction about our story. The Police in Portugal appeared fairly supportive but were not particularly interested in protecting us, in fact, it seemed that some were giving the press our address. It was starting to feel ugly again.

We were feeling a little like prisoners again. Jessica became increasingly frustrated at being hemmed into the house when she wanted to be up and out enjoying her life. It was almost impossible to explain to her and make her understand. We talked to Jack and Angie about going back to England, but thankfully they wouldn't hear of it. We wanted to stay, and we felt in time things would calm, surely as no editor would let his reporters spend too much time in Portugal when the search for Barbara was still in the U.K, and by wasting time in Portugal could evade eventual capture. At least that's what we hoped would happen.

One afternoon we got a call from Wilson. "Have you found her? I asked, not really believing that was why she was calling, and I was right. "I've been dropped from the case," she said in a resigned tone. "That's crazy," I said. "No one knows this case, more than you do." "Well, that's not what they think she said. "The pressure from the press has been intense. "I think the powers that be feel things would be easier for the police if I was removed from the investigation. "It's like a witch hunt I said. "Yes it feels a bit like that, but I think they are doing what they think is right, besides in one way they are right. We let Burns escape, and we haven't managed to apprehend her yet. "What do you think has happened to her? "Well I'd love to tell you that I thought she had got on a ferry, and jumped off, but sadly I think she's smarter and deadlier than that. "I'm sorry Bex I've let you and Michael down. Perhaps this is all for the best." I didn't really know how to reply. We were all in a terrible position. Wilson sounded sad, but more than that, she sounded tired. "I've put everything into this case, but I've failed. "A very dangerous individual is out on the loose, and I haven't managed to make things right. Again, I'm sorry. "Don't apologise Sally. It's not all your fault." "Maybe," she said. "I am being replaced by Detective Superintendent Paul Linette. "He's a very experienced Scotland Yard Detective, "maybe new eyes, and ears will help the investigation, maybe, she said almost to herself. "Will we see you again I said, amazed that our fractious relationship had changed into a basic understanding. She had made my life a misery for a while and had made errors in Jessica's case, but she was always at the end of the phone, no matter what time, day or night, would this Detective Linette be that accommodating? I doubted it.

"Will we ever see you again," I asked.

"If Burn's is ever captured and there is a trial, believe me, I will be there, to see she goes down.

"They will find her won't they," I said desperately. There were a few moments of silence. The answer was what I expected. "I hope for all of our sakes that they do"!

Chapter 48.

As the weeks went by the press intrusion did start to calm down, and there were definitely less of them around. Cautiously we started going out little by little. First to a small private beach, that the kindly owner of, had let us use to get some peace. This calmed Jessica down, as she began again to enjoy the wonders of the beautiful Algarve scenery, beaches and warm water. We were into September, and lovely though it was, a chill was beginning to set in, not like the chill in England, but a swifter more powerful breeze, which made our days at the beach slightly shorter. Back at the house though, outdoor living was still the everyday joy that we all appreciated and loved. We still had balmy evenings, but now we would as night fell wrap ourselves in a shawl or long sleeves, as we drank red wine and watched the sunset. Still, though the evenings were clear, and it never ceased to amaze me, when looking up at the night sky, to see, few clouds, and a blanket of stars.

It was at this time however that Melissa's health began to take a turn for the worse. We had two instances of grand mal seizures, which required her to go to the hospital. It was at this time, however, that we found how wonderful the hospital services were in Portugal. The staff were amazing and welcomed Melissa as one of their own. At the end of September Melissa came down with, what was initially a cold, and as always she was put on antibiotics immediately. This time, however, she did not recover as quickly as she usually did. She was becoming too ill to be left alone at night, so we were all taking it in turns to stay with, and monitor her. One evening I found her breathing was becoming very laboured. I woke Michael "We need to get her to the hospital, I said as calmly as possible. "I think this is turning into Pneumonia. Both on high alert, Michael slipped in to see his parents, to say where we were going and would call them as soon as there was any news. We told them to go back to sleep. But it was unlikely that they did. We drove in the car, on quiet streets, listening with increasing panic at Melissa's laboured breathing. When we arrived we were ushered into the emergency room. Doctor Avril, who had been amazing with Melissa, since we had come to Portugal was on shift. He prescribed strong intravenous antibiotics, and she was given oxygen to improve her breathing. Within two hours she had stabilised, much to our relief. "We will keep her in for a couple of days at least, said Doctor Avril. "She is responding well to treatment. You should both go home and try to rest. "There is nothing more you can do. "No, I said. "I'm not leaving her; please can I stay? "The Doctor smiled. "Of course Mrs Schaffer, we will set up a cot in Melissa's room for you. "Thank you I said tears of relief filling my eyes. "Michael, you go home. "you can come back tomorrow, with a few things for me and Melissa. Michael didn't' seem too sure. "I think I should stay too Bex. "No Michael, that's crazy, it doesn't need two of us here, besides Jessica needs you. He pulled a face like a disappointed child. "Okay, he said finally, if you're sure. "Yes, I'm sure I said smiling. He gave us both a kiss, and Melissa an extra sloppy one. Usually, this would have produced a pulled scrunched up face, full of amused disgust. This time there was nothing. Not even a flicker. "Night, my two angels he said blowing kisses as he went. I stayed in with Melissa for a while, before they moved her to her own private room. It was large, too large really for just the two of us. Melissa seemed calm, so I settled beside her in my put-up bed and looked up at her for a while till sleep began to overcome me, and I dropped off.

I was woken with a start, the alarms were beeping, Melissa's breathing was very hoarse and difficult. I got out of bed. "Melissa are you ok?" She was beginning to struggle. I ran outside to get a nurse. She was already on her way, took one look at Melissa and ran out of the room. The next thing I knew, was that the room was suddenly full of people. I could hardly see Melissa as they surrounded her. Her heartbeat was slowing down. Tubes were being inserted into her throat. I was transfixed with terror. I couldn't move or speak. She's bradycardic one of the doctors said. Suddenly her heartbeat stopped. I couldn't move. I must have been in shock as I wasn't crying, just watching the horror unfolding in front of me. They began CPR. It seemed so harsh. "Be careful?" I said in a whisper, please don't hurt her, but they kept on. I watched the monitor, it's line flat but sharp. "No breath, try again! On and on and on. Suddenly! "I've got a heartbeat." You could hear the cry in the room, and it wasn't just me. The line no longer flat, the heart rate increasing. Still, the doctors worked on my baby. For the first time, someone turned in my direction. "We are just trying to stabilise her ok?

"Yes, I replied meekly. After about ten minutes the doctors and nurses started to disperse. The doctor on call, whose name I don't remember said. "She's going to be ok. "Are you okay Mrs Schaffer?" "Yes," I said without thinking, "I'm ok." "Good, the nurses will do obs every fifteen minutes okay. He left the room, and we were alone. I was almost too scared to walk up to her. As I looked at her it was impossible to see what had just happened. Her cheeks were rosy, and she looked calm and peaceful. At that moment I just broke down. The horror of what I'd witnessed finally became clear. I dropped to my knees and sobbed and cried in a way I had not done since the hours and days after her birth. I was wailing in agony at what and why did my baby have to suffer in this way. "Why" I cried to God. "Why." A nurse came in, and her arms enveloped me. I wanted my Mother, I wanted her so badly. Why did she leave me? Why am I all on my own? The nurse carried on comforting me like a baby, and at that moment that is exactly how I felt. A baby lost, damned and alone!

The next day when Michael returned I did not tell him of the nightmare of the night before. There was no need. He did not need to know. It would help no one. He came armed with too many things I didn't' want, and not enough of the things I did. It didn't matter, I was just happy to have him here with us. Melissa stayed for five days before she was deemed well enough to leave. An ambulance took her, and I back home, To our wonderful haven of peace. Jessica was ecstatic when we returned, and within a day, the sad atmosphere had dimmed somewhat, with hope recurring within me, after the ache of pain, that we had both encountered. As the days wore on, I did see a change though in Melissa, and it was not for the better. She was more tired than normal, but more than that, there was a sense, and I can only say sense, because there was no proof, that Melissa was slowly slipping away. Not dying, at least that's what I told myself, I remember thinking, but slipping more into another world, maybe even another dimension. As a baby, she showed me on numerous occasions her strength and desire to live. She fought for life, and I could see it. Now I felt almost the opposite. There was a feeling of her giving up. When I talked to her, she always used to turn towards me, straining to understand what I was saying, and what was happening. Now when I spoke, she turned away, too tired to bother. Where she went to in these times I didn't know, it was though as if to Somewhere else, where the calmness was more inviting, where her pain was diminished. I knew now, it wasn't here, with us. This filled me with dread and sadness I was worried as to the choices, that my distant beautiful daughter was now choosing to make.

I prayed at night that her decision would be to stay, but deep down inside me I feared our lives together were numbered, and the sense of dread prevailed in my every waking moment. I didn't discuss my fears with anyone. If Suki were here I would have told her, but of course, she wasn't. I sat thinking and wracked with guilt about Suki, her life, death, and the discovery of her body on that terrible day, and then the finding of my Pendant, worn nearly every day, since the day I discovered it, in Suki's Jewellery box. There was also a guilt that I would never be able to shake from my heart and mind. It was my fault that Suki had been murdered by Barbara. I had involved her in my life, and troubles, now a good caring mother had been taken away from Ramon, and also Rajesh, as I knew he still loved her. I felt ashamed for believing she had stolen my necklace. It was another Barbara trick. Put the blame on someone else. Where there was goodness, she replaced it with wickedness. I would never forgive myself for Suki's death. A part me wanted to know exactly what had happened? How had Barbara had got into Suki's house, and why? It was a mystery I wondered if I would ever know the truth. I knew one thing though. I had blood on my hands.

I spoke to Michael for the first time about, what I think had happened to Suki. He was as horrified as me, knowing that it was "her" all along, but there was nothing we could do. "Maybe one day I said, Barbara might admit to what she's done? "Maybe said Michael, but to be honest Bex, I doubt Barbara has any thoughts about alleviating the stress and pain of others. "Yes I know you're right, Suki only ever wanted to help me, and she paid with her life. I cried again for a dear woman who had been taken, for daring to care for me.

Chapter 49

My restless sleep was permeated with nightmare flashes of Suki's body when I found her, and nightmares of Barbara chasing me. Each time I thought she would catch me, I managed to get away. I saw a knife shining in her gnarled hand, as I was cornered, Suki appeared, like a rotting corpse, trying to grab at me. I was drenched with her bodily fluids, and I screamed as the thick congealing sludge engulfed me. Barbara's laughter echoed in my brain, holding Melissa in her cold wicked vice-like grip. I screamed for it to disappear. "Melissa I screamed "Melissa".
"It's alright, Bex, calm down, I'm here. Michael was at my side holding me, and I succumbed to my now conscience cries of fear and despair. After I had calmed, Michael went downstairs to make me some coffee. The percolator smells drifted into my senses, making me feel calmer and more relaxed. When Michael appeared with the coffee, accompanied by croissants, butter and jam, I luxuriated in the simple pleasures, brought to me, by the man I loved. After eating I got dressed, and just as I was ready to go downstairs the phone rang, and I immediately grabbed it. "Hello said a voice I didn't recognise, this is detective Superintendent Linette, is that Rebecca Schaffer. "Yes I replied, but please call me Bex! He coughed as if feeling uncomfortable with familiarities. "Yes Bex, I am handling your case. "I have some information for you, and it is imperative that precautions are taken. My heart jumped. "What's happened? Mr Linette. "This morning we have had some information

brought to our attention, and it is vital you are informed. "Why do these People always have to talk as if it's come straight from the police officer's manual, I thought? "Yes Mr Linette, please tell me what has happened? Mrs Schaffer, two days ago a woman under the name of Barbara Burns, got on a flight, heading for Portugal! I felt as if I'd been punched. She was coming for us! I think I had always known this would happen. "Mrs Schaffer? "Yes, I'm sorry. "I'm sure this must be a terrible shock for you, and I really think that under the circumstances, you and your family should return to the U.K, We can't protect you here." It sounded like the right thing to do, but I knew for us it wasn't. "No, Inspector, we are not running away again, we are happy here." "Please Mrs Schaffer please reconsider, you and I both know how dangerous, this woman is, and there is only one reason that she has gone to Portugal. "Yes Inspector I know her, and I know why, but we are staying." Linette sounded frustrated. "I have already spoken to the local Police, and if you are determined to stay there, I will do what I can to ensure your safety." "Thank you, Inspector, I said. "I know this seems crazy, to you, but we have been running from her for so long, I refuse to do it anymore. "I don't agree with your decision Mrs Schaffer, but I have to respect it. "Mrs Schaffer there is one thing also that I need to inform you. "We believe, although we have no proof, there is a likelihood that Barbara Burns was involved in the death of your aunt, Mrs Saunders." I choked, but I knew. "Yes" I replied tears in my eyes, "I think I always knew it was not a suicide." "Again "Bex we will do what we can to find and convict this woman. "Yes I replied resigned, I'm sure you will. "Thank you I replied, relieved that the persuasion to leave had stopped. "Please Bex, if you change your mind, we can have you back on the next plane to the U.K. "Thank you," I said, I'm grateful. "Please feel free to call at any time," said Linette. I put the phone down and realised I was not alone. Michael was standing in the doorway. "How much of that did you hear?" I said. "Enough", he said. There was a sad look on his face, and I was expecting an argument. "There's some fresh coffee downstairs if you want some. "okay," I said surprised, I'll be down in a minute. Michael smiled at me and walked back downstairs.

After coffee, I decided to get a book, and try to read, in the quiet of Jack and Angie's substantial garden, as I walked out into the large garden alone, I wandered through and around the Lemon and lime trees, and breathed in the heady aromas of the sea, sand and fresh flowers. I was thinking about everything that had happened to us over the last year. If it wasn't true, I wouldn't believe it. I went to sit down on a garden chair, one of many dotted across the garden, as I glanced to my left I could just see a grey Renault Clio parked further back, on the street a few yards from the house. At first, I decided it was one of the security police, watching over the property and us, but as I stared, it didn't look like a police car, so I ducked down, fearing once again, that the press was still watching us. I stayed in the chair, the trees and shrubs disguising my presence, as I carried on watching. For a moment I considered confronting the person in the car and telling them to "piss off, "and leave us alone. I was pondering this when someone got out of the car. It was a woman. Her hair was covered by a sun hat, she went to the boot of her car, retrieved something, and got back into the driver's seat. I couldn't determine her age, but her body language sent a shiver down my spine, and I felt the pressure in my ears and head, that told me we were in danger! I was rooted to the spot. Was it her? No it couldn't be, but why wouldn't it be, I thought. A complete and utter sense of misery and foreboding enveloped me. She's come for us, I thought. What do I do now? I again considered going up to the car, but I my legs wouldn't move. My fear had rendered me rooted to the spot, unable to put one foot in front of the other. I tried to breathe. "come on Bex breath in, breath out". I started to feel the blood flowing back into my legs. I started walking. Then walking faster, until I was running, I wasn't going to be scared. I wasn't going to hide away. Enough I thought, as I realised I was getting closer to the car. Just as I was thinking what the hell I was going to do when I got there, the car suddenly started moving, and drove off, at breakneck speed.

The relief was palpable. I realised I had stopped breathing, so I gulped in fresh glorious air. I was dying of thirst so ran back into the house, as if I had been lost in the desert for days.

Michael caught me as I stumbled into the kitchen. "What's happened Bex, tell me"? I explained what had happened, trying to play it down, and saying I was sure it was a mistake, and I was just paranoid. Jack said "We have to call the police", even if you are wrong, we can't take the chance. We all agreed, so Michael went to the phone, to call the local police station, and inform Linette in the U.K. We all became paranoid after that. I was upset that I had caused them all to feel such fear when I could easily have made a mistake, or gone back to England. We could have been back there by now, and she trapped in Portugal! The woman's hair was very dark, but then Barbara would have had to disguise herself to get out of England. I'm not sure if the build or walk was the same, but deep down, I knew it was the same. She was here, I knew it, watching, but as I felt fear, I also began feeling a sense of strength. Whatever was to happen next, she was not going to win. I would never again let her hurt my children. If there was going to be a fight, it would be a fight to the death, and at that moment I knew it was a fight I could win!

Chapter 50

We tried to carry on with life as best we could, the local Police patrolled around the perimeter of the house on a regular basis, while all the while we were alert to our feelings of fear and dread. We all felt it but were all too exhausted to admit it or to even talk about it. It hung over us. The darkest of clouds, that pervaded our very souls. Jessica had no inklings as to our fears. She didn't notice, how much closer we stayed to her. We never left her alone. If she wanted Jessica she wasn't getting her, I would die to protect her! About three weeks after the supposed sighting, on a cold but bright late October evening. We had all had a lovely dinner of chilli linguini and shellfish. Jessica loved seafood, which was a wonderful surprise, with a child, with such limited food tastes. Angie had toned down the chilli in Jessica's portion, but ours was hot and luscious, made even more so, by washing it down, with homemade Sangria. That evening Melissa was not in good spirits. No matter what I did, or how we held her, she seemed unhappy. She seemed upset about something, as she spluttered and coughed in discomfort. "What's wrong baby I asked? For a moment she was still, her eyes stopped moving, and she seemed to be looking straight at me. I knew this wasn't possible, and thought perhaps she was having a petit mal, but I returned her gaze, a tear in my eye, as I drunk in her immense beauty. "I love you, Melissa. "I will never leave you or let anything bad happen to you. I promise". The arching of her body relaxed, and the upset seemed to diminish. Her eyes lost their stillness, yet the rest of her body seemed calmer. I was relieved. I kissed her on the lips, and she scrunched her face up, in disgust. It was noted by us all and we laughed. She was such a madam, such a strong child. I knew no one really knew how strong she was, but I knew. A shiver went through me, like someone walking over my grave, and it made me pick up my shawl from over the dining chair, and wrap it around my shoulders. "I think this young lady must be tired, said Michael. "You think", I said, not wanting her to go to bed. I think she is, said Angie, and to prove it Melissa yawned the biggest yawn ever, again we laughed. I could tell she didn't understand why she made us laugh so much, and gave us so much joy. If only she knew, I thought. Michael insisted on taking her to bed, said he wanted "Daddy time" with his big girl. We all gave her more sloppy unwanted kisses and Michael took her up to bed. "Do I have to go to bed too? Said Jessica in a whiny fashion. I looked at my watch. It's eight o clock I said, almost to myself. Alright, Jess. One more hour ok. "Yes, Yes, she cried happily, as she skipped around the garden porch. I knew at one time we may have to leave Portugal, and decide what we were going to do with our lives, but not tonight I thought.

Jack, Angie and I, sat drinking a little too much Sangria, whilst watching a deliriously happy Jessica. Michael joined us after about thirty minutes. "Someone's a little tipsy methinks, he said in a mocking voice. "I beg your pardon, Mr Schaffer, I have hardly touched a drop", and to unprove the point I hiccupped. Laughter again. I was so happy at that moment. I had lost my dear mother but had gained this incredible, though small loving family. Just for a moment though I thought of Sam. I hoped he was o.k. I could never repay him for his support for me, and I determined that when we went back to England, although I would never see him again, I would thank him in a letter. I was more than a little drunk and becoming emotional. "Bex said Michael, in an amused tone, I think it's bedtime for you. Jessica was sitting on Angie's lap, snuggling up. "I need to put Jessica to bed I protested. "No, I think that's my job tonight said Angie with a smile. "Oh ok, I said slowly, not really in any position to argue. Michael took my hand, he had to almost carry me to bed. I don't remember him tucking me in, but I do remember the softness of the cool sheets, as I wrapped them around me, and fell into glorious tipsy sleep.

I heard a cry, a deep from the soul, agonising cry! I was still half asleep, and still more than a little drunk. I almost fell out of bed, pulled myself up, and started following the screams, as they increased in tempo and ferocity. I was at the top of the stairs, looking down, and trying to get my bearings before I fell down. Michael was at the bottom of the stairs looking up. I will never forget the look on his face. "Jessica I screamed. "What's happened to Jessica? "Oh my God. It's not Jessica! For a moment, that almost released the tension surrounding me, but then he cried. "Melissa is gone. "She's gone!
I stumbled down the stairs bashing my knees on the bannister, rushing into Melissa's room, and lurched across the room, she must be here. "Oh no, maybe she has fallen off the bed. I ran around to the other side of the bed. The barrier was down. We never

left it down when we weren't in the room. The
window was open; she hadn't fallen out of bed.
BARBARA HAD HER!
Angie was crying hysterically. "That woman has
taken her. "I know she has. "Oh God, please. It took
all of Jacks strength to hold her and calm her. "I'm
calling the Police, said Michael desperate. I almost
ran to the back door. Looking out at the darkness.
"Where have you taken my baby"! I screamed into
the darkness. I ran into the house, grabbed the keys
to Jacks BMW and headed outside. I was just in
pyjamas. Michael ran after me. "Where the hell are
you going, Bex? "We have to wait for the police,
and you can't drive, you are drunk! "I have to go
Michael. I have to search, "but where? "I don't
know Michael, but I have to go!" I got in the car.
Michael didn't stop me, but I could hear his cries in
the distance. I started the engine and stalled it.
"Damn fucking damn, I screamed, as I started the
engine again. This time it fired and I sped off. I had
no idea where I was going, but the beach was
calling me. I didn't know what was in the mind of
that sick demented bitch. The moon was full,
casting its light on the deserted beach. Without any
understanding or thought of where I was going, I
followed the light of the moon, leading me to the
beach, dark and cold. Suddenly I saw it! The Grey
Clio, the only car parked on the beachfront. I
stopped the car, got out and just stood at the brow
of the sand dunes, and the wooden walkway that led
to the beach. Frantically I started looking across the
beach, thankfully lit up by the all-powerful moon.
Suddenly I saw her! She was about a quarter of a
mile away. She was walking slowly as if carrying

something heavy. "Oh God help me" it has to be Melissa, I ran across the bridge, and found my way to the flat sand, and I ran, faster than I had ever run before in my life. I felt, though, as if I were running uphill, like those nightmares, where no matter how fast you run, you feel as though you are continually going backwards. I started to scream using every fibre in my body "STOP, STOP". I watched as she turned, realising that I had found her. She tried to pick up speed, but I was carrying nothing, I was, younger, faster, and I was going to get her! I realised she was heading from the sand further and further into the waves of the sea. I panicked but carried on. I couldn't stop now.

I was almost in touching distance of her, and I could hear her panting, as she held fast to a heavy Melissa. She was up to her knees in the water, when she stopped and turned around to face me. I ran the last few yards until I was about ten feet away. She looked triumphant, she could hardly breathe, but she was holding Melissa tightly, I had to be clever. She looked at me. Her evil, sucking the life out of me. "You stupid bitch" she hollered finally. "Did you really think I would let you get away from me! You are such an idiot!" "What do you want from us" I screamed at her. "What have we ever done to you?" "Your fucking mother, she thought she could force me to have an abortion, because of her I was never be able to have children, then the hypocrite that she is, gets herself pregnant with a little runt like you - she stopped me having children, so I will stop you from having children" "What are you talking about" I shouted in disgust, "my mother did nothing but try to help you, and you have never had an abortion, that's just a fantasy, and a lie, that you have cooked up to get sympathy. You had children. Two little girls, whom you got bored with, and then you murdered them!" "That's a fucking lie" she screeched. "I never hurt a hair on their heads. "They were my babies, and they were taken from me. I didn't do anything!" "Yes you did" I said, "you are a narcissistic, evil murderer. You killed your own flesh and blood, and you killed your own sister, and you killed Suki!" Melissa's feet were now in the water, Barbara started laughing, almost hysterically. "My little sister Jill, my god, what a stupid cow she was. "She never helped me at all, if it wasn't for her, Flo would still be alive. "You are fucking mad," I hollered at her. "Jill was just a kid; she didn't want anything to do with your sordid disgusting life! Suki, my friend, why did you hurt her? She was so gentle; how could you have done such a wicked thing to her. She was innocent! The light caught her face, and it was as though looking at the devil himself. "That silly little do-gooder, she laughed again. She found out about me didn't she, and I couldn't let her go to the Police. "Oh my god, and she laughed and laughed. "That sari wearer would have believed anything I told her, she thought she was so clever, "She thought she could get the better of me, but she was a fool. "So easy. "She came to help her little friend, but it didn't take her long, to come over to my side". "She believed every fucking word I told her! "Yes of course she did, that's because she was a good person, who had never come into contact with such an evil manipulative bitch". "She cared about people. She was kind, and you killed her" "Yes of course I killed her. She broke into my home. She had no right, so I went to her home and hung her up high, with one of her stupid ugly scarves! So damn posh, looking down her nose at me, and she thought she was so clever! Well when I hung her from the bannister, she didn't look so posh, or so clever then!" Oh my, said Barbara, as she revelled in the wickedness, the look in her eyes, was priceless, just priceless" She carried on, manically laughing…

I wanted to grab her now. Kill her now! but I stood waist deep in the water considering my next move. "You know Rebecca, Melissa is going to die tonight, but you won't die, because I want you to suffer. I want you to feel all the loss that I have had in my life. I would rather have killed Jessica, as well, but you kept her so close, you kept your favourite, and I've had to make do with this one!" She held Melissa up high, as if she was nothing. I started to move forward to get her.

Melissa suddenly and inexplicably arched her body in a strong spastic grip. She slowly turned her head deliberately, but not in spasm. Not in seizure. Barbara and I were both transfixed. What was happening. Melissa turned to face me. The moon lit up her green-grey eyes. they were completely still, there was no flickering, she wasn't having a fit. Melissa truly looked at me. Not moving, but looking at me, with a calmness, I had never seen. She opened her mouth, and with a sound of angels she said gently.

"Mummy I Love You".

I let out a scream. The shock was more than anything, that I had ever witnessed in my life. Barbara also screamed. I watched in awe as Melissa started turning her head back towards The Hate. The fear in Barbara's evil eyes, filled me with euphoria. I realised though that Barbara was losing her grip. I screamed, "hold on Melissa, hold on! Barbara screamed again, as she let go of Melissa. Melissa tumbled, and fell with a loud splash, as she was plunged into the sea. "Noooo, I screamed as I dived through the freezing water. I ploughed on, in a desperate state. I managed to grab Melissa's pyjama sleeve, pulled her tightly into my arms and turned, moving through the waves toward the shore. Just as I believed we were getting to safety, a hand grabbed me and pushed us both over. I felt myself going down under the black water. It took all my strength to fight the hands that held us down. I managed to free myself again, as I frantically slammed my hands into the water, desperately trying to pull Melissa free again. Suddenly I had her, and this time I managed to drag her to the shore. I lay her down, safely away from the waves, and turned back to face my demon. I ran back into the waves towards The Hate, grabbing her by her hair and pushing her down under, with all my might. I suddenly felt a terrible sharp pain piercing my stomach. I screamed in agony, and let her go. She emerged from the foam like a shark, ready to attack again. I was wounded. She pushed me down. I was being held by a force that seemed greater than me. I felt myself giving up, but something drove me on, "Melissa" I screamed under the water to give me the strength I needed. I managed to get myself above the waves. I grabbed the demon's face and squeezed with all my might. I heard the horrible pop, as her eyes burst in their sockets, a river of blood covering me. She screamed like a tortured, fatally wounded animal. "You have to die" I screamed, and I pushed her down again. She still fought for life, able to come up for air, before I pushed her back down again. I could hear her screams fade as the salt water was coursing through her lungs, filling every orifice of life preservation. There would be no saving her this time, her life force was so strong, but even as I felt myself weaken, I drank in every moment, as the life ebbed out of her, as her struggling became less, she calmed, then just when I thought I had won, she would struggle some more. The gaps between her movements got longer, until she struggled no more. I didn't trust myself to let her go yet, so I held her down longer, my fingers still embedded in her skull. I had to be sure that the beast was dead. I knew, that this all had to end tonight, on this beach. I screamed with relief. "We've won Melissa"! We had fought in shallow water, but I feared letting her go. She was not human to me, so even now, I still believed she could be alive. With one hand I loosened my grip and waited. I feared removing my other hand, and as I did so I had to remove them, with all my might from inside her evil skull. When I finally released myself from her forever, her blood, dripping from my hands, she floated like flotsam in the waves. I stood beside her for a while, as she bobbed up and down within the ripples of the ocean. I suddenly came to my senses and looked towards Melissa, and I began pushing through the water, back to the beach. I realised I was in pain, and with each breath, each moment, the pain increased. She had cut me, but with what, I had no idea, and I didn't care. I forced my way back to the sand, to my Melissa, and held her close. Tears filled my eyes as I cried. "It's okay my baby. It's okay my love we're safe. I cried as I held her. Her wet hair hung to her face, so I pushed it back to see her. Her eyes were wide open. "I heard you Melissa" I cried! "I heard you!" I waited for her to talk to me, to say she loved me again, however there was nothing but silence. "Melissa" I cried, stroking her beautiful face.

The day was dawning, and I could see Melissa in an almost ethereal light. My arm, that was cradling her, moved slightly, and her head fell backwards. There was no spasticity in her. She was too calm and still.

Her eyes were open but without life. I pulled her closer to the safety of my body. I stroked her face and combed her hair with my fingers. Suddenly a cry like a wounded animal emitted from my body, the realisation that my angel, my baby,
Melissa was dead!

Chapter 51

I woke from what felt like the deepest of sleep. For a moment I hoped everything was just a dream. I sat up, my head hurting. My stomach hurting, from where I had been cut. I felt drugged. The realisation hit me. It wasn't a dream, Melissa was dead. Every action felt like I was moving through molasses, thick and dark. A blackness had descended, that would never lighten again. We were bereft. Jack and Angie seemed to take over the everyday activities that Michael and I could not contemplate ever doing again. We knew that we had to go back to England. It was our home, and it was the only place where we would bury our beautiful daughter. We had to endure the fact that there would be an autopsy. We could not take Melissa back home before this. While we waited, we lived in a twilight world. The results revealed that Melissa had died from a massive epileptic seizure, and not from drowning, as we had suspected and feared. Nothing was of any consolation to us, now though. Jack and Angie organised the repatriation of Melissa's body, back home. It was a nightmare sitting on the plane, knowing our child's beautiful ravaged body was in the hold. Michael was inconsolable. Sometimes I just held him. We couldn't speak. Jessica was so quiet, and her grief, without truly understanding it, was unbearable to witness. When we arrived back at Gatwick, there were only a few journalists there. We had assumed that they had listened to our wishes, to be left in peace, to grieve for our loss. It was hard to be back in our old house, with all the memories, good and bad surrounding us. I remember when the Undertaker came to the house, to help organise the funeral. We were calm, in shock, robotic. I remember he thanked us at the end of the appointment, saying we had made the ordeal of organising our child's funeral easier for him. It was interesting to see that even someone who dealt with death on a daily basis, found the death of a child so difficult.

Michael and I didn't talk much. Sometimes I felt he was better being on his own, which was difficult for me, as I needed, and wanted him. I would lie with him, my arms wrapped around his body, but mostly he seemed alone in his grief, and cried openly, most of the nights, unable to carry on. I thought he would break, and I was scared, for him, more than myself.

Chapter 52

The day of the funeral was the day I had feared the most. This was the day, we finally had to admit, our baby girl was dead. It was decided that the funeral would be too much of an ordeal for Jessica, so Angie offered to stay with her for the day. It was for the best, as far as Jessica was concerned, she needed time to heal. As the hearse arrived, its white coffin inside, I almost collapsed with the shock. Seeing it there, covered in flowers, knowing that Melissa was finally at peace. We followed behind the hearse. There were many people driving behind too, and as we drove along, there were some people lining the street, tossing flowers at the hearse. We were touched. The whole country seemed to have followed our story, without us knowing, and this was its horrible conclusion. The church service went by in a blur. I didn't know the Vicar, but he said all the right things, and I believed he meant them. I looked around at all the people there. There seemed to be hundreds. Michael cried throughout, his head was rested on the shoulder of his father. Jack was trying to console his beloved bereaved son. I felt in that moment, that he would never be free again. As for myself, I didn't know. I felt lost and somehow detached from my body. When we left the church, it was only a short drive before we arrived at Ashford Cemetery. Although large, and somewhat impersonal, it was still a beautiful and peaceful place. Although the day had dawned with rain, the sun now blinked through the clouds, as if to light the way, for our final goodbyes. We waited in the car, as the coffin was taken from the hearse.

Michael had wanted to be a pallbearer, but his grief was all too consuming for him to do so. It all seemed surreal. How could this have ever happened to us? We were just ordinary people. All I had ever wanted was a family to call my own. We had suffered the tragedy of Melissa's birth. We had survived, and carried on, and tried so hard to have a normal life, but normal had always alluded us.

We stood at the graveside, with the deep void waiting to take its gift to the earth, as the Vicar spoke, Michael broke down. I tried to comfort him, but it was Jack whom he clung to, where the outpouring of his grief was directed. I looked above and watched the leaves of the trees swaying in the breeze. I looked around, seeing more people than was usual at a cemetery, there must have been many souls being laid to rest today. I looked at the congregation present and realised that amongst our relatives and friends, Sam was there. My heart lurched. He was still as handsome as I had remembered him. Our eyes met, but he seemed to look through me, tears streaming down his face, I believed, feeling our pain.

Suddenly I could hear laughing. Not loud, just gentle girlish giggles. I remember thinking how strange it all was. To hear that in a cemetery, especially whilst a funeral was going on. To be honest I almost found it comforting. I looked around to see where the sound was emanating from. At first, I saw nothing in particular, just the hundreds of headstones, for all the souls residing there. I carried on looking, and then behind a bold, solid, beautiful willow tree, I could just see her! It

appeared to be a child, hiding behind the tree. I was holding Michaels' hand, but I let it go, as I inched towards the sound, and what I thought was a child. As I got near to the tree. I called: "Hello, is anyone there". I could see golden hair blowing in the breeze, revealing the whereabouts of the mischievous child, playing hide and seek. "I can see you," I said cautiously, as I didn't want to frighten her. Slowly a peek from a little eye came from behind the tree. "Come on," I said in mock admonishment. "You know you shouldn't be here playing in the cemetery. Where are your parents?" The child emerged, wearing what looked like a bridesmaids' dress of ivory and gold. It matched her complexion completely. As the child stood before me, there was a sudden recognition. That dress! The dress we had chosen to bury her in.
"Melissa" I said in a stunned whisper.
The little girl stepped forward cautiously, as if not to frighten me. "Mummy, I love you," she said. It was what she had said to me, that last time, on that terrible beach. "Melissa" I stammered. I stepped towards her and wrapped my arms around her. This time she held onto me, her hands and arms gentle, yet strong as she returned my love. Tears streamed down my face. "My baby" I cried, "you're not dead" I picked her up in my arms, and I ran towards Michael. To the grave, where I wanted to scream. "Tell them all, Michael!" I cried. "Look, she's alive! Melissa is alive" Michael, however, ignored me completely, as if I wasn't there. Still holding Melissa, I stared back at the coffin once more. I had been surprised initially, why was it so much larger than it should have been? I had

reasoned, because there were so many special things put within it. Soft toys, books, pictures, paintings and drawings from Jessica.
The vicar carried on talking.

"As we say farewell to Melissa and Bex, we know that their souls are in heaven, where one day, they, and their family will all be together once again. A world without end."

I blinked back tears as I looked at Melissa. The coffin, I now realised was adult size. "Are we in there together Melissa? I whispered. "uh huh, she said, nodding, and smiling, "but we are not really there are we Mummy, we are here". I looked at everyone there. "Michael, can you hear me"?
I knew now, that he could not. I put Melissa down on her feet, her hair blew in the wind, golden and beautiful.

"Have I died?" I said stunned.
"On this earth, you have Mummy, but we never really die, It's just a veil we pass through. One-day Daddy and Jessica will pass through it too, and come home, and we will all be together" A lump rose in my throat. "Jessica! How can I leave Jessica?" "Daddy, Nana and Grandad will look after her, they will never let her forget you" "but Melissa, I don't know if I can leave them?" I said tears rolling down my cheeks. "I love you, but how can I leave them behind?" "We can visit them, Mummy," she said. To hear Melissa, speak, her gentle dulcet tones, filled me with joy, as well as sadness. "We will be with them whenever they need

us. We will watch Jessica grow. She is strong, and she will have a good life." "Will she?" I pleaded. "I don't want her to suffer." "she won't suffer Mummy". "You died, so she could live. Her life will be good, with love and laughter, and we can be there, watching for always".

I looked back at them all, engulfed in their grief. "We need to go home now Mummy", said Melissa brightly. "But sweetie I don't know where that is?" "that's okay mummy, Just follow me" she laughed, "I know the way. There are so many people who want to see you. Some have been waiting for ages", and she rolled her eyes.

Completely in control. Intelligent, beautiful and funny, as I always knew she was.

"Is my Mother there," I said hesitantly. Melissa giggled again, "of course Mummy, they are all there". "I'm a bit scared," I said. "I know what you mean Mummy. I was a little scared when I first came here, but then I realised, that I had been coming here often while I was alive, so I know lots of places where we can go".

I took hold of Melissa's hand. This was it, I thought, this was how it was always meant to be. I was lost without her, now we would be together forever. We, I realised, had so much to catch up on.

"Is Suki there", I said suddenly, my heart lurching, just thinking of her! "Yes Mummy, she is here, but she is in a Special Place, as her passing was so difficult, so she needs some help to get better, but she knows you're here, and she can't wait to see you."

I smiled, and Melissa's beauty smiled back.

We began walking away. I turned one last time, just to see them all.

"I'll visit you soon" I whispered. "I love you".

I turned back to Melissa. She let go of my hand, and skipped in front of me, as I had always wished she would. "Come on Mummy". "Hurry up"!

I walked faster, "I'm coming, Melissa, Mummy's coming".

~ ~ ~ ~

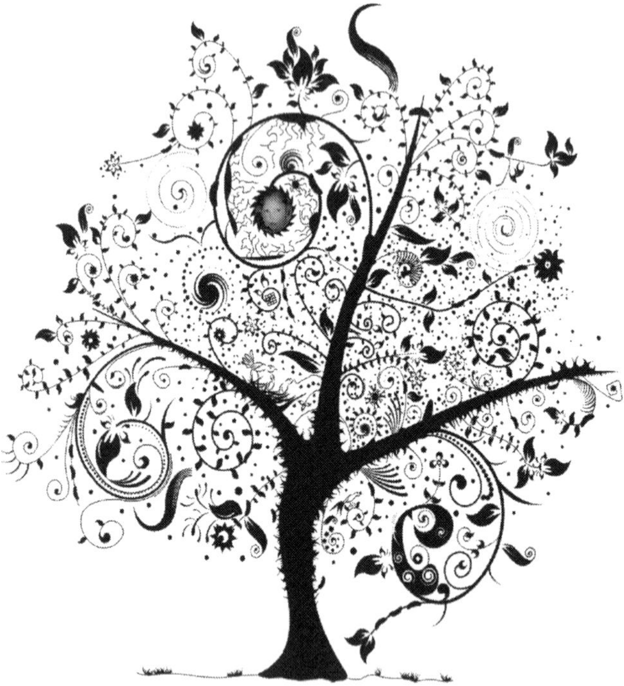

About the author.

Susan Bolden lives with her family in Maidenhead, Berkshire.
She is married to Peter, and they have two children, Jenny and Tom.

Their eldest daughter Lucy,
died in on St Valentine's day 1998
aged six and a half.

Dental Practice (for Sunday)
0118 9043888
9:00am — 111 referal.

Printed in Great Britain
by Amazon